THE COLOR GONE

QUEST FOR ANSWERS

Rian Mileti and Marlene Bryan FHD

Written by Rian Mileti
Cover Design by Rian Mileti
Edited by Dane Cobain
Illustrations by Rian Mileti

Dedicated to my grandmother and inspiration,
Marlene Bryan, born July 17th, 1961.

Her last words were "I love you," and they were spoken to me at 10pm on August 22nd, 2020.

It was the day we completed this book series.

Connect with me and learn more at
TheColorGone.com

Contents

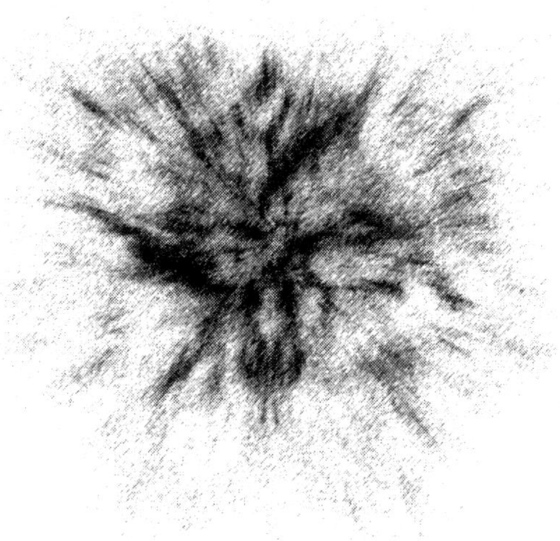

PROLOGUE: THE BIRTH OF EARTH

SOON LOOKED AT his young students as he remembered the brilliant kids of days past. There were several incredible minds amongst the group, and at least two of them could be a challenge to teach. But Soon loved a challenge.

He looked with more intent at the colors that the children had chosen for their uniforms. Soon had learned years earlier that when he let his pupils select the colors, they had a sense of self and were happy even though their outfits were identical.

A soft breeze caught his long, dark cloak, briefly revealing the soft flicker of faint silver symbols hidden in the fabric. Soon was a tall, slender man with vibrant energy. All seven of his students stood at half his height, and the tall grass came up to their shoulders. Soon looked out, scanning the horizon and watching the wind brush against the verdant, spring green grass as it blew across the endless landscape. There was nothing to see but the waving plains, which stretched from horizon to horizon.

"We have nothing to fear on this world," Soon said, looking out over the plains. As he spoke, he heard the children's laughter while they continued to explore. Laughter bubbled up from the curious group because the grass was so tall. The children started trying to scare each other by hiding in the tall grass and playfully springing up.

After some time, Soon announced, "It's time for everyone to make the world brighter. It's time to learn how to maintain happiness through our laughter and how everything in the universe began."

As the children settled down, one of the little girls paused and popped her softly curled red head into view.

Those are some of the brightest uniform colors, Soon thought, briefly. *How did she find so many orange roses to combine with that shade of hot pink?*

He looked at her left shoulder and noticed a rainbow-colored rose opening up.

I'm amazed that all of the colors in her uniform are in this one rainbow rose. And can I smell those roses as well?

"No one's ever done that with their uniform," Soon whispered quietly to her, so that the other children wouldn't hear his surprise.

"Master Soon," she asked, eagerly. "How did something come from nothing?"

"How did something come from nothing?" Soon repeated, smiling at her. "Aurora, let me show everyone how everything began."

Soon looked up and raised his palms to the deep, black sky. His students eagerly followed his gaze towards the endless blackness above.

His brilliant blue eyes changed to a silver-gray as the sky erupted with light.

Author's Thoughts:
I wanted to join you as you read through this book. From time to time, I'll add onto the story as I read through as well. This story begins before the Big Bang and Master Soon and his students are a part of the colony that created everything...

CHAPTER ONE: NEW HORIZON

RADIANT SUNSHINE broke through the cobalt blue curtains and shone down onto Kayden Mile's 15-year-old face. The gentle ocean breeze carried a refreshing smell of fresh saltwater into the room through a window that had been left open overnight.

Kayden sat up on the edge of his bed and yawned, rubbing his eyes. From the kitchen, he could hear his dad laughing and teasing his mom as she cooked them breakfast, and it brought a smile to Kayden's face. But better than the sound was the smell – his mum's cooking was enough to make anyone jump out of bed. She was making toasted raisin bread, his favorite. No one made breakfast like his mom did.

Oh, boy!

Kayden scurried down the hall and into the kitchen. His mom – Star – was setting the table when he hurried in, his tired eyes hunting for the raisin bread. Once he saw it, his hand reached out automatically to grab at the pile.

"Morning, Kayden!" his mom said. "Good timing. I was about to wake you up. I made you some raisin bread because your dad ate all the bacon."

Smiling playfully, his mom swatted at his dad's hand, which was reaching out for a slice of the raisin bread. Then she kissed Kayden on the forehead like she'd done every morning for as long as Kayden could remember.

Kayden slid onto one of the tall stools by the kitchen island and stuffed a slice of bread into his mouth before immediately reaching for another piece. A small frown appeared on his mom's eyes, but a gentle half-smile teased across her lips.

"Kayden," she scolded, flashing a loving glance across at Brian. "Where are your manners? You're eating as though you're starving, just like your dad. What's gotten into the two of you this morning?"

"I'm just hungry," Kayden said, turning to look at his father. "Hey dad, are we still going out on the Merry Miss today?"

"You'd better believe it, bud," his dad said, winking at his wife with a glint in his eye. "I just found out that dolphins are around this time of year."

"Dolphins?!" Kayden exclaimed. "Dad, can we swim with the dolphins? Can we?!"

Kayden turned to the hallway as he heard little footsteps running towards the table.

"Mom, did you hear that?" Brooke asked. She was Kayden's 10-year-old sister, and she celebrated by jumping into her mum's arms. "We might get to see dolphins! Oh, I can't wait to see them!"

As Brooke hugged her mother, happiness beamed out from beneath her messy brown morning hair. Her dark chestnut curls danced.

Then Brooke dodged her mother's lips as Star leaned in to kiss her. "Yuck, mom! You're making kissy fishy lips. The only fishy lips I want near me are from dolphins." They both laughed.

"Eat your breakfast," Star insisted. "And don't forget your sunscreen!"

She looked over at Kayden's dad and added, "Now, don't you lose your phone in the water, and take lots of pictures for me. I'm going to stay here. I might look around some of the shops while you guys go out on the Merry Miss."

Then she leaned in close to Kayden and whispered, "Make sure your dad puts on your sunscreen, okay? I'm depending on you for that."

Star handed Kayden and Brooke their apple juice and then wiped down the counter.

It was their fifth day in their new home, and Kayden was excited to get to know the neighborhood. California was a whole new world compared to what they'd been used to in North Carolina. His dad had said that there weren't enough jobs to support a family back there, so when he'd been offered a job as a journalist on the west coast, the Miles family moved to California.

Kayden didn't mind the move because he was shy and would rather play on the piano or do some drawing than worry about making new friends. Kayden had liked a girl since third grade, but he was so shy he never told her. Now, he was looking forward to all the new things he'd experience in California.

***

After everyone had gobbled down their breakfast, Brooke skipped down the hallway singing her favorite song as Kayden walked behind her towards his room. Their bedrooms were across the hall from each other. Star watched as they both made their way down the corridor.

"Brooke," Star called, "brush your hair and I'll put it up for you. What are you planning on wearing?"

She followed her daughter into her bedroom and saw what Brooke had in her hand.

"Oh no," she said, "you're not wearing that worn-out purple swimsuit. No more! You've worn all the good out of it."

"But mommm," Brooke whined, "it's my favorite swimsuit!"

"I know, Brooke," she said. "That's why you've worn it out. Here, put your new yellow swimsuit on. You can be daddy's sunshine girl. Now get your hair brushed and I'll put it up for you. We'll look for a new suit when we're out shopping."

Secretly, Star hoped that Brooke would forget all

about it, but she was glad that Brooke was excited about Brian taking them out.

***

Kayden figured that if his mum had said no to Brooke's purple swimsuit, he'd better not choose the holey shorts that he'd been planning on wearing. Instead, he grabbed a pair of green swim shorts and climbed into them. Then he slipped his old tennis shoes on and went running down the hall. Brooke was right behind him with her yellow ponytail holders shining against her precious, dark brown curls.

As the children ran out, they were followed by the sound of paws across the wooden stairs. Bobo was a black and white cocker spaniel, and his coat glistened in the sun's rays as he skittered around the corner and out the door, not even stopping for bacon.

The kids ran down the hill and started clunking down the long dock with Bobo beside them. Kayden hopped into the BowRider and helped Brooke and Bobo to board the boat.

The boat was made for families, with holding rails down each side. The kids loved sitting up front when they got out on the water, and they immediately started pretending they were sailing the high seas and looking for adventure.

Kayden looked over toward the house and yelled, "Dad, hurry up! We have to see the dolphins before they all fall asleep!"

He reached down and secured Bobo's doggy

lifesaver vest.

"I'm not going to have you swimming with the dolphins before I can," Kayden said, looking down at Bobo.

A sharp whistle cut through the air, and Bobo pulled free from Kayden's grasp, bounding onto the dock so quickly that he was almost a blur. The dog's racing paws slipped on the wet dock as he rocketed toward Brian. Bobo's feet scrambled under him, paws and fur a blur. Sliding sideways, Bobo, careened towards Brian's knees. Like a wax statue, Brian's reaction froze, arms raised, mouth agape, one foot hugging the dock, the other carelessly lifted, trying to make room for Bobo. Brian was holding towels in one hand and a small cooler in the other. An in one cacophonous calamity Brian and Bobo crashed into a heap. The cooler popped open. Towels fell across Brian's eyes, leaving him groping for the dock. And scooping up a sandwich in his mouth, Bobo emerged victorious, running to the house, tail carried high.

"What was all that about?" he murmured. He climbed breathlessly into the boat, grunting as he eased himself over the side. "Oh, my back."

"What's wrong, dad?" Kayden asked.

"Ah, nothing," Brian said. "My back always hurts when there's a storm coming. And, no, it has nothing to do with our pet bulldozer."

The kids looked across the water and watched the sunshine dancing across the soft waves that were being formed by the gentle ocean breeze.

"But it's a beautiful day!"

"That it is," Brian admitted, bending down to ruffle Kayden's hair and drawing his attention away from the gentle ripples across the water. "Perhaps your old man is just getting a little… well, old."

He sighed and then added, "Alright, I just have to untie us from the dock and then we'll be on our way."

Brian untied the mooring rope and pushed the Merry Miss away from the dock. Brooke plopped down on the seat next to Kayden as they started to drift out to sea.

"Oh yeah," Brian said. "You forgot to put your sunscreen on." Brian tossed the sunscreen to Brooke.

"Hey, dad. Why do bananas wear sunscreen?" Brooke quipped.

"Why?" Brian shot back with a tease.

"Because bananas peel!" Brooke laughed.

Tapping Brooke on the nose Brian added, "What do you put on a pig's nose if it gets sunburned?"

"Oinkment!" Brooke blurted, pretending to squirt her dad with sunscreen. But she stealthily pivoted and squirted Kayden instead, as he reacted with a yelp.

"Brooke, get him!" Brian said. "Rub that on your brother, since he's too much of a big baby to do it himself."

Brooke started wildly smearing the lotion all over Kayden's back, increasing the rocking of the boat. Her father leaned in and rubbed some lotion on Kayden's arms and shoulders.

"Kayden, don't forget to rub some on your face and ears," Brian said. Then Brian turned his white, coated hands towards Brooke. She peeled off a scream, trying to get away. "Brooke be still while I get you finished. I don't want it to go in your eyes."

Once he'd finished, Brian lifted the captain's chair and pulled out some lifejackets that were hidden inside. He tossed one to Kayden and tightened another around Brooke.

"I like your outfit," Brian said, motioning to Brooke's yellow swimsuit. She smiled at him.

Brian put his jacket on over his simple red t-shirt, then stood back and put his hands on his hips. He surveyed the boat, patted the pockets of his gray plaid shorts and gave the nod.

"Done," he said. "Now let's go."

He sat down and cranked up the boat with a noisy roar of the motor. The kids grabbed hold of the rails and the Merry Miss lunged forward, skipping across small, breeze-blown waves.

The wind flowed around Kayden's face as the sun's bright rays bounced off the wake around the boat. The ocean air brought out his excitement as they rounded the point, encountering choppier water than in the bay. A pod of short-beaked common dolphins began leaping out of the water and landing with a splash around the boat.

Kayden looked back at his dad, who had one hand on the rudder and who was holding his phone with the other. He was filming Brooke, who was bursting with laughter. The dolphins glowed in the sunlight as they leapt out of the water, playing in the wake of the boat as it skimmed across the ocean. Kayden extended his arms, enjoying the breeze. The dolphins splashed water up at him as they raced the family towards the open ocean.

Brooke held her hand up in the air, looking at the sky through her fingers. She giggled and said, "New Horizon!"

> *I would love for that to become popular. A greeting for hope and peace*

A bright light suddenly filled the sky as an object fell through the atmosphere and plunged into the ocean, sending a massive geyser into the air that blocked out the sun. An enormous wall of water climbed into the air as the wave raced toward the motorboat.

Wide-eyed, Kayden sank behind the rails. The family BowRider lifted nearly ten feet into the air as the wave overtook them.

***

Kayden's hands welded themselves to the railing around the bow as the wall of water curled the boat into the air. His father's phone dropped from his fingers as he sat up tightly, gripping the wheel. He frantically turned the wheel to bring the boat to a forty-five-degree angle against the giant wave.

"God, please," he murmured. "Help me to keep my babies safe."

The phone flew over his shoulder, tugging on the strap around his neck. Brooke stumbled back, landing on the padded seat as the wave slammed the boat back into the water and down the other side of the wave.

Brooke screamed, and Brian stared blankly as he fumbled to grab the phone, which was still recording as it swung around his neck. Kayden's stomach fluttered as they drifted up and down in the aftershock as smaller waves hit the BowRider's port side. The pillar of water turned into mist as it fell back to the ocean, bringing the sun back into sight amidst a rainbow of color.

"Dad, what the heck was that?" Kayden demanded, letting go of the rail.

"Daddy, I'm scared," Brooke stuttered, jumping off the seat and running over to jump into Brian's arms. Her face was ashen and her entire body was trembling. She buried her face into her father's neck.

"Don't be scared, honey," he replied, pulling her close against his shoulder and automatically starting to rock her back and forth. "I won't let anything happen to my little sunshine girl."

He kissed her temple and her trembling stopped, tears slowing but still rolling freely down her face. Brian moved back to the rudder, slowly turning the boat towards where the geyser of water had been. The front of the motorboat lifted into the air as they moved forward. Skipping over a few waves, they picked up speed as they cruised through the cool fog.

Kayden stared into the depths while Brian cut the engine and the boat settled back into the water. He spotted another boat approaching them and pointed to it.

"Dad," he said, "it looks like we have company."

The boat floated alongside them, and a group of men shouted over to them. Brian stood up and held Brooke with one of his arms.

"Good morning," he said.

"Are you all okay?" This came from a tall man who

was wearing a hat and sunglasses with a navy and white Hawaiian shirt. He was smiling warmly and looking around the BowRider. "We saw that wave hit you, and I sure thought your boat was going over. Did you guys see what we just saw?"

"We saw something," Brian said, chuckling. "But we have no clue what it was. Everything happened rather quickly."

The man shook his head and said, "Yeah, we want to get a dive team out here tomorrow to go down and take a closer look. See if we can figure out what fell from the sky."

"I've got some gear of my own," Brian said, looking across at the boat crew. "When are you guys thinking of getting started? I live just around the bay."

"Probably early in the morning," the man replied, glancing at the other men in the boat. "I'm thinking around eight. Let me give you my card."

He reached into his pocket and pulled out a plastic bag with his wallet and keys in it. Opening the bag, he took out a business card as their boats drifted closer together. The boats collided, causing Kayden to lose his balance and almost fall over. Still holding Brooke, Dad reached over and took the card from him.

The man quickly turned his head as a voice called to him over the radio. Then he tipped his hat to everyone and the boat started drifting away.

***

Brian stopped the recording on his phone and walked over to the front of the boat. Then he looked over the side, checking for anything that could have caused a geyser the size of the one they'd just witnessed. Sunlight danced across the surface, but a faint white glow hid beneath the sea.

Thank God it didn't topple the boat, Brian thought. *Thank God the kids are safe.*

Then he returned to the captain's seat and started the engine. Glancing at the business card in his hand, he slipped it into the pouch with the phone.

Brooke scurried to the front of the boat to sit with her brother. It was a quiet ride back to the dock, and no one had much to say because no one had any answers. Brooke curled up in Kayden's lap and they shared the boat's bow for the whole ride home.

"I hope the dolphins are okay," Brooke said. "I wonder if they were as scared as I was."

Brian saw that she was getting misty-eyed as she snuggled deeper against Kayden. Kayden wrapped his arm around Brooke and held her tight until they pulled into the dock.

Brian tied off the boat and lifted Brooke onto the pier. The kids raced up the steep hill towards the house, still wearing their life jackets.

"Mom!" they called, leaving the sliding glass door wide open as they ran into the house, their father a couple of steps behind them. "Mom!"

Star rounded the corner of the living room with a box from upstairs in her hands. She dropped the box to the floor and looked at the kids.

Why Was Star Upstairs?

"What's wrong?" she asked. "I thought you guys

would be gone for longer than that."

"Mom!" Brooke cried out excitedly. "Mom, a star fell into the ocean. A star!"

Mom looked first at Kayden and then at Brian as he caught up with them.

"It's true, Star," Brian confirmed, pointing to the phone around his neck. "We saw a star. I caught it all on camera."

"It made a huge splash that blocked out the sun," Kayden added. "It nearly turned the boat over. The wave must have been 100 feet tall, and it even blocked out the sun. It was huge! We saw it fall from the sky, but it fell so fast that we couldn't see much."

Star reached down and scooped Brooke into her arms.

"Now, Kayden," Brian said, "it wasn't 100 feet tall. If it had been, the Merry Miss would have capsized. It was more like a ten-foot wave, which is plenty big enough."

"But dad," Kayden protested. "It blocked out the sun! Ten feet of water wouldn't have blocked out the sun, would it? And it was the whole sun, not just part of it."

"Son," Brian said, "that was from the geyser made by the meteor or whatever it was, not from the wave that hit us. That was way smaller, and that's good for us because if it had been any bigger, we would have turned over."

"Are you guys, okay?" Star asked. She looked concerned and her eyes were scanning over them to make sure that they were safe and sound. "My babies are safe. Thank God, my babies are safe."

"Honey, you've got to see this," Brian said, holding up his phone. "I'm glad you insisted on getting me that waterproof case."

Star snuggled in close to Brian as he flicked through the phone to pull up the video. He handed the phone to Star, watching her eyes widen. Suddenly, she shuddered, dropping the phone, disbelief etched into her features. "But..but… that couldn't be," Star stuttered.

CHAPTER TWO: THE VISITOR

Twenty years later…

Dr. Mile is Brian Mile's son. This chapter introduces what happened to the family after the star entered their lives

DR. MILE'S HEAVY EYES were in search of answers and on the hunt for truth. He grabbed the towel from the open metal door just above his black, wavy-haired head and wiped the sweat from his face.

"How are you feeling?"

He turned to look at Jessica, his lab partner, who was outside the tank. The gentle, compassionate expression in her pretty green eyes complimented the soft smile on her face as she looked at him.

It was an old routine, and one that both of them were

used to. Jessica started working through the list of questions that she insisted on asking after every stay in suspended animation. She had to make sure that he didn't overlook anything because it could cost him his life. Dr. Mile knew that she was terrified of losing him. No one else would want to continue the research.

"I'm blissfully dissatisfied at the moment," Dr. Mile replied, smiling at Jessica through the glass. He handed her a towel.

He was the first reported scientist in history to successfully stop the process of aging by experimenting on himself. The last time Jessica had taken his blood sample, they'd confirmed that he hadn't aged during the last few months of testing – and they'd secretly discovered that he was younger.

They'd also discovered that nausea was a side effect of the suspended animation used to slow aging. He placed his hand on his stomach as it churned beneath his skin.

"How are you feeling?" Jessica asked.

"I'm feeling better this time," Dr. Mile said, spotting the concerned look in her eyes. Then he looked down at his feet and flashed a thumbs-up signal so that they'd turn on the tank. As the liquid poured into the bottom of the tank, he reached up for the breathing tube and put the mouthpiece between his teeth, closing the lid of the chamber and locking it.

There was a knock on the glass and it brought his focus back to Jessica.

"New Horizons," she said, laying her palm flat against the glass with her fingers and thumb spread apart.

Dr. Mile reached up, matching her palm and mumbling through his mouthpiece.

"New Horizons," he said.

Then she walked away. He stared after Jessica with warmth in his eyes, realizing that this was her way of saying "keep up the excellent work" and "I've got your back", all in one expression.

Over twenty years ago, the video his dad made that day when they chased dolphins, had caught the crystal orb falling from the sky, hitting the water, and it went viral, along with Brooke's "New Horizon" phrase.

He had flashbacks of Brian, his father, jumping into the water with the dive team all those years ago. They'd found the crystal sphere that had caused the geyser and the wave that had narrowly missed capsizing the Merry Miss.

After some study, they'd realized that the orb was a star map that glowed in certain places. The star cluster inside the sphere was an actual location in space. Dr. Mile was trying to make the journey across time and space to learn more about the beings that had sent it. That was why he was doing the cryonic suspended animation tests. He wondered idly what he'd need to work out next as he watched his feet go under the liquid.

Jessica walked over to her desk to grab her clipboard and spotted an envelope with her name on it. As she lifted the envelope, her eyes went to the tank and a caring expression settled on her face.

Dr. Mile's life had changed a lot since the orb had fallen from the sky. The flood of scientists and astrophysicists that kept knocking at the doors had inspired him as a child. It had also given him the connections he needed to make the experiment possible.

Jessica had been helping him to crack the cryogenics by monitoring him along the way. She had an analytical mind and was taking detailed notes on everything they tried and the results of each trial. Those records were why they were as close as they were.

She reached over, picked up the letter and gently opened it.

Dr. Mile had made it his mission to crack cryogenics and had dedicated the last few years to it. Jessica had been under contract to never release any information about the project outside of the lab. No one in the scientific community had believed that the previous test findings were real anyway.

"On the morning of May 6th, 1954," Jessica said, smoothing out the letter as she read from it, "British athlete Roger Bannister achieved the impossible and became the first person to run a full mile in under four minutes."

Dr. Mile watched her from inside the chamber, feeling the liquid close up around his legs for the 439th time. They were dissatisfied with the methods of modern cryonics. Other labs were freezing patients at low temperatures in the hope that they'd figure out how to revive them in the future.

There are many cell types and differences in the body, he thought, for the umpteenth time. *Unavoidable, microscopic ice crystals form, resulting in memory loss and brain damage. I can't risk damaging my mind or body. I've got to figure this out without any other lab's help. Solving aging is a priority and a must!*

Jessica's white lab coat floated back to reveal her soft pink blouse and black business skirt. She was holding the letter so he could see it as she smiled through the glass and nodded her head. He noticed her long, flowing tresses looking like mature corn silk waving in the breeze. He smiled lazily as he felt his body temperature drop.

He knew that a living person couldn't be successfully frozen and thawed without killing them because of the amount of time it took to freeze and thaw them. When he was younger, he'd read a comic from 1931 about a professor who shot his frozen body into space. In the story, an alien race revived him. The practicality was a different matter altogether, but it was an intriguing idea.

It's called "The Jameson Satellite By: Neil R. Jones"

The liquid that he'd created for the test touched his fingertips and sent a slight shiver down his spine. He closed his eyes and started taking deep breaths.

"If I don't expect it, I won't find the unexpected," he whispered to himself. "For it's hard to find and it isn't easy."

Jessica knocked on the glass and held up a science magazine. Dr. Mile recognized it. It contained an article about how he'd been given the green light to go into space after his successful experiments in suspended animation.

The Science Magazine: "By Design" Is a fictitious piece that is based on the real science of aging

"That's about you, Doc!" she exclaimed, flashing him a smile. "Are you ready to go to Wonderland?"

"We all just want to be happy and to progress, right?" he said to himself, feeling the liquid rise over his chest.

Over the last 20 years, Dr. Mile had received more than his fair share of press coverage. There were dozens of articles and videos online about him having a "beautifully crooked" mind. He took some comfort from the fact that "crooked" was mostly used to describe how he was creating a new path, all on his own. It wasn't necessarily a bad thing, and he was thankful for that.

His real secret was that he wasn't impressed by his own achievements. Lost in his thoughts, he told himself, *as long as I'm hydrated extensively and go through oxygen therapy, my cells will be fine. Thankfully, my memory has passed all the exercises.*

He took a deep breath, aggressively bit the mouthpiece and shouted, "So, let's do this!"

A rush of liquid poured into his lungs. It was part of the plan. He knew this. *I should be okay with this,* he told himself. But he started to panic anyway, as his vision went dark.

CHAPTER THREE: THE GIFT OF LIFE

DOC'S PERSPECTIVE

I PUSHED THE METAL DOOR away, feeling the outside air as the icy fluid spilled into the room. The liquid poured onto the floor as I struggled to breathe. I must have been having a nightmare. It felt like I was suffocating.

I quickly slipped off the table and onto the hard floor, gasping as the cold air pricked the inside of my airways when I coughed, trying to drain my lungs of the bubbly liquid. I started rubbing my eyes, but all I could see was a white blur as I coughed up more from my lungs.

I sat up slowly, pressing the sides of my head with

my hands. I could hear my pulse as I tried to regain my breath.

"Kayden..."

The male voice called out as I coughed and slowly sat up. My vision began to return as I heard my name again, this time from Jessica, whose voice sounded concerned as it echoed around the room.

"Kayden," called a third voice, another female who I didn't recognize.

I coughed into my hands, still emptying the liquid from my lungs. The blurred white surroundings were all I could see.

"We're so grateful you're alive."

I nodded, unable to speak, still catching my breath and gesturing for someone to bring me water. Sensing someone beside me, I raised a hand, urging them to keep their distance.

"It's going to be okay, Doc," Jessica said. "Here, drink this glass of water."

I nodded at her and gave her a thumbs up as she handed me the glass. I drank it quickly and then set the glass back down onto the floor. I reached up and grabbed the edge of the table, stumbling as I pulled myself up. My blurry vision slowly began to return as I fumbled around in search of my glasses.

I lay down on the bed and focused on my breathing as I started to drift off to sleep.

"Kayden?" It echoed through the room as I opened my eyes and felt the bright sting of light hitting my pupils. "Kayden?"

"Jessica?" I said, straining to get my voice out as the

bed slowly began to raise me into a sitting position. Jessica looked at me with worry in her eyes.

"I'm aware that your body isn't faring well," she said. "I'm going to give this to you so you can write on it for me. I don't want you to harm your vocal cords while I assess your physical state."

She handed me something that felt like a whiteboard.

"I'm so grateful that you're awake."

I swing my legs off the end of the bed, trying to stand up. She put her hand out, insisting that I stayed where I was.

"I need to assess you to make sure that you're in good health," Jessica said. "I want you to relax. Try not to move or speak or get up just yet. You hit the floor pretty hard. Can you nod if you can see my finger?"

I watched as Jessica held her index finger in the air. I followed it as it moved and then nodded.

"Take a deep breath for me."

"Hey Jessica," I said, looking across at her. "I feel like I've got a sour stomach is all."

"What was the last thing you ate?" she asked, staring into my eyes.

"Eggs, I believe," I said, breaking the eye contact and resting my head back on the pillow. "Not much."

"What's the last thing you remember doing?" Jessica asked, looking at my hands. Her voice sounded strange, and I followed her eyes and glanced down at my hands, still suffering from stomach cramps. I saw that there was a black film all over my body.

"What's this on my hands?" I asked.

"Hey, look at me," Jessica said, leaning in towards me. "You're not in the same clothes you were in. Close your eyes and lie back for me. Just breathe and describe your day as best as you can."

I let out a sigh and closed my eyes, leaning back against the raised table.

"I was in a panic," I said. "I remember a terrible feeling as my vision went black. Honestly, it seems like a bad dream. I was drowning as I pushed open the metal doors. Liquid went everywhere and I'm guessing I was moved out of that mess and into this room?"

Then a thought caused me to open my eyes. Where was I? I traced a line across the ceiling before I reached up and touched my face. Softly, I whispered, "Jessica?"

"Yes? What is it?"

"I can see!" I exclaimed, looking over at her in shock. I couldn't feel any glasses on my face. It seemed to be the real deal.

From over Jessica's shoulder, I saw a man in a long black cloak appear out of nowhere.

Master Soon, is the great teacher and helped create the Big Bang from 14 billion years ago. Soon is also an author in real life

"Hi," he said, as he strolled to the end of my bed. "My name is Soon, as in when will we go for ice cream?...soon," he said smiling. "I don't have much time. I hope you like not having to wear glasses."

"No glasses? That's the best news I've heard all year!"

"It's because of that film you're wearing," Soon

explained. "It's surrounding your entire body. The film currently looks gray, as opposed to being clear or any other color, because you haven't fully activated it yet. Still, I wanted to give you some insight into the film before you started to worry about it. The film, Kayden, can take on any appearance. Simply visualize what you want to look like whenever you're ready. Let's take a moment and properly get to know each other. What do you remember?"

I looked more closely at the dark film covering my body. It looked like someone had dipped me in paint. Confusion overtook excitement. Jessica had somehow disappeared, and I didn't recognize the white room I was in. Looking down at the film on my feet, I thought back to the voices in my head and mutter, "Kayden?"

"Well, Kayden," Soon said. "The film on your body is made from what I call electric-dust. I'll teach you about electric-dust and macro-systems later. It's a suit I designed to maintain your body during recovery."

"Doc" The main character, is trying to figure out if he should trust Soon or not

I carefully examined the paint-like substance on my hands, then reached over to try to pull it off my fingers. I held my hands up and stared at my palm, watching it melt from my fingertips. The dark film slipped slowly away from my hand as if it knew precisely what I was thinking. I closed my hand into a fist, watching the electric-dust slide effortlessly through my fingers and down around my wrist. I opened up my hand but couldn't see any of the scars that I used to have. Then my eyes widened as I watched my scars slowly reappearing. I looked over at Soon, but I didn't know what to say. It was like something out of a science fiction movie.

Soon smiled from across the room.

"I want to relieve as much confusion as I can," Soon said, walking over to a white chair that I hadn't noticed before. "In 1906, radio frequencies traveled from Earth at roughly the speed of light and were sort of lost in the background noise of the universe. However, we've found those frequencies and were able to piece the choppy data back together fairly well using samples from multiple locations."

Soon sat down and said, "In 1977, NASA launched V–"

"Voyager 1," I interrupted.

"Yes, of course," Soon said. A smile brightened his face and he stood up, adding, "Follow me, Kayden, and bring your gift. Oh, and let's see what you look like. Turn your whiteboard over and take a look in the mirror."

I looked down at the board that Jessica had given me, then turned it over to reveal my face. I leaned in and realized that it was as imperfect as I thought it would be.

Thought it would be?

"What's going on here?" I asked Soon, looking over at him.

"I like your shirt, Kayden," Soon said.

I looked down, confused, to see that I was wearing a familiar floral shirt, along with jeans and a pair of sneakers.

"Soon," I said, "I need to know what's going on."

"Good question," Soon said, walking towards the blank wall of the room. "Let's figure it out together. I left a gift for you at the end of your bed that should bring some more clarity, and I'm not talking about the water either," he said smiling.

I followed his outstretched finger and saw a glass of water with a white ball beside it.

"What is it?" I asked. I turned my head to look towards Soon again, but I couldn't see him. I walked over to the wall and started to knock at it, my panic growing with every passing second. "Soon?"

I felt my way around the walls, but they all seemed solid and I couldn't find an opening or an exit. I stared blankly at the orb, then lifted the glass of water and took a sip. Then a familiar noise caught my attention as a vibration made its way around the room.

I turned in a full circle, seeing nothing but blank walls. The eerily familiar sound of a cell phone humming echoed around as I set my glass back down before patting at my body and checking my new pockets.

"Call from Jessica."

His cellphone would tell him who was calling when it would ring, like he just heard. But...where is his phone?

The sound was coming from the glowing white ball, and I turned my head to take a look at it. My eyes widened as I picked it up and brought it closer to my face.

Suddenly, the ball turned red in my hands, and everything drifted into darkness.

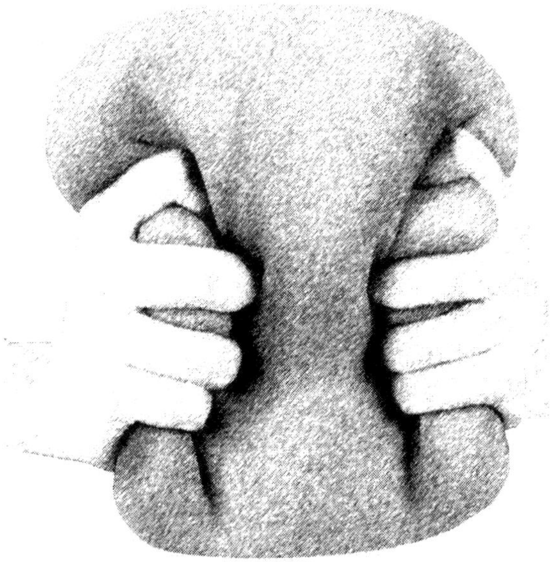

CHAPTER FOUR: DISCOVERING

THE PHONE VIBRATIONS faded away and Doc found himself surrounded by blackness. He felt the ball between his hands getting bigger as he tensed his entire body, feeling the floor disappear beneath him. His grip tightened as a rush of crunching noises took over his hearing, his hands curling into a ball as it grew. The ringing in his ears was broken by the sound of sirens filling the air.

A sting covered his face as he lifted his head from the airbag. His eyes traced the fuzzy cracks across the windshield as he let go of the steering wheel. He felt a pinch across his nose and brought his hands up to his face to adjust his glasses. Groaning, he pushed away the airbags and tugged on the car's door handle, sliding out onto the glass-riddled asphalt.

"Soon!" he yelled, the ringing in his ears preventing him from hearing anything besides the sirens. "Soon, what's going on?"

Two men walked over and shone a flashlight in his face. The light combined with the ringing in his head and caused him to ball up. He pressed his palm against his forehead, trying to figure out what was going on and why his face hurt so badly.

"What's going on?" he repeated, as he was rolled onto a stretcher. He winced in pain and felt the stretcher tilt as he was carried. His head was secured to the stretcher's pads and then he was loaded into the back of an ambulance. As the doors shut him inside, he looked over at one of the EMTs.

"What happened?" he asked.

"You ran into an intersection," the man replied.

Doc closed his eyes again, overwhelmed by the pain in his face and shoulder. He was only distantly conscious of the ambulance's movement as it howled towards the hospital. He heard a female nurse say something about x-rays as they wheeled him through the halls.

"I'll get you checked in," the nurse said, as his stretcher rolled to a stop.

Doc looked over, taking in the hospital room he was in. He noticed that at some point, as he'd been drifting in and out of consciousness, he'd been transferred from the stretcher and into a chair. He could hear children talking excitedly to each other. Briefly, he opened his eyes to see who chattering just inside his door.

"Woah," a young voice said. "What do you think happened to him? Maybe he was skiing and tried to wrestle a bear to save a little kid who was rocketing out of control."

"Yeah, make that all on one ski," another young voice said and chuckled.

"Who am I kidding," said the first voice. "Just look at me." "What about you? How did you end up in here?"

"My old man told me not to play where the barbecue gas tank was," the second kid said. "I guess I didn't listen. I was outside and I fell over, breaking the gas line. Gas started pouring out, and the hickory smoking chips popped and lit the gas. I was engulfed in flames really fast, man. You should have seen it! Whoosh! I was on fire everywhere. If it wasn't for the pool, I'd be dead. Dad grabbed me and jumped into the water."

Doc shifted in his wheelchair, tensing up as a few sharp pains cut through his shoulder. The itchy tape on his bandage set his mind racing. It had been tough for everyone, lately. He was grateful they were all still there.

The first kid's voice added, "I'm here 'cause my big brother chased me into the kitchen and tackled me. He threw me against the stove and spilled mama's stovetop deep fat fryer on me. She'd been frying the fish we'd caught for dinner. She grabbed the dishwater and washed off the oil while the ambulance was on the way. Guess we both got pretty lucky."

"You sure are funny-looking," they both said almost simultaneously, sharing a big laugh as an attendant walked up to Doc and wheelchair.

"Have the kids been keeping you entertained?" the attendant asked, as she rolled Doc out of the room and pushed him down the hall.

"Owww," he whimpered.

The kid's story is based on a real story. Marlene added this into the book to share her insights on handling burns and to open Doc to talking with her personal favorite character "Williow" later in this book

As he listened to the heart rate monitor, he looked down at the IV in his arm, as confused as ever. The last few hours had been confusing and he was having a hard time putting everything together. He replayed the vibrating ball over and over in his mind, looking for an explanation.

Where's Jessica? Why did she disappear? And what about Soon? Where did he go? Did he run into the intersection? Which intersection? Why am I hurting so much? Why am I in a hospital? What happened?

Life can sometimes make me feel lost, how about you? Have things happened to you that entirely changed your own life? Doc actually woke up in an unfamiliar white room & is now trying to figure out how he got there. Could this strange accident just be a dream? It sure feels real...

"Knock, knock, son," Brian said, rounding into the unit as the nurse pulled back the curtain. "How are you doing?"

"I hurt a lot," Doc responded, touching the bandage over his eye and stating the obvious.

"Nothing is broken," the nurse said, bringing Brian

up to speed while providing Doc himself with a refresher. "And he doesn't have a concussion, just some bruising. The tests came back negative for alcohol."

The nurse handed Brian a plastic bin containing the clothes and personal belongings from the accident, and then he closed the curtain.

"How did you get here so fast, dad?" Doc asked, looking at the bin in his dad's hands.

"Your cousin Jimmy was the EMT," Brian said, walking over and looking at the IV in his son's arm. "He said you didn't recognize him. Your glasses were broken but he brought them in anyway, which they don't normally do. You were on your phone and you ran a red light. You're lucky to be doing as well as you are. Come on, let's go."

Saving your life is their priority. →

"The doctor hasn't come back yet," Doc replied, reaching up and holding the patch over his eye.

"Look, the longer you're here, the bigger your bill is going to be," Brian said, gesturing for a nurse to come over and escort them out of there. "Trust me, I'm only looking out for you."

***

Not long after, Doc was sitting in his dad's truck with his head against the glass, watching the streetlights pass. Brian was talking about all the times that he'd gone out of his way to help him.

"You've been bad since you were a kid," Brian said. "Remember how many times you had to change schools? And how bad your grades were? You used to waste time chasing girls instead of studying."

"Dad–"

"This isn't the first time I've gone out of my way to help you," Brian continued. "You need to start focusing more on what you're doing. You need to get a grip, son."

Doc sighed and started to tune his father out. His father's complaints were nothing new. The old man had always thought of him as a failure.

The small pickup turned off onto the gravel road and bounced across a few potholes as it circled the trailer park. The truck pulled into the driveway and slowed to a stop. After they disembarked, Brian pointed Doc in the direction of the back bedroom as they approach the trailer in the dark.

Doc hobbled inside and weaved around the trailer before collapsing onto the bed. He felt like a failure.

What happened? Where did Soon go? Great. Now dad thinks I'm a druggie, sheesh!

He lay his throbbing head back and slipped into a painful sleep.

***

The following morning, Brian woke with the dawn and immediately grabbed his cellphone. He scrolled through his contacts to find Doc's office number and then hit the dial button. He started talking as soon as the call connected.

"Hello," he said, "this is Brian Mile. I'd like to speak to the manager. My son works for your company and

I'm afraid I need to report that he was in a car accident last night."

"Oh my goodness," the operator replied, and Brian registered dimly that she was a woman. "Is he okay?"

"He got hit pretty hard," Brian said. "He's recovering at home with me."

"What's his name?"

"He goes by Doc," Brian said. "He's the head of the lab."

"Oh Doc, thank you, sir," the receptionist said. "Please hold."

Brian held the phone up to his ear and listened as he walked over to the window and pulled back the curtain. He looked out over the trailer park as he talked on the phone, and something didn't add up about what he heard. A frown crossed his face.

Brian's life had been tough. The kids had arrived earlier than he'd expected and then he'd lost everything in the divorce. He'd pushed his kids through school so that they'd and live better lives because of it. He'd known that simply having a professional designation made a big difference to a person's credibility, if nothing else.

When Doc finally got a job, Brian had felt like he'd succeeded as a father because he'd only ever wanted to see his son do better in life than he had himself. Brian's parents had screwed his life up, and that was why he didn't have anything. That's what he told himself, at least.

Brian hung up the phone and made his way into the bathroom. He waited for the water to warm up, took off his robe and then got into the shower to calm himself down.

***

It was still the early morning when Star started crying in front of her makeup mirror, her black nightgown showing the tremors throughout her whole body. Tears ran down taking lines of mascara with them as she looked through her phone and responded to her nephew Jimmy's texts from the night before.

She made her way over to the spiral staircase and sat down on the bottom step. As she looked up into the sky, the mascara running down her face intensified the morning glow from the skylights. Scrolling through the contacts, she found Brian Mile and hit send.

***

Brian had just got out of the shower and was buttoning up his shirt when his phone started ringing. He walked over to it and saw that Star was calling. He sighed and picked up the phone.

"Yeah?"

"How's my son?"

"I'll let you ask him," Brian said, turning out of the bathroom and heading down the hall. When he reached the door to the back bedroom, he swung it open and flipped on the light. A groan came from a broken face behind a bandage that needed to be changed. Brian held out the phone.

"It's your mom," Brian said. "She wants to know how you're doing."

Brian set the phone on the bed and switched it to the speaker.

"Hey, mom," Doc said, his voice crackling as he lifted his head and revealed a large bruise across his cheek.

"Did I wake you?"

"Nah," he said, yawning as he looked up at his dad, who was leaning against the doorframe. "I'm just lying here."

"I bet you're sore," Star said. "Did you break anything?"

"No," Brian said, jumping into the conversation. "He doesn't have a concussion either. Jimmy put him on the stretcher last night."

"Oh gosh," Star said, laughing softly. "I bet that was a fun ride in the ambulance."

"I called his work this morning," Brian said. "As if things weren't bad enough, now he's unemployed as well."

"For getting into a car accident?"

"No, not for that," Brian said. "He was a no show a month ago, and they assumed he'd quit!"

"A month ago?"

"Yeah," Brian said. "I called his office this morning, and that's what they told me. He's got to be on something. Last night, he was out of it."

"I wasn't on anything," Doc insisted, glaring up at his father. "I don't remember last night at all, but my drug test came up clean. You heard the nurse the same as I did. No alcohol and no drugs, just some chemicals. And before you ask, I don't know what kind of chemicals. I don't remember anything."

"Let me talk to your father," Star said. She sounded upset, as though she was fighting back tears on the other end of the line.

Brian picked the phone up and switched the speaker off. Then he walked out of the room.

***

There was a dull pain in Doc's shoulder, and he closed his eyes tightly to take his mind off it.

Has it really been only a month?

Doc opened his eyes back up and looked over at the dusty blinds again.

"I have to get out of this room," he murmured.

He flopped onto the floor and grabbed his shoes, straining to put them on. Hobbling into the bathroom, he flipped on the light and looked at his swollen, bruised face. He stroked his hands across his bandage, seeing that it needed replacing.

"Dad?" he shouted. "Do you have any bandages I can use?"

He heard his father's footsteps as he approached the bathroom, followed by a knock on the door. Doc opened up the door and took the bandages.

"That's all I've got," Brian said. "I guess I'd better go back to the store for more bandages. I'll be back soon."

"I need my glasses," Doc said, turning from the mirror and looking at the door. "I can barely see."

"I tossed the bag with the glasses in beside your bed while you were sleeping," Brian said, walking away.

Doc slowly exited the bathroom and made his way back to the bedroom, then started rooting around the side of the bed for his glasses. Once he'd found them, he headed to the bathroom and took a shower, then carefully dried his face before examining the damage above his eye, figuring out how to redress it with the bandages that his father had given him.

***

Once he'd finished ordering the cellphone, Brian closed his laptop and stashed it in its carrycase before climbing into his old pickup truck and hitting the road. He was hungry, and he knew the perfect place to grab a bite to eat.

The trip to the sandwich shop only took him twenty minutes or so, and he was soon back inside the trailer and looking at Doc who, with a bandage over his eye, was hard to miss.

"Looks like you found your glasses," Brian said, noticing the tape that was wrapped around one of the hinges. "I see you got that bandage replaced."

"Yeah," Doc said, vaguely. "Listen, do you know where my phone is?"

"It's over there with your wallet," Brian said, pointing towards the belongings that the paramedics had returned. "Don't bother getting up, though. It's been smashed to pieces."

"What am I going to do?"

"Lost without your phone, huh?" Brian said. "Don't

worry, I ordered a new one. It's nothing special, just a cheap, disposable phone, but it's better than nothing."

"Thanks dad."

"Oh," Brian said. "I almost forgot. I called Jimmy and he said he's going to check on your car to see if you left anything behind. We wouldn't want something being taken or going missing."

"Thanks," Jimmy repeated.

There was an awkward moment of silence between the two of them, which Brian broke by offering Doc one of the sandwiches.

"I bet you're hungry," he said.

***

The lifted 250 truck slowed to a stop in the parking lot, its mud-lined tires crunching against the asphalt.

Jimmy disembarked from his vehicle and walked into the office, smiling at his old high school crush, who was working behind the counter.

"You look hot today," Jimmy said, still wearing his EMT uniform.

"Hey, Jimmy," she replied, smirking alluringly at him. "How you doin'?"

"Well, looks like my day is almost over," Jimmy said, resting on the counter. "My cousin's car was totaled when I put him on a stretcher last night. Is Kenny here?"

"Yeah," she said, picking up the phone and dialing a number. "I'll get him for you."

She spoke a few words into the handset and then

replaced the receiver. Jimmy waited impatiently, pacing backwards and forwards in front of the reception desk, until Kenny finally opened the door to the left of the desk and stuck his head through the doorway.

"I've got to show you this, Jimmy," Kenny exclaimed, beckoning him over and ushering him down the narrow hallway. "I've been in this business for 15 years, and I've never seen anything like it. Man, you aren't going to believe it."

CHAPTER FIVE: THE FLICKER

KENNY LED JIMMY into a room full of surveillance monitors. Jimmy was mildly surprised at how free of dust the security room was compared to the rest of the building. Static filled the computer screens that lined the walls. Kenny slowly closed the door with a quiet click, engulfing them in silence.

Kenny pointed to a squeaky office chair and said, "Have a seat, Jimmy."

They both settled into their chairs and rewound the surveillance footage from the night before. Jimmy noticed that Kenny had got a new uniform. He'd put on a little weight.

"Is your wife feeding you properly?" Jimmy joked.

"Oh, yeah," Kenny bragged. "She's a good cook."

"How far along are you?" Jimmy joked.

The black and white surveillance video showed the wrecker pulling up to the gated fence and bringing the car inside. Jimmy leaned forward, squeaking the chair as he looked closer at the screen.

"Yeah," he said, looking at the crushed passenger doors. "His car got hit pretty hard."

"That's not what's bothering me," Kenny said, looking over at Jimmy. "Watch what happens."

They turned back to the screen, where the cab of the car had started lighting up as it was dragged into the lot. There was a flickering white light that appeared to be coming from the driver's seat.

Switching angles, they watched as the wrecker lowered the car onto the lot in the back. They fast-forwarded the footage and watched the wrecker pull away. Jimmy watched time tick by on the corner of the screen, his confusion mounting with every second that passed.

"Kenny, what am I looking for?" he asked.

"Keep watching your cousin's ride," Kenny said, his attention focused on the car. The vehicle's headlights had started to flicker.

"What's going on with the car?" Jimmy asked, his confusion still growing.

"You needed to see that before I showed you the car," Kenny said, standing up and leading them out of the room and into the dark hallway. The smell of old oil and grease filled the hall, and the stench grew stronger with every step they took towards the end of the dark corridor. The heavy metal door let in a gust of air as they made their way out to the car.

Dust kicked up as they walked between the wrecked vehicles of the gated lot. As they slowed to a stop in front of the car, they looked up at the barbed wire fence that surrounded them.

Kenny pointed towards the driver's seat as Jimmy peered in through the shattered front window. Walking around the side of his cousin's auto, Jimmy stepped up to the door and looked inside again. A light in the floorboard caught his eye, and he reached up to the handle and pulled the door slowly open.

"Look out!"

Jimmy jerked his hand back and fell to the ground. The car's lights were flashing, and the horn blared while Kenny rolled about with laughter.

"Dammit, Kenny!" Jimmy yelled, his feet still in the air. "You almost gave me a heart attack!"

Kenny was still laughing as he cut the alarm off, dangling the keys from his hand. Jimmy climbed back up and dusted himself off before snatching the keys from Kenny's hand.

Jimmy went back over to the car and started looking around, opening up the different compartments and recording it all on his phone. He took a few photos and then grabbed a jacket and a college tie from the trunk, as well as a cup of coins from the center console.

"Thanks, Kenny," Jimmy said, walking off the lot and back to his vehicle.

Jimmy climbed up into the driver's seat and tossed everything into the empty seat beside him. Then he pulled out his phone, scrolled down to the name Jessica and pressed the call button.

"Hello, Jimbo!" Jessica said, as she answered the phone.

"Hey, Jess," Jimmy replied, clutching the phone to his ear as he cranked his truck. "Real quick, where are you right now?"

"I'm leaving the lab with my best friend," Jessica said. "We're going to the mall. What's up?"

"My cousin was in a car accident last night," Jimmy said. "I loaded him onto the stretcher myself. He was delirious, kept murmuring something about someone called Jessica calling him. It wasn't you, was it? Did you talk to him last night?"

There was a pause on the other end of the phone line.

"Who was in a car accident?" Jessica asked, cautiously.

***

Brian had paid extra for same day delivery, and Doc's new phone had arrived early that evening. Brian had handed the parcel over and then sat down to read the newspaper while Doc played with the settings and got the device up and running.

Brian turned over the final page of the newspaper, looked over at his son and said, "Have you finished setting up your new phone, son?"

"I think so," he replied. "Give me a call and let's try it."

Brian did so. The phone rang and Doc grinned and then cut the call. He nodded at Brian, who walked off into his bedroom and closed the door after excusing himself for a nap.

Doc sat back on the couch and stared into space as the day passed slowly by. Suddenly, his phone vibrated, and he was woken abruptly by the buzzing in his pocket.

"Dad, are you trying to call me?"

Brian didn't answer, and Doc guessed that he was still asleep. He pulled his phone out of his pocket and answered the call.

"Hey, Kayden!" the caller announced. "You disappeared on me!"

"Who is this?" he asked, his eyes widening.

The caller chuckled and then said, "It's Soon."

"Soon?" Doc repeated, standing up suddenly.

"Kayden, are you okay? Are you safe?"

"I–" Doc began, but his phone died in his hand before he had a chance to reply. "Are you serious? Right now?"

He plugged the phone into its charger, then dropped into his dad's recliner and leaned back, giving the phone some time to charge.

After a few minutes, he heard the sound of tires crunching on the gravel outside. He stood up and walked over to the window, then looked outside.

He watched as Jimmy's bright blue truck rolled into the parking area. The sunshine reflected off the chrome strips down the truck's side and its 20-inch rims wrapped in mud tires. Jimmy slid out of the driver's seat and started gathering something from the back of the truck while Jessica climbed down from the passenger side, her flaxen hair looking like a ripened wheat field with a breeze blowing across it.

Jimmy walked over to the door and pulled it open, catching his breath as he saw Jessica smile.

"Hey," Jimmy said, handing over Doc's belongings. "Your dad asked me to see if there's anything you need from your car."

He held up the orb and added, "Where did you get this?"

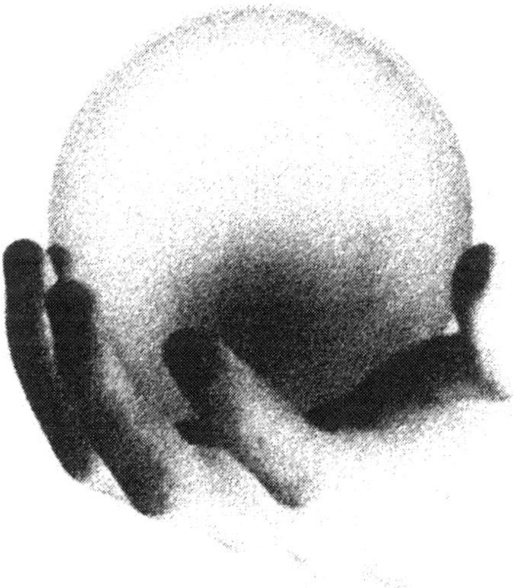

CHAPTER SIX: THE STEP

JESSICA WALKED FLUIDLY over and sat down in a chair beside the recliner.

Doc noticed that her flaxen hair was cascading over her pale green shoulder as he lowered himself into his father's recliner. His eyes were glued to the orb that Jimmy was carrying with his other belongings. It filled his head with questions and reminded him that he needed to call Soon.

"Where did you find this?" Doc asked as Jimmy handed the glowing sphere over to him.

"This snow globe was on the floor beneath your driver's seat," Jimmy recalled. He looked as though he was about to say something more, but then his phone rang, and he put the rest of his cousin's belongings on the table before stepping outside.

Doc leaned back in the soft chair and then held the orb out to Jessica, who took it.

"What's this?" she asked.

"I was hoping you could tell me," he murmured, watching her roll it around in her hands.

The ball flickered from its usual white to a dimmer pink and orange a few times before returning to white again. They stared curiously at it and then she handed back the orb.

"It was given to me by a man you work with," Doc said.

"He may be the best person to ask about it," Jessica said.

The orb started vibrating in Doc's hand and he looked back to Jessica.

"Do you hear that?"

"Hear what?" she replied.

Doc opened his mouth to say something more, but then he was interrupted by a knock at the front door. Jimmy was smiling at them through the window, gesturing for Doc to join him on the porch. He still had his phone to his ear.

Who's Jimmy talking to? Doc wondered.

He felt the orb buzzing in his hand again, and then the ache in his shoulder came back. He turned the doorknob, and the light pressed its way around the door as it opened.

***

DOC'S PERSPECTIVE

I stepped into the blinding light and turned my head away, closing the only working eye that I seemed to have left. For some reason, it felt like someone was shining a flashlight in my face. Hearing the click of the door behind me, I opened my eye and asked, "What's up, Jimmy?"

As I rubbed my eye, my vision came back into focus. I stumbled abruptly backwards and a hand reached out and stabilized me. I was shocked by who I saw.

"Soon?" I spoke. "Thanks, I'm still a little off from my accident."

I reached up, adjusted my glasses and felt the bandage that was still over my eye. Looking around the room, I saw that everything was the same as I remembered. My head was swimming with thoughts. I shook it and let out a sigh.

"Last time I saw you, you'd just got out of bed," Soon said, his voice deep and slow-paced as he slowly sat down in a chair beside the table. "I understand that you need me to clarify a few more things, and I can't imagine what you're going through. It seems as though you feel lost, Kayden."

"I don't know what's happening," I said, shaking my head again. I looked slowly up at him. "I was in a car accident."

"A car accident?" Soon said, tilting his head in curiosity. "Where were you going?"

I paused and looked at the orb in my hand. I'd been

trying to figure out where I was and what was going on for a long time. "Where did you go, Soon?"

"You know how your clothes change through your thoughts? It's like having psychic clothing, and it looks like you're a medium." Soon said, laughing. He continued, leaning forward out of the chair. "The orb can do the same thing for your environment."

I grew cold as he added the final touch to the picture he was drawing in my mind.

"Toss me the orb," Soon said. "I don't want you getting into another car accident."

I tossed it over to him and watched as the orb slowed down and floated above his hand. It started buzzing, and I heard "call from Jessica", which chilled me and slid an icy finger down my back. The orb turned red as the room went black, and we both suddenly appeared at an intersection.

A traffic light above us turned red and Soon gestured for me to get out of the road. He had the orb in his hand. Out of the corner of my eye, I noticed my car barreling down the road while we stepped up onto the curb. I turned around and faced the intersection, staring towards the headlights of an oncoming truck in the distance.

Soon lowered his hand and the orb pulsed in different colors as both vehicles entered the intersection. The truck smashed the passenger-side window of my car as Soon flicked his wrist, causing the orb to slowly fade from one color to another. The sands of time drifted into a slumber as the squeals of the rubber tires on the asphalt faded eerily away.

I watched the vehicles as they slowly pressed together, metal crinkling and crunching against the glass. Cracks crawled across the windshields as the cars' airbags bloomed for a few lingering moments. I looked over at Soon, who was casually walking towards the slow-motion collision as time finally froze altogether.

This is Doc's last memory, before he woke up in the white room.

"Let's go see what happened to you," Soon said, stepping out into the road.

Soon rounded the car while I looked around at the late-night intersection. I knew it well, because I'd grown up nearby and walked through it hundreds of times when I was younger.

"Are you coming?" Soon asked, playfully popping his head over the car. "Just run with it and learn as you go, Kayden. A strong character comes from continuing to seek truth. I could be wrong, but isn't this experience something new for you?"

"Yeah," I said, shaking my head. I slowly eased myself off the curb and limped out into the street. Rounding the car, I reached out and touched it. The cold steel shocked me, as did the smell of rubber and metal. I knocked on the panels of the car I used to drive, then lifted my

hand back off it. "Soon, I'm uncomfortable. I didn't expect it to feel real."

"When did this happen?" Soon asked, smiling and pointing into the car.

I followed his gaze and saw myself holding the steering wheel with both hands.

"Last night," I said. "Shortly after you disappeared."

Soon held up the orb, and it slowly turned white as the environment misted away like sand and the room turned white again. He held out his arm and handed me the orb,

"Kayden, try not to get into another car accident," he said softly, shaking his head as I took it back from him.

"Soon," I replied, pausing to gather myself. "Am I dreaming, or is this real life?"

"Welcome, Kayden," Soon said, opening his palms. "You made it!"

"And where did I make it to, Soon?" I asked, trying to make sense of it all.

"Join me, Kayden," Soon said, gesturing to the empty room and walking out into the space. After a couple of steps, Soon paused and turned back towards me. "Remember, just run with it, Kayden."

I slowly stepped forward as Soon looked towards the ground in front of us. My eyes widened as a faint shadow appeared across the floor, which seemed to have been caused by a white fog that I could barely see.

The fog seemed to be condensing into solid-white

objects, and several white metal vines started growing out of the mist on the floor. After a few moments, I realized that the vines were being woven into two chairs that were facing each other. Soon sat down on one of them.

The fine haze disappeared as I arrived at the other chair and admired how solid it felt. The smooth, braided metal chair rolled under my hand as I touched it. The seat didn't contain a single straight line, as though artificial intelligence had grown them from the floor. I sat down in it and noticed that it was perfectly formed to my body, like it was made for me.

"What do you know about the universe?" Soon asked, from where he was seated across from me.

Silence descended upon the room as Soon looked over at a black window on the wall. There was a lot that I didn't know. I looked out the dark window with him, rolling the orb in my hands. "When I look up at the stars," I break the silence. "I know that it goes further than I can imagine. The universe is expanding, and it's getting bigger every second. Long distances change a lot in space, once you get out there. When you look up and out at the stars, you're seeing out into the past. After that I get lost, Soon."

"The vessel you left your home world in was brilliant and was born from true imagination," Soon began. "You were preserved in an incredibly creative way. I've been looking forward to this opportunity to welcome you. It's bananas to imagine the level of sophistication that it took to get you here. You could hold your biological state for thousands of years. Your lab was one of a kind."

"We didn't like the technology we had access to," I said, carefully. "So we did what we could."

"Imagination is intelligence," Soon said, smiling at me. "I've always wondered if the speed of light is the loading speed of the universe. Maybe a mind like yours can help me to figure that out. Settlements in space are so far apart that I've got to ask you something."

He gestured at the sphere and I looked down at it, noticing that it had started to flicker.

"What would happen if you left your home to go to a far-off land and then returned to realize your home was farther along technologically than the civilization you discovered?" Soon asked. "A world changes as quickly as the most creative individuals in it."

"Is that why advanced space civilizations don't regularly hang out in the Earth's atmosphere?" I asked, taking my eyes off the mesmerizing ball and looking back at Soon.

"Yes, exactly," Soon said. "It's a big sacrifice to spend millions of years in space away from home. That much time away makes it difficult to readjust to society. So, I created this room for you, as well as the orb and the moldable fabric you're wearing, as soon as you arrived. Our planet isn't habitable with you as you are, so when you go to sleep, we don't want you getting hurt. Your dreams can affect your suit, and I want to make sure that you stay safe at all times. Since your biology is different from ours, I thought it best to give you the freedom to decide what you want to do, rather than choosing for you. The orb you're holding can create anything you can imagine, just like this room can recreate an environment or a memory."

I felt the orb in my lap and raised it into the air, holding it out towards Soon as it continued to flicker.

"What's this?" I asked.

"That's a ball," Soon said, looking at me with a smirk. I laughed, dropping my hand into my lap, not knowing what to ask. My mind was full of questions, but that simple answer had diffused a lot of the tension.

"It's good to see you smile, Kayden," Soon said, nodding at me as he took in the moment.

"I don't do that enough," I replied.

"How would you feel about yourself if you smiled more?" Soon asked, raising his eyebrows. He leaned forward in his chair, looking up towards the ceiling at what appeared to be a small, blue dot, waiting on me to answer.

"Happier," I replied, following his gaze and smiling as I stared at the dot on the ceiling.

"It's okay to feel what you feel when you feel it," Soon said, taking a deep breath and then letting it back out. "Toss me the ball."

I threw the ball into the air, and as it left my hand, gravity seemed to lose its hold on it and it floated up to the ceiling, sticking itself to the blue dot.

Soon was just sitting there looking up at the ball. He leaned back in his chair. I remembered watching astronauts in space, and I tried to wrap my head around how the room was manipulating gravity.

"If you took a cellphone back in time to people hundreds of years in the past," Soon said, "wouldn't it look like magic?"

I agreed and looked up at the ball. The orb attached itself to the ceiling and started growing in size. A white hand fluttered its fingertips out of the bottom of the orb. The hand reached out through the ball and into the room.

"This isn't magic, Kayden," Soon said. "It's just part of the world that's waiting on you outside of this room."

Standing up, I approached the hand, which was reaching down from the ceiling.

"Your mind is designed to protect you by making you think twice about doing anything outside of your daily routine," Soon explained. "The only way to truly change your life is to make new decisions every day. The first step towards that is to grab that hand in under five seconds. Four... three... two..."

I jumped up and grabbed the hand that was hanging from the orb, and fire flooded into the room. Time seemed to slow down as a layer of glass crawled across my body, protecting me from the heat. Soon was nowhere to be seen.

I was lifted slowly into the air through a growing ring of blackness, and then I was plunged into darkness as the crackling sounds faded away. Silence echoed as the hand let go of me and I began to fall.

CHAPTER SEVEN: FIRE

JERKING AWAKE, Doc realized he was in the recliner in his dad's living room. He opened his eyes, dripping with sweat and shaking. The orb was lying in his lap and his heart was racing.

"Hey, son," Brian said. "Did you have a good nap?"

Doc looked at his dad, who was crossing the living room in front of the recliner.

"How long have I been asleep?" he asked, looking at his trembling hands as he slowly sat up in the chair.

"A few hours," Brian said, looking through the stuff that Doc's friends had dropped off. "Jimmy said you passed out in the recliner when he was called into work."

"I'll take that stuff back to the bedroom, I guess," Doc said, grabbing the orb and sliding his phone into his pocket. He climbed out of the recliner and Brian started to hand him his belongings.

"Son, it's getting late," Brian said. "I need you to start calling around some local businesses to look for work. Maybe you could go online and look for job opportunities."

"I guess," Doc said.

As Brian started making dinner, Doc walked into the back bedroom and laid everything out on the bed. His jitters continued as he tossed the orb towards the pillow and headed into the bathroom. His clothes were drenched in sweat, and he took a deep breath as he walked over and turned on the shower.

He slowly removed his shirt before peeling off the bandage over his eye. The dressing came off clean and didn't stick to his wound, showing that it hadn't bled any further.

Good, he thought.

He removed the rest of his clothes and then stepped into the shower to wash the sweat off. As the water ran over him, it sent pain flaring up in the random cuts that forcibly reminded him of the accident and how real the world was around him. Shivering despite the warm weather, he stepped out of the shower and made his way over to the sink. He reached over and grabbed the worn towel and wiped down the mirror in the trailer's humid bathroom. For the first time since the accident, he could see the damage that had been done. There was a cut and a swelling around his eye from where the airbag had mashed his glasses into his eyebrow.

Snapping out of his endless staring, he started drying himself off. He sighed, feeling a small puddle of water under his feet as he knelt with his towel and started to mop it up. A gust of heat blew through the vent in the bathroom. The warmth from the vent comforted him as he wrapped the towel around his shoulders and sat beside it, slowing his shivers. A familiar buzzing sound caught his attention. He scrambled into the bedroom and looked at the orb as it vibrated on his bed. With the towel wrapped around his waist, he reached over and grabbed the ball, which quickly faded into a deep black color.

"Kayden..."

The voice seemed to come from somewhere inside his head. He looked around the room uncertainly and whispered, "Soon?"

"Yes," Soon said. "The orb allows you to hear me while you're holding it. I wanted to help you along as quickly as possible."

"Soon, where am I?" he asked, sitting down on the bed.

"You're still in that white room," Soon said.

"So, I get I arrived at a different settlement in space," Doc said. "But why am I living in my world again?"

"We're glad you arrived at our settlement, Kayden," Soon replied. "You're currently in a mental reconstruction of your home as you understand it. Your biology requires you to eat and sleep, and our world isn't set up for anyone to ever do that. As you learn more about our world, you'll start to understand. For now, you're essentially living out an everyday life. You can even reach your dreams by sticking to one path until you see it through or slowly working to become who you want to be. Everything you know about where you came from is programmed in your reconstruction. Your learning also affects the world around you. The laws of physics and intelligence are integrated into everything. It's a second life while you recover from your journey."

"So I'm living two lives?" he asked, looking around at his room in the trailer.

"Exactly," Soon said. "You're living two lives because you're not fully merged with our technology. In this new world, everything is controlled by your thoughts. Imagine that the world changed while you slept because of your dreams. Imagine that one day, all of your thoughts just started randomly happening in reality. We decided that it would be best to give you the freedom to be yourself. Falling asleep in this world causes unknown side-effects for you, Kayden. In the simulation you're living in now, everything is based on your actions. Try not to get hurt in another car accident."

"I'll do my best," Doc grumbled.

"Perhaps you could describe your life back home with your family as an Earth simulation," Soon continued. "What you do matters because you need to eat and survive from day to day. My world is controlled by thoughts and emotions, and thoughts here are more than just the seeds of change. This world is more dreamlike because our minds control the surroundings."

"So," I wondered aloud, "I can dream and imagine

anything I want when I'm here in my Earth simulation without worrying about my ideas controlling my surroundings. But in your world, all my thoughts will become real?"

"Yes, you'll need the Earth simulation to live with us here, especially when you're asleep," Soon said. "I'll explain more next time I see you."

Then the black orb turned white. Doc carried it back into the bathroom, shutting the door behind him.

After setting the ball on the counter, he opened the medicine cabinet. Glancing over at the floor, he noticed that there was water on his only pair of clothes. He reached down, picked up the wet floral shirt and put it on the counter beside the orb. He bent back down again to retrieve his pants, which were dripping wet, and then he placed them on the counter only to discover that his shirt had disappeared.

"Where in the world?" he murmured.

He glanced around the bathroom and then looked back at the orb when he spotted movement. It absorbed the pants like a fluid as he instinctively reached over to grab at them, chasing his pants as they disappeared into the orb. A floral fabric snaked out of the orb and around his body as he dropped the orb back onto the counter.

How is this real life? he thought.

The fabric stretched across him as his pants melted down over his legs. Shocked, he admired his fresh, dry outfit. He pulled the floral shirt away from his body and felt it in his fingers. He shook his head in disbelief.

Just like new, he thought.

He centered himself in front of the medicine cabinet.

Opening it up, he sorted through it until he found the bandages that his dad had picked up. Slowly, carefully, he started replacing the dressing on his face.

"Son," Brian yelled from the kitchen. "I made you some dinner."

Finally dressed, Doc joined his father in the kitchen and started scrolling through his phone, looking for restaurant openings and random job opportunities in the area. Random bills and pieces of mail were scattered across the dining room table. Brian stacked some of the envelops into a pile, making enough room for them to eat together, and then he brought the food over.

"How's the job-hunting going, son?" Brian asked, sitting down at the table.

"I've filled out three applications already," Doc said.

"You should go and volunteer at the museum again," Brian said. "If you do a good job, they might hire you. I'll take you there in the morning and we can talk to them about it."

"I want to swing by my old job," Doc said, glancing first at his phone and then at his father. "Something doesn't add up about why they let me go."

"I talked with Brooke while you were asleep," Brian said. "She told me that Jessica has been calling a lot. It seems like the two of them are getting close."

"I haven't talked to Brooke in a while," Doc said. "I've been adding contacts to my phone, but I'm missing some. Can I see your phone?"

Brian tossed Doc his phone and then sifted through the mail until he found a pad and pen, which he also handed over. Doc scribbled circles on the pad until the ink came out, then started scrolling through the contacts. He wrote down numbers for Star, Jimmy and Brooke, then started copying them off the sheet and into his phone.

"Do you think Jimmy and Brooke would say that they're not family if it helped me to get a job?" he asked.

"I'm sure they'll help you out," Brian said.

They got up from the dinner table and went to their separate bedrooms. Doc took the notepad with him and sat down by the window, looking out at the gravel road that weaved its way through the trailers and which was lit by streetlights. The orb flickered a white, glowing light on the bed behind him.

Doc kept working on applications throughout the night. As the early morning sun crept over the horizon, he reached over and grabbed the orb.

He walked down the hall with the notepad tucked under his arm, lighting the way with the faint glow of the orb in his other hand. Reaching the kitchen, he set the ball and notepad down and collected a glass from the cabinet. Quickly drinking a couple of glasses of water, he found new energy even as he heard a rustling behind him.

His father was opening his bedroom door, fully dressed and ready to start the day.

"Go and get in the truck," Brian said.

Looking at his father and noticing the dark circles under his eyes, Doc grabbed the orb and notebook. As they got in the truck and started bumping around the gravel driveway, his father glanced down at the notebook.

"Are those the places you're going to apply to work at?" he asked, looking back at the road.

"They're all the places I applied for last night," Doc said, yawning and trying to fight off the urge to sleep.

"I can't believe you walked out of a job I would have killed for at your age," Brian said, shaking his head. "What's wrong with you? I can't support the both of us like this."

Silence descended upon the cabin of the truck as they pulled into the museum's parking lot. Brian cut off the engine and parked the truck.

"Get out," he said.

***

Star looked out over the ocean, her ears filled with the sound of glasses clinking and light music playing in the background. Her cherry red peignoir fell softly open with the morning breeze as she looked over at her husband, Blake Grayson.

Blake had just closed another early morning deal, and the two of them were in the mood to celebrate. It had been an international deal that he'd worked hard on for months, and he was satisfied with the final outcome. But a ghost hung over her, and her concern for her son was etched onto her haunted face.

"Any news on the accident?" Blake asked, pulling his sunglasses from his pearl-gray morning suit and slipping them on before readjusting the white jade dragon tie tack that he'd worn as a compliment to his clients. "You haven't told me much about it."

"Brian went to get him from the hospital," Star said. "But I need to bring him here. He's miserable in the trailer park, but I don't want to see Brian."

"He's your son," Blake replied. "This isn't about Brian."

"Brian used to take him out onto the boat when he was young," Star said, looking intently at him. "Do you remember when the crystal sphere fell from the sky?"

"Yeah," Blake said. "The sphere is being held at the lab up the street, isn't it?"

"Yes," Star said. "Brian was the reporter who almost got hit by the orb out there on the water. His career took off after that."

"Sounds like it took him right to the trailer park," Blake said. "I heard the story on the news, but I didn't know you were his wife at the time."

"That's me," Star said. She set down her glass and sighed deeply as she pulled her phone from her purse.

"If Brian recorded the orb," Blake said, "then was Kayden the boy at the front of the boat?"

"Yes," Star replied. "Brian had taken them out on a boat ride to see the dolphins. I'm going to give Brian a call."

Star dialed Brian's number, but there was no response and after a couple of seconds, it went to voicemail.

"Hey, Brian," Star said, once the voicemail started recording. "It's Star. I wanted to offer Doc a room here at the house if it's needed. You know, until everything is running smoothly again. Call me back."

Then she put the phone down and looked across at

Blake, who shrugged.

"Well, hey," he said. "You did what you could. Are you alright to talk about what happened?"

"Yeah, sure," Star said, slipping her phone back into her purse. "It's been years."

"After the orb hit the water, did anything happen that didn't go public?"

"Oh yeah," Star said. She picked up her glass and finished off her mimosa. "But it's something I don't talk about much because it's pretty difficult still."

"You don't have to talk about it if you don't want to," Blake said. "It's a long time ago, now."

"I was standing here when I found him the next morning, Blake," Star said, her glass shaking in her hand.

"Found who?" Blake asked, his eyes widening. "I didn't know anyone got hurt."

"He was so young," Star said, pouring herself another mimosa and taking a sip from it. "He was never the same after that."

"Never the same after what?"

Star looked over the ocean and sighed.

"He saw the glow in the water, and he couldn't swim," she explained, a tear running down her face. "I found him soaked on the shoreline. I never told Brian because I didn't want my son to be all over the news."

"What happened?"

"It was my son," Star said, turning towards him. "He jumped in to save someone he saw underwater."

"Someone else was underwater?" Blake asked, incredulously. "I didn't know any of that."

"I'll never forget when I first found him," Star said, reaching into her purse and pulling out her phone. She scrolled through it and loaded up Jimmy's text messages, then started to read them aloud. "'He was yelling 'Soon!' and something about a phone call from Jessica while I loaded him into the stretcher. Brian's on his way to the hospital now.'"

"I'm lost," Blake said.

Star looked at him, her eyes swimming with tears.

"That was what my son was yelling on the shore that morning when I found him," Star said, crying visibly and trembling all over. "He was shouting, 'Soon! Soon! Soon!'"

CHAPTER EIGHT: FLOWING MEMORIES

A NOTIFICATION LIT UP Brian's phone as he drove through town.

"Stay in the truck," he said to his son as he got out and went inside to pick up a couple of sandwiches. As he shut the door, he pulled out his phone and saw a voicemail from Star. Shaking his head, he pressed he play button. He listened to it, deleted it and then ordered a couple of subs before carrying them back out to the truck.

"Any calls yet?" Brian asked.

Doc was scrolling through his phone and fighting sleep, which hung heavy on his face. He looked up at

Brian.

"Not yet," Doc said. "But I'm cleaning the museum tonight. Let's get home. I don't want to fall asleep while I'm there."

Doc dozed off during the journey and didn't wake up until Brian bumped across the gravel road that wound between the trailers. After he parked the car, he watched Doc as he dragged himself up the steps before wandering towards the back room of the trailer.

***

DOC'S PERSPECTIVE

My breathing got heavy as I fell into the soft spring of the bed. A comforting feeling flowed over me as I sank into the sheets, sliding into a cocoon of heat next to the window. Looking at the orb, I felt lifeless as I let out a sigh.

"Soon, what am I doing wrong?" I said to the ball.

The orb flickered softly and then faded to a soft blue. My energy started to return as I rested against the pillow. The orb slid out of my hand as I relaxed. There was a soft thud as it hit the floor, and I softly jerked my head, noticing that the orb had fallen. I reached for the blankets but didn't feel any, as my tired mind slowly faded away behind my eyelids. Thoughts started hitting me as I tried to get some sleep. I wondered where my blanket went and why my clothes were warm and fuzzy.

Compelled by curiosity, I peeked over the edge of the bed, but the orb was nowhere to be found. The

warm sunlight fell through the window, dressing the dusty bedroom with an ember glow. Motionless, I noticed the curtains flutter open, letting a few pink petals dance their way into the room. The petals drifted through the sunbeams and shadows cascaded softly down the wall. I looked towards the curtain and wondered which tree the petals were coming from.

Then I noticed that the orb was flickering blue and sitting on the window ledge, its soft, blue light shining out of the window.

I pulled myself out of bed to go after the orb. Once I'd stood up, I noticed that I felt weightless, and I was relieved that I'd got so much done. I climbed out of the window, not realizing that I'd left it open, and cast my eyes down the long gravel road out of the trailer park, scanning for the orb's glow.

Once outside the bedroom, I saw a frayed seam zigzagging across my body. Still dazed, I got the idea that it was a result of my sleepless mind trying to patch and shape the blanket around me, like a tailored suit. Walking down the gravel road, I kicked at the rocks.

"Soon," I whispered to myself. "Where are you?"

The orb's blue light disappeared and then reappeared further down the road, invisibly jumping a few feet when I got close to it. The road turned and dipped down into the valley, out of view.

I followed the path along and a huge weeping willow appeared. The beautiful, light green tree looked like it had lost its leaves to the wind like a living fountain. The blue, glowing orb slowly flashed at the tree's base as the road forked, with one path going up the mountain and another leading towards a stream. I walked up to the orb and picked it up as a familiar voice caught my attention.

"So tell me," Soon says, walking down the mountain path towards me. "How has your relationship with success been?"

"I've burned myself out, Soon," I replied, looking up at the twisting branches of the willow tree. "Nothing I do ever seems to be good enough for my father."

The leaves rustled in the wind, creating an elegant pause as Soon smiled.

"I like what you're wearing...a new fashion trend? What would you call that? The blanket you're wearing. Ah, it doesn't matter, I'm warming up to it," he said wiggling his eyebrows. "It's out of the norm for you."

"What don't I understand, Soon?" I asked, looking to him for insight.

"What are you doing wrong?" he asked me. "Have you burned yourself out? Are you doing more than you're used to?"

I thought back over my day as Soon looked towards me for clues. I'd done exactly what my dad had wanted me to, but he hadn't said anything positive or reassuring.

"I feel like I'm doing something wrong," I said, reaching up to my eye and feeling the bandage over it. "I feel stuck and... emotionally, I feel nothing at all."

I leaned up against the tree, and a couple of popping sounds caught me off guard as the tree leaned with me. Stumbling to find my balance, I looked up at the tree's limbs. They lowered themselves around us like an umbrella and then smoothly lifted back into the air, pulling in a cool gust of wind.

Turning around, I pushed away from the tree with my hands. Black lightning darkened the tree as it fell back to the ground, trying to get away. Cracking and snapping sounds rang out from overhead as I scurried backwards across the ground in a sitting position.

The tree let go of all of its green leaves, creating a rainfall of color and causing alarm to rise up within me. The tree's limbs fractured themselves and twisted black as it scared itself into a haunted maple, the kind found dark and leafless in the middle of winter. I looked up at Soon from where I was sitting and watched as he reached out and caught a spinning leaf.

"Wow, would you look at this tree?" Soon said, stretching his hand towards me. "That was amazing, wasn't it, Kayden? Have you ever seen a flowing willow turn into a dark maple?"

"No, I haven't," I replied, looking up at Soon and grabbing his hand. "What just happened?"

"Are you overheating at all?" he asked, pulling me up and then twirling the leaf in his fingers.

"I'm sweating in this blanket, to be honest," I replied, looking up at the tree with a slight scowl. Soon grabbed my shoulder and pointed up at the tree branches with the leaf.

"The tree was leaning back for you so you could rest," Soon said, dropping his hand from my shoulder. "Its limbs pulled a cool breeze around us because it knew you were overheating So when you pushed the tree for trying to help you, you passed along the emotion you felt in that moment."

A feeling of empathy fell over me as I looked up at the tree, releasing the scowl from my forehead. My clothes slowly turned into a simple shirt and jeans. I looked around at the mound of leaves.

"Am I dreaming again?" I asked, looking out at the rolling grass and pure blue sky. "Or am I still in a box? That felt like the trailer park that my dad lived in. Like I stepped out of the window, and now here I am."

"That's what happened," Soon confirmed, walking toward the tree and placing his hand on it.

"How am I standing here?" I asked, shaking my head. "This world doesn't make sense."

"The world changes with the ideas in your mind," Soon replied, turning to look at me. "So what you think changes everything."

Soon stepped back from the tree as a mist collected around his feet, forming into a chair.

"This world has completely merged and you can interact with everyone in it," he explained, taking a seat in the chair. The wind over the hill moved the grass around like water as my mind raced. "It's all connected, like one being or program."

"I don't understand the way everything is connected here," I said. "So it bothers me, Soon."

I watched another chair form beside him as he looked out over the waving plains. I walked over and took a seat, then watched a bird as it flew across the sky.

"Do you remember watching the chairs magically

forming in the white room?" Soon asked, calmly. "Or when we went back and watched your car accident and were knocking on the car? All of the things you touched were created by our technology. The new world that you're now living in does just that."

I raised my eyebrows and thought about my mom and dad on the phone and how real everything felt.

"I believe the most advanced thing you've experienced is virtual reality," Soon said. "To summarize, our imagination and personality is our actual and personal reality."

I took a deep breath as I started to realize how out of place I felt.

"Your clothes are compiled of bots that are smaller than grains of sand," Soon continued. "They conduct energy through each other and are made from various materials and clear alloys. Each independent bot can interlock with the ones around it. They can change colors and glow, and their secret is their ability to build and transform materials. With this ability, our bots can create anything you can imagine at the speed of thought. Just like the chair you're sitting in right now. Watch the leaves on the ground, Kayden. The ones that fell from the tree beside us."

A fog formed around the leaves, and I watched as they turned into dust and flowed across the ground and back into the roots of the tree.

"Our entire planet isn't made of dirt," Soon continued. "It's made of electric-dust or bots. We can't have you falling asleep here because you'd still control our world while you were dreaming. Your reality would be the same, whether you were awake or asleep, and you'd be extremely vulnerable. Just do the best you can and you'll teach yourself along the way."

Soon looked towards the sky and added, "Just in time, too. Our friends are coming over the horizon."

I looked closely, but I couldn't see anything in the air. I could see a large, grassy field, but I couldn't make out any details. I noticed that the lush green grass around us was offset by a crooked black tree behind us. Sorrow drifted over me as I looked up at the brittle branches before turning around and examining the gravel.

"You know bumblebees?"

"They sting, don't they?" I said, turning towards Soon.

"Not here," Soon said, laughing. "Conveniently for the bees, every time they land, this world makes a flower for them."

"That's cool, I guess," I said, wondering why he was talking about bumblebees.

"I see how tired you are, Kayden," Soon said. "I've got a story for you that came about long before our technology. Want to know a secret that will help you?"

I settled into the chair and nodded, interested in any help I could find.

"Progress only meets achievement if you never quit," Soon said, pointing towards what I could finally make out as a few bumblebees. "So what happens when progress isn't found but you still refuse to give up?"

"Are those bees our friends?" I asked.

"Yes, those are our friends," Soon replied. "And they're a part of the secret. Imagine young eyes watching a bumblebee flap its wings in a futile attempt to force its way through a pane of glass. The bee's whining wings sang the story of its history. The bee believed that it had to keep trying harder. Interestingly enough, there was an open window only a few feet away, and if the bee had given up altogether and gone in the opposite direction, it could have gone out of an open door. Sadly, they couldn't tell the bee that there was an easier way. It had to discover that all on its own."

Above our heads, the bees landed upon the black limbs of the trees. At their touch, the trees sprouted pink flower petals, reminding me of the petals that had brought me out of my window.

"What's even worse," Soon continued, "is that the bee might never realize that there's another option, because the relentless approach makes perfect sense to it."

We both watched the bees dancing around the dark tree and bringing life back to it.

"Regrettably," Soon said, "there's no promise that trying harder will cause a goal to be obtained. Things that take longer than expected are often wrong because more of the same, stays the same. Like Einstein said, the definition of insanity is doing the same thing over and over again and expecting different results. It's often the question that's the problem, not the result that we find ourselves with. Putting yourself under more pressure to get things done can end up just costing you your motivation. When you set out on a goal, keep it to yourself. It's good to be a humble bumble and to look for an easier way forward. Don't ever give up on your word."

The tree behind us started moving as I stood up and watched the bark brighten. The limbs thinned out and the bees flew away as it morphed into an elegant cherry tree.

"Well," I said, looking over at Soon, "I need to find a job to make some money so I can eat, since that world is still real in my mind. I need to get out of my dad's house because he can't support us both. I'm only volunteering at the museum until I can find something better. I can make money after that. The only thing I can count on is that I can work two or three jobs to make more money."

"I can't imagine," Soon murmured, standing up and starting to walk down the gravel path towards the river as I followed him. "I'm sure even the museum will lose its luster eventually. Let's get you out of your financial loop as soon as possible. Does that sound like a plan? And with your bandaged face, I guess a career in modeling is out."

"My feet are okay. Is there such a thing as a foot model? I'm down for anything that gets me out of the trailer park," I chuckled.

"Well, on that note, put your best foot forward. And just be the best you can be until you find something is working, then run with it," Soon said, as we both arrived at the water's edge. "I'm going to teach you how to soar out of that trailer park, my friend."

I paused as Soon walked into the water. My shirt started to pour water as I began coughing. My hands and hair dripped as I collapsed onto the riverside. Water ran off me into the river as Soon turned and looked down at me. My upper body was lifted up as my mom held me in her arms.

CHAPTER NINE: THE RIGHT TO HAPPINESS

DOC'S PERSPECTIVE

WATER DRIPPED FROM MY HAIR and I tasted a familiar saltiness on my lips. The saltwater feeling flowed into my eyes. The grassy bank next to the stream slipped away as stiff sand formed underneath me. I was lying there with my legs out, and my mom was holding my torso in her lap, her satin pajamas getting wet. The blue sky was slowly cast with a gradual morning hue as I looked up at my mom.

"It's going to be okay," she said. She looked older than I remembered, and tears were cascading down her cheeks. "Honey, you can't swim. What are you doing? Why were you in the water like that?"

I heard a rush of water as I looked over at Soon, who was standing in the river that was flowing along the new sandy bank. I remembered my mom holding me like that long ago, after the orb had hit the water. It had been early, and a dim light had lit up the middle of the ocean. I'd kept it secret that I'd seen the glowing light out in the water. I remember watching it late at night under the stars, slowly getting closer to the house while I was upstairs looking out of the window.

I looked over at Soon, who was still standing in the stream while I reminisced. I remembered running down to the edge of the ocean before the sun came up and watching a few flickering lights blinking in the water before changing to a calming blue glow. I'd looked back at the house and guessed that everyone was sound asleep before I'd decided to jump in.

“What are you doing out here?" my mum asked, as I looked up at her and coughed.

Water gushed around my body and splashed over my feet while I gasped for air and looked out over the ocean. My mom was still holding me when I noticed that the river had turned into the vast ocean that I remembered,

"Soon!" I yelled, frantically thinking back to when he'd said that I controlled the world through my mind. "Soon!?"

I worried that my reminiscing had swept him out to sea. My back fell onto the sand as a faint mist flowed around me. A sense of being away from home set in as the memory of my mother disappeared. It was followed by a wave of sadness as I remembered her concerned expression and the tears running down her cheeks. I'd never told her the truth, and she still didn't know what had happened.

"Hey Kayden," Soon said, walking across the beach towards me. "Your ADD is an amazing creative gift, you know. Some of the most creative people I know unintentionally create squirrels and butterflies when they talk. A random butterfly enchants a conversation."

Soon helped me up to my feet.

"With you," he said, "I need to keep picking you up off the ground. We all fall when new things come our way. I know I do. But can you imagine what your life will be like once you have the hang of this? I see the water brought back a memory."

"Yeah," I said, sighing. "Now I'm cold."

"You won't be cold for long, my man," he replied.

A warm feeling washed over me as the water began to evaporate from my body and to disappear into the air. I looked out at the vast ocean in front of me and shook my head.

"My mind is all over the place," I said, squinting at the sun as it rose over the sea. "That memory was a big one for me."

A little sadness washed over me, but I kept my eyes and my mind focused on the beach so I didn't activate another scene.

"A big memory for you?" Soon asked, as we started walking down the beach toward the sunrise. We left footprints in the sand as the sparkling ocean crashed into the beach in front of us. The amber sun shone with speckles of decorative purple as though the sky was a canvas. Dolphins were jumping out in the water.

"What's a group of dolphins called, Soon?" I asked, as I watched them in the distance.

"A pod of dolphins," he said. "I know a few people who create the wildlife here, and we share consciousness, which I hope to teach you more about later. Kayden, I'm proud of you for staying up all night and filling out so many forms. I'm grateful to have met a hard worker like yourself."

"No one has ever told me that before," I said, glancing over at Soon. "Thank you, Soon. So what's this place called?"

"I'd call it a beach," Soon replied, smirking. "But you can call it anything you like. We don't have a name for this settlement, Kayden."

"Oh, really?" I said, looking at the sun beaming through the sky. The sun's rays were dusted with various colors. "I wasn't expecting that answer."

Soon put his hand on my shoulder and we stopped walking. As I turned around, I noticed that there was gravel in place of sand inside my footsteps.

"What are you thinking about right now?" Soon asked.

"The trailer park," I replied, studying the gravel. "And volunteering at the museum."

"Let's take a moment," he said, as we both sat down in the sand and looked out at the sunrise.

"Your imagination is amazing," Soon said, looking admiringly over the landscape. "I've never seen such a beautiful sunrise with so many colors accenting the sky."

"What does this place look like from a distance?" I asked. "I can't imagine a planet that can change forms like this being stable at full scale."

"Well done," Soon said, laughing. "Yes, you're in another room, Kayden. I need you to keep better hold of this."

He pulled the orb out of his cloak pocket and held the baseball-sized sphere up to the sun. The light shone through it, illuminating a crystalline structure inside it. He pulled out a piece of paper by clicking on the ball with his finger and then pinching it.

"This orb does a few things you're not aware of yet," he said, handing me the paper while pulling a pencil from the orb. "Set those in the sand in front of you."

Once I'd done it, he rolled the ball towards the objects, and they were sucked up inside the orb. My eyes shot open in disbelief at what I was seeing. I looked at Soon, seeking answers.

"What else can the ball do?" I asked.

"It's a macro-system of electric-dust," Soon explained. "Up to ten pieces of this dust can fit on top of a single strand of hair. Let's call them bots instead of pieces of dust for a moment and say that they can all work together as one macro-system. Even though they're too small for you to see, I encourage you to take a look around us at what they can do. It's amazing that bots so small can create an entire world by working together. That creative power is inside the ball."

The wind picked up and blew a few butterflies

past us.

"It looks like we have a visitor who wants to get to know you better," Soon said, holding out his palm as a butterfly landed on his hand. "Since you still have the same body, I encourage you to let your ideas become an extension of yourself."

Soon gently pulled the butterfly close to him and watched it change through a rainbow of colors. A soft pink and orange blend settled across the butterfly's wings.

"Can the orb remember things for me?" I asked, looking down at it.

"Yes," Soon replied. "The macro-system will be able to remind you about things when you need to know them. It's a great idea to make an occasional note to yourself."

The butterfly fluttered from his hand and Soon dipped it into the sand. The orb magically slid across the sand and up into his palm. He pulled out the pencil and paper and set the sphere in the sand. Slowly, Soon started writing at the same time as he spoke.

"I see a lot of people losing the best moments of their lives," Soon said. "They wait for a specific feeling to go away so that they can enjoy the moment they're having. I'm writing this down so I can give you this message again in your future. It's not because you'll forget, it's because I want it to be remembered."

Soon rolled the paper around the pencil and dropped it back onto the orb. It absorbed everything as it fell, becoming a part of the orb once again. He picked up the sphere and looked it over.

“This doesn't have to stay as an orb,” Soon said, setting it in my hand. “Just look at your sunrise, Kayden.

"I used to watch the sunrise from my bedroom a lot as a kid," I explained, looking out over the water with Soon and feeling the ocean breeze. I noticed the dolphins leaping in front of us and saw someone riding on the back of one of the dolphins as it jumped into the air.

"Soon," I said, “is that the visitor you were talking about?"

"Aurora looks like she's having a blast today," Soon said as the dolphins turned and started leaping towards us.

A loud yell came from the ocean as a wave crashed into me and pushed me back onto the beach.

***

Brian flipped on the light and watched as his son jerked awake in his bed. Doc looked confused.

“It's time to go to the museum,” Brian said.

CHAPTER TEN: THE MUSEUM

DOC PULLED BACK his blankets as his father walked away down the hall. A sharp pain shot across his shoulder and he settled back, breathing deeply. Frustrated, he let out a gust of air.

"Really?" he murmured, taking a breath. A puddle collected in his eye as he struggled to motivate himself to proceed.

Looking down at the orb in his hand, he fumbled around in bed in search of his phone. When he found it, he took a breath of relief and looked into it to see his reflection.

Can you imagine what your life will be like once you have the hang of this? Doc thought. *That's what Soon asked me.*

It's gotta be a good enough reason to get out of bed.

"I've got five seconds to get out of bed," he murmured, staring at his bedroom door. "Four seconds... three..."

Abruptly, he rolled over and climbed out of bed, then stood up and stretched.

"Got it," he groaned, yawning expressively as he gathered his thoughts.

Standing there in the dusty back room of his father's trailer, he lost himself in thought with his phone in one hand and the orb in the other.

These are real cuts, he thought. *Real abrasions, and real bruises all over my body. I have to start paying more attention. Soon keeps saying to "just go with it", but I think he means to be willing to take action.*

Doc shook his head, looked at the orb and whispered, "A ball of bots? Alright, Soon, what am I going to learn tonight?"

He took the corner of his phone and slowly pressed it into the orb. A childlike wonder washed over him as the orb rolled around the corner of his phone like a balloon. He turned the phone slowly over and the orb stretched like glue on the back of the phone. The surplus of liquid machines formed a paper-thin pair of white ribbons around his wrist. Studying the phone case, he admired the design as it adjusted into a form-fitted, radiant white phone case.

"So my actions are the only thing that changes my reality in this world," he murmured to himself. "Got it."

The light emanating from the phone case illuminated his way as he hobbled into the bathroom.

The cold thump of his socks on the floor slowly grew softer. Stepping into the bathroom, he flipped on the light and watched a rubber material form on the bottom of his socks before gliding across the tops of his feet, forming a leather shoe.

He slipped his phone into his pocket and watched his jeans fade and morph into dress pants. Straightening up his hair, he eyed his floral shirt in the mirror, watching as it morphed into a solid black polo. He flipped off the light, the room falling into darkness. The glowing white ribbons on his wrists shone brightly, and he could see the faint glow of the phone case through his pants pocket. Darkness surrounded him as the bots slowly faded to black.

"Aurora says hello, Kayden," Soon said.

"Oh, hey," he whispered, exiting the bathroom and feeling his way down the hall towards the light in the kitchen. "I got up because my dad is taking me to work."

"The liquid bots have formed earpieces on either side of your head," Soon explained. "You can hear me and I can hear you, but no one else can hear my end of the conversation."

"I should tell my dad to take me to a tech company," Doc said. "I could make a fortune off these things."

"That sounds like a great idea, doesn't it?" Soon said. He paused. "The problem is, it wouldn't work. The Earth simulation you're in is limited, so you can dream. Everyone in your Earth simulation sees the orb as a snow globe or as something familiar. When you change cloths, they see you as wearing the same thing, but they may notice a spring in your step. The orb creates your ideas and is one with of you. No one can see your ideas on Earth, unless you make them real, right? Also, our technology knows when you're fully conscious and when you are dreaming so that you can exist in and out of your Earth simulation."

"Oh," Doc said. "Jimmy asked about my snow globe earlier. Let's see how far in life I get today."

As he left the bathroom, he saw his father searching through the refrigerator. He was holding up Doc's sandwich from the night before, and it reminded him that he hadn't eaten.

I'm glad I still have it left, Doc thought, looking across at his father. *I'm starving now. How many dusty blue t-shirts and khaki pants does dad have, anyway? Note to self: buy him some new clothes. If I ever have the money...*

Brian handed over the sandwich and tossed Doc a bottle of water, and then they both went outside and climbed into the truck.

"If you do good job, they'll hire you to clean up at night for good," Brian said, as the car pulled out of the gravel driveway. "It'll be a good job for you until you find something better."

They cruised along the roads in silence until they got closer to town, when Brian started to complain about the other drivers.

"Does everyone have to jack their trucks up so high that you need a ladder to get into them?" he grumbled. "Plus those new lights are too bright, and they never bother readjusting the beam angle, either."

Brian reached up to his rearview mirror and adjusted it to stop the lights of the car behind him from blinding him.

"Why is it that every time I go out, especially at night, someone acts like if they tailgate me for long enough, I'll speed up?" he complained. "Every time."

As they pulled up to the museum, Doc stepped out and approached the front door. The museum had closed a few hours ago, but Ms. Nova M. Rain was still there and she greeted him with a smile as she opened the door.

"Text your sister when you've finished," Brian said. "Brooke told me she'd pick you up."

Doc watched his father drive away and then followed Ms. Rain into the building. Her burgundy business pantsuit gave a slight swish as she walked him through the dimly-lit entranceway. Once inside the museum, his eyes were overwhelmed by countless relics and heirlooms that were stacked from floor to ceiling.

"Are you well enough to work?" Ms. Rain asked. "I don't want you hurting yourself."

"It's just bruises, there's nothing broken," Doc said. "I'll be fine."

"You're a fighter," Ms. Rain said, a look of admiration crossing her face. "I can tell. Most kids won't help out here these days, and you're here doing it despite being in pain. Once you're healed, nothing's going to hold you back with that attitude."

Ms. Rain led him to a tiny doorway at the end of the corridor that was tucked away behind some well-worn war jackets. She opened the door to reveal a closet of cleaning supplies.

"Start over there and work your way across," she

said, pointing towards the end of the long room. "I want you to dust and clean everything as best as you can. A box of old stamps has just been donated to the museum by a local gentleman. I'll be labeling and putting them in a case around the corner if you need anything."

Doc's invisible wristband faded into a black color as he turned and looked at Ms. Rain.

The band is like nature, because it uses colors and sounds to communicate. We only have to witness and listen. Soon, is speaking with Doc which is why it turned black.

"What does your name mean?" he asked. "I've never met a Nova Rain before."

"I haven't been asked that in years," she said, smiling in admiration. "Everyone looks it up online instead. It means new blessings."

"It's unique," Doc said. "I like it."

He turned around and started reaching into the closet, grabbing a dustpan, a broom, a roll of paper towels and a bottle of cleaner. Then he walked towards the end of the room and set to work, spraying the cleaning fluid onto the glass cases. He left it to soak as he started sweeping. His phone pinged with a low battery notification as he started to polish the display cases, noticing as he did so that they hadn't been cleaned for a long time.

A couple of hours later, Doc rounded the corner and said, "Ms. Rain? I don't mean to bother you."

"It's quite alright, dear," Ms. Rain said. "You've been here for long enough today. Most kids don't even show up. Let's take a look at what you've done."

She followed Doc back to where he'd been working

and took a look over the freshly polished exhibits.

"I've never seen the museum looking this bright," she said, beaming at him. "That's all I needed you to do tonight. You exceeded my expectations. Thank you."

"If you want the museum to stay this clean, let me know, Ms. Rain," Doc replied. "Would you like me to do anything else?"

"That's all I have for you, tonight, dear," she replied. "I'll call you soon."

"Looking forward to it," Doc said.

***

"Brother!" Brooke yelled, her voice hurting Doc's ears as it made its distorted way through the speakers of his mobile phone. "Are you ready?"

"Yeah," Doc said, sitting down on a public bench in the museum's foyer. "I just finished up."

It feels like I'm an exhibit, Doc thought. *Like I'm on display here at the museum. Am I sitting here for the public?*

"I'll be there in five minutes," Brooke said.

"Sounds good," Doc replied, noticing Ms. Rain passing him and standing up. "I'll see you soon."

He cut the call and followed her to the front door.

"I should take a full tour of this place," Doc said as they reached the door."

"We can do that next time," Ms. Rain said, unlocking the door for him. "There are some amazing pieces of history in here. What are some of the things that you enjoy?"

"I can't play anything, but I like music," Doc replied

as a set of headlights lit up the front of the museum.

"I'll call you soon," Ms. Rain said, as she swung the door open. Doc stepped out and she closed and locked the door behind him.

The sound of a car door shutting echoed out from in front of him, and he turned to see his sister's yellow skinny jeans as she walked around the car. A tie-dyed shirt was tied around her waist, complimenting her dreamcatcher earrings. Her ever-curly hair bounced off her shoulders as she ran over to him. Her toe caught on the edge of the curb, launching her right into him. Their heads briefly smacked together as he bent down to grab her. He pulled her up, and she hugged him, both of them groaning a bit as they then rubbed their heads.

"Oh, sorry," she said. "At least I smacked the good side of your head. Are okay?"

"I'm getting better," he said as they walked up to her four door sports-car. As he climbed in, he noticed that the back seat was full of random clothes and paper lunch bags. It smelled of fresh burgers and fries.

"Sorry about the mess," she said, as she sat down beside him and clicked on the interior light. "I need to clean out my car. So, what happened?"

"She wants me to help out at the museum again," he said.

Brooke looked him up and down and pointed at the scrapes and bruises, as well as the bandage on his face.

"I don't mean *that*. I should just smack you up both sides of your head," Brooke said. "I mean *this*. Your accident! You've lost your cover girl flawless complexion. How did you get like this?"

There was a tense moment of silence as Doc considered the question.

“I don’t know,” he said, eventually. “I was texting and driving, I guess.”

“You guess? That’s what people do on a game show. C’mon. Tell me the truth,” she pressed. "I know that it probably won’t help if you’re feeling low, but I love you. I’m going all hot breakfast cereal on you…you know mushy! So what happened?”

“I don't remember,” he insisted. “Honestly!”

“Were you on something?” she asked, looking out of the window.

"No!” Doc insisted. “Why does everyone keep asking that?”

“Because you kept it from the family!” Brooke replied, her eyes cutting across to look at him. “I haven't heard from you for months! It feels like if I don't ask, you won’t tell me anything. You were in an accident and Jimmy said he didn't know how you walked away from it. Would you have called any of us if Jimmy hadn't been the EMT? Are we even good enough for you to call us if you needed to be bailed out of trouble? You’re my big brother, and I’ve always looked up to you.”

She paused for a second to wipe a tear away, but she still had her eyes on the road, as though she couldn’t bear to look at her brother while she talked to him.

“I'm not perfect, just look at the inside of my car,” she continued. “There are things that you don’t know about me, but I want you in my life. Remember when the crystal sphere splashed down and scared me witless? Daddy held me until those men came in the other boat, and you know how things got between me and dad. I only felt safe with you after that. You disappeared a month ago and now, out of nowhere, you're volunteering at some museum!? Like who does that? Dudley Do-right? I'm proud of you for finally looking for work, but I want to know that you're going to keep going!"

"I–" he began, but Brooke cut him off.

"Look at yourself," she said, reaching over and flipping down the passenger-side visor. "You were meant to do something great, not waste your life or have your life wasted in a car accident!"

He looked at himself in the mirror. The tape on his glasses and the abrasions on his face popped out beneath the yellow glow of the lights inside the car.

"What do you want to become? And I'd guess sweeping up around relics was never your dream as a kid." she persisted, wiping another tear from her face. "What are you trying to do to yourself? You need to accept where you are and take responsibility for where you want to go. People think that being uncomfortable is a bad thing. Not many people understand that if we want to develop ourselves, we need to risk being offensive and put ourselves in uncomfortable positions. Ever tried yoga? Talk about some uncomfortable positions. But you know what I'm saying, right? Do you think I'm being mean?"

"No, I think I do need some help sometimes but I am just struggling," he admitted.

She checked her mirrors and flicked on her signals before taking a right, pausing momentarily to focus on the road.

"Gyms are a great example of that to," she continued. "Or even difficult conversations with the people we love, like this one. If you're seeking truth and you're already upset about it, you have to get uncomfortable if it's important to you and you want to find answers. Like you can't be afraid of what other people think. Just look at me. Tie-dyed and dream catchers. At first being different was uncomfortable. But it was me. Now I love the skin I'm in, and my happy hippie clothes, too. So like, if you're comfortable at the gym, you're not building muscle. When you get tired, you quit, but you've already put the effort in. If you give up after doing the hard work, it takes away the reward that you deserved for doing it."

"What do you mean?" he asked, as a puzzled look crossed his face.

"Are all these bruises just temporary inconveniences?" Brooke asked, leaning towards him and pointing at his injuries. "Or are you going to let them take you down? When you look at your face, do you realize what you're looking at? Is that image of you the best that you can be?"

"I..."

"What are you going to do with your life?" Brooke continued. "Believing that you can think your problems away is called depression, and it usually comes with a trip up the old river denial. You have to *behave* your way out of a feeling."

Suddenly, abruptly, she slapped the visor back up in front of him.

"Live a life worth living, brother!" she said. "Your life is about the step you're taking right now. You'll never, ever be stuck in a feeling or situation."

She crawled the car to a stop outside her house and cut the engine, then applied the handbrake and turned to look at him. Then she reached over and hugged him, the tears still in her eyes, and snot running out her nose. As she pulled back, looking him in the eye, wiping her nose with her sleeve, "It didn't get on you. Promise," she said with a bit of her winning smile.

"You're a genius and I love you, Booger," she said, her voice softening to breaking point.

"I love you, Brooke," he said. "I'm sorry for everything."

"Don't mention it," Brooke said. "I'm going to try to be more open with you from now on. Welcome to my crib."

The apartment complex had several units both upstairs and downstairs. Brooke's place was on the bottom floor at the end. She walked over to the door and put the key in the lock, then turned around.

"Stay away from my roomie," she said, unlocking the door.

Doc followed her inside.

The first thing he noticed was a tie-dye blanket which covered the window of the dimly-lit room with purples and yellows. The couch was surrounded by giant beanbags, each of which was a different color. Doc saw an acoustic guitar leaning against a wall and started humming to himself.

"You can go back to Dad's later," Brooke said,

tossing him a television remote. "I'm stealing you for tonight. I told him I was going to. Help yourself to the fridge, the bathroom is right there, and the couch is yours. There's a blanket at the end for you. Goodnight, bro. Don't worry about your ex. She lost a good one."

Brooke walked away down the hallway towards her bedroom.

The lamp in the corner was his only light source. He looked over at the guitar and continued to hum to himself. Then he walked over to it and picked it up.

I wonder if Jessica would have listened to me if I could play, he thought.

He tapped his fingers against the wood of the guitar to make a beat and started to develop his humming into lyrics, which he sang softly to the backdrop of the percussion.

If he was me
If she was me
If I was him
If I was them

Have you been living day to day?
I've seen the look upon your face
Watching our time slip away
Just waiting for you to notice me

You're caught up in a memory
I'm caught up in what we could be
I've heard you say you're not ready
No time for us to be complete

If he was me
We'd make footsteps in the sand
We'd get lost just 'cause we can
Around the world again and again

If I was him
If I was him
If I was him
If he was me

We'd make footsteps in the sand
We'd get lost just 'cause we can
Around the world again and again
If I was him

We'll have too much so we can give
We'll be happy wherever we live
'Cause home is where the heart is
Spending all our time with

My angel in clouds just soarin'
Your hair in the sky just a-blowin'
Looking up at you just knowin'
My heart for you is overflowin'

If he was me
We'd make footsteps in the sand
We'd get lost just 'cause we can
Around the world again and again

If I was him
If I was him
If I was him
If he was me

We'd make footsteps in the tires
We'd get lost just 'cause we can
Around the world again and again
You can't even imagine

He sighed and looked down at the guitar, then leaned it back against the wall. Then he heard a female voice from the hallway.

"Who's that about?" Jessica asked, walking confidently into the room.

CHAPTER ELEVEN: THE RABBIT

DOC'S HEART POUNDED out of his chest as he sat on the couch. He turned his head quickly, knowing that he must have gone red and looking at Jessica's delicately sandaled foot. He didn't dare look up, because he knew he wouldn't be able to speak to her.

The soft tendrils escaping from her ponytail framed her face, acting as the perfect finish to her softly-draped body. The pink silk blouse caressed her over the form-fitting black tights that had left him speechless. He didn't know if he'd spoken to her back at his dad's or whether he'd just passed out when Jimmy brought her over.

"That's a beautiful song," Jessica said. "Goodnight."

Jessica turned around and walked back out of the room, closing the door behind her. Doc fell to the couch, his blank face slowly returning to its natural color. He stared up at the ceiling, whispering to himself.

"I learned that Jessica lives with my sister," he murmured. "Right before…"

His eyes widened as he felt a buzz in his pocket. He pulled his phone out, but it died as he went to answer it.

"I've got to sleep this one off," he muttered, flipping his shoes off with his feet.

Doc pulled his charger from his pocket and stretched over towards the outlet to plug his phone into the wall. It struck him as ironic that he was pouring more effort into plugging it in than he would have if he'd just got up. Reaching over, he grabbed a blanket from beside the sofa. He threw it over himself, ignoring the trembles in his hand from seeing Jessica. Then he settled back onto the comfortable couch and slowly drifted off to sleep.

***

It felt like he'd only slept for a couple of minutes when he woke back up and reluctantly dragged himself off the coach towards the bathroom. Brooke watched him from beside the kitchen countertop, where she was drinking a morning health shake. He nodded at her and opened up the fridge, looking aimlessly for something to eat, and then he went to use the bathroom.

When he wandered back into the living room, his sister was sitting in an armchair and scrolling through her phone. She watched him as he slid his way back onto the couch. Then she stood up and mechanically stepped over to one of the beanbag chairs, before slinging it over her shoulder and then bringing it down onto his head.

"Ow!" he shouted. "What was that for?"

"Just trying to knock some sense into your head. You're already awake," Brooke said. "Why are you going back to bed?"

"Huh?"

"Why are you going back to bed?" she repeated, pulling the beanbag chair off his head.

"I'm still tired," he complained.

"You need water, and I need your help," Brooke said. She was standing with one hand on her hip and clinging onto the beanbag with the other. Brooke's white tennis shoes accented her lavender shirt and purple jeans.

"What do you need me to do?" he asked. He groaned inwardly, wishing that his little sister wasn't so chipper and full of energy.

Why couldn't she have slept in?

"Get in the car," she said, throwing the beanbags back on him. "I've been waiting for you to get up."

"Fine!" he shouted, sitting up on the couch and letting the beanbag flop slowly off his head and onto the floor. "I'm up already."

Doc reached over, putting on his shoes and grunting because he could still feel the bruises from his accident.

"Looking at your hair, I'm just glad I'm not the cow," she joked, as he reached up to smooth down a sprig of hair that was out of place. "Come on, Booger, you've thrown away a million dollars already."

A "Cowlick"

"A million what?" he asked, caught off guard as he fumbled with his shoes.

"Let's go," she said. "Are you gonna let a lady beat you out the door in the morning?"

"Oh, you're a lady now, huh? Well, I'm not a morning person," he grumbled.

"Noooo," Brooke said, laughing at him. "You're just not good at mornings yet. People only hate things they suck at."

"I guess."

"Here," Brooke said, as she feigned throwing water on him then handing him a glass. "Have some water. A lot of people feel groggy in the morning, but drinking a glass of water can make a big difference."

Doc eyed the water suspiciously and then drank it.

"That's weird," he said. "Why is it room temperature?"

"Our guts have to adjust it to body temperature before we can absorb it," Brooke said. "The closer to our temperature the water is, the faster it gets into our system. We should always drink liquids at room temperature when we can, especially in the morning when we haven't had anything to drink for a while. Personally, I think that's how the marketing of coffee got started. Hydration works even though we get adjusted over time to drinking coffee in the morning. It's a brilliant sales model."

Brooke finished her shake and gave him a hug, then took the glass from him and headed back towards the kitchen. Doc watched her go before being distracted by a white glow from beside the wall.

He scurried off the couch and knelt to unplug his phone, which was fully charged. His glowing phone case immediately lit up the bands that were hidden on his arm. Looking over to Brooke to see if she'd noticed anything, he watched her lazily as the lights faded away. Then he rolled up the phone cord and stashed it in his pants pocket.

"Kayden," Soon said, catching him off guard. "My man! I called as soon as I could," he chuckled.

"Good morning," he whispered, turning to an empty room. He watched Brooke walk to her bedroom to get her car keys.

"Did you sleep well?" Soon asked through the earpiece.

"I wasn't expecting to wake up on the couch," Doc admitted.

"You didn't expect to wake up where you fell asleep? You are funny!"

"I'm ready for some changes," Doc whispered, looking down at his phone case.

Brooke came back out of her bedroom and they got into the car. He pulled down the visor and fixed his hair. Brooke laughed at him as they drove down the road and headed into town, eventually pulling up at the Department of Social Services. She cut the engine.

"Go and get a list of where to find free local food," she said.

"Like food stamps?" he asked, a confused expression settling across his face.

"No, not food stamps," Brooke said, resting back in her seat as she cut the engine. "But you'll need a list of places you can get food from if things get tight. The worst-case scenario is that you'll have to ask a homeless person for help, but I'm going to do everything I can to keep you off the streets and going through what I had to go through."

He got out of the car and walked inside, strolling past mothers with children and random men in the waiting room and going straight up to the desk.

"Hi," he said. "I'm unemployed and I was wondering if you have a list of local food banks."

"Sure," she said. As she walked off to find him an information sheet, his wristbands turned black.

"Thank you so much," he said, smiling at her. Then he walked out and got back into the car.

"Wow, look at you," Brooke said. "Seeing you smile for real rather than just seeing your teeth makes a big difference. Are there any food places open today?"

She cranked the car as he looked down at his wristbands, just in time to see them fade away.

"The only thing today is that a church is giving away a free meal," he said, pulling out his phone. "They'll start serving at 217 Fellow Beings Road in ten minutes."

"So," she said, chuckling. "A beanbag chair to the face made sure that you ate today?"

"Yeah," he said, sighing and leaning over with his

head against the glass.

"What's that about?" she asked, turning her head to the side.

"No one's got back to me about my applications yet," he said, slipping his phone back into his pocket.

"Okay," she replied, rolling down the car's windows. "Can you ask the lady inside where that church is?"

"Yeah, I can do that," he said, climbing back out of the car and strolling inside. The woman on reception smiled at him, showing no surprise that he was back so soon, and she was more than happy to help, writing him out a list of directions.

"It's a ten-minute walk away," she explained. "Just make sure you take that second right and you can't miss it."

Doc thanked her again and re-emerged from the building, then jogged back over to his sister's car, which was parked just outside. He reached for the door handle and tried to swing the door open, but nothing happened. He tried again, and his hand slipped from the handle as he discovered that the door was locked.

"I want you to promise me that you'll stay positive and won't give up," she said.

Her brother leaned into the window to listen and looked back toward the doors.

"I'm going to make you do the things you don't want to do so that you'll be the person you want to be in life," Brooke said. "I could watch you struggle, but I could also help you. Will you go on this quest to better yourself with me and give me a positive attitude for a few months? C'mon, next to failure, my offer is looking pretty fly, like my purple pants. I can hook you up with some purple pants, too."

Doc looked at her, gauging the situation he was in, before replying.

"I can do that. No pants, though. Thanks," he said.

Brooke unlocked the car and he got in. As they wound their way through the roads, he started thinking to himself.

What choice do I have? I need to be able to eat. What's my little sister going to teach me? Oh well, if I don't play along with her, I'll probably end up walking.

Several minutes later, they pulled into the parking lot of the church that was serving the free meals.

"I'll be back in a few minutes," Brooke said, dropping him off outside. "See if you can get something to go."

She waved to a few people as she pulled out of the parking lot, still beaming with energy. Doc's wristbands vibrated and faded to black as he listened to Soon in the headset. Turning and walking up the steps, he approached a lady who seemed excited to see him.

"Can I get something to go?" he asked, raising his eyebrows. "I got a ride here."

"Just for you?" asked the lady behind the counter.

"Could I also get some food for my driver?" he asked, his smile feeling fake and forced on his face.

"Sure you can, sweetie," she said, filling up a couple of Styrofoam containers and handing them to him.

Doc walked outside with the containers and sat down in front of the church. There were hundreds of people there eating food, and he was astonished that the church was able to do it every week.

His phone vibrated in his pocket and he reached in to withdraw it. When he checked it, he saw a text from his dad asking whether he got the job at the museum. He tapped out a quick response to say that he was waiting for Ms. Rain to get back in touch with him.

A red sports car pulled in and he stood up and started walking over to it. As he got in, he noticed that Brooke had a familiar-looking bag of food on her lap and that her backseat was clean.

Doc remembered Brooke's backseat being full of the same kind of lunch bag. pg 102

"You can keep the extra food and put it in the fridge for dinner," she said, waving at a couple of people as they pulled out of the parking lot.

"Do you know those people?" Doc asked, opening the top container of food.

"No," she said, smiling. "But I'd hate to build a habit of not saying goodbye or waving. It's my way of practicing, so I never forget."

"Never forget what?"

"So that I never forget that my friendly gesture might be the only kindness that they have offered to them today," she said. "And so that I never forget that they matter to someone, so they should matter to me. At the very least, I can remember the circumstances that they're in, because I could be in them too at any point."

A couple of miles down the road, she pulled over near the ocean. The siblings got out of the car and walked towards the water.

"So," Doc said, as they settled on a bench facing the sea. "What do you do, Brooke?"

"I'm a reseller," she replied, reaching into the bag.

"What's a reseller?" he asked, putting a spoonful of food in his mouth.

"I find deals for things online, buy them and sell them on," she explained, unwrapping her food. "I like to think I'm helping those things live their best life. It's easy to find stuff on clearance and to see if you can make a profit or not. Especially at yard sales or markets, when you're first getting started."

"So, you're like a junkie," Doc said, earning himself a shove from her. "How did you get into that?"

"Before grandpa passed, he took me to auctions with him," she explained. "He shared a few tricks with me, and I taught myself from there."

"Could you teach me?" he asked.

"Yeah, but it'll cost you. Promise I'll always be your favorite sister," she smiled. "But you need money to go to an auction. Luckily for you, Booger, I can teach you how to get it. Anyway, Jessica told me you were playing a song last night. Who was it about?"

"I'm so confused when it comes to women," Doc said, shaking his head. "And I'm so broke that no one will want me anyway."

"You could get any woman you want," Brooke replied. "If you seem uninterested but if you smile just to watch it appear on her face, that is being useful and honest, and you'll do just fine. What separates the impossible from the possible are your skills so, become good at something. Everyone thinks that compliments are the key to finding a mate. That's why they're usually the first thing out of a person's mouth. Instead, try just giving her a smile and saying something true before you cut it short and calmly walk away, leaving her wanting more. Being fun doesn't work but being fun and something else keeps you interesting. Trust me, if you see her all the time, this works every time."

"It does?"

"Yeah," Jessica replied. "Tell you what, brother. I'll teach you how to get all the girls you want if you stay single for long enough to get off my couch. Honestly, I hate to see you like this."

"Sounds like a plan," he said as she hugged him. "Are you a millionaire, Brooke?"

"You say that like you don't think you'll ever become one," she replied, sitting up and grabbing a handful of sand, which she trickled through her fingers and watched as it blew away in the wind. "How's your credit?"

"Honestly, I don't know anything about credit or why it matters."

"The key is to have as much credit access as possible," Brooke said. "Just remember that credit cards are only used for collecting the cashback bonus that they pay out, and not for spending money. You risk going bankrupt if you don't immediately have the entire amount to pay them off."

"I feel like you don't want me to get a job and just start my own business," Doc said. "But I don't know what to do besides work."

"I don't like the idea that you need a job to get

somewhere in life," Brooke said, a small wrinkle forming between her brows. She leaned over towards him. "I own the apartment complex where you're sleeping on the couch. I make more than I need from those buildings. You spent years studying at college to get a job and then got fired from it. What a slap in the pocket book. Most billionaires drop out of college and most restaurant franchises cost the same as college tuition."

She got out of the car and stood up to stretch her legs, then looked out across the ocean.

"You'll need a job to get to where I am," she said. "But you'll also need to do what I tell you. Hey, no eye roll. Finally, it's kid sister's turn to be the boss. And on that note, you need to start building passive income. Because of that apartment complex, I can spend my time here on the beach and still bring home more money than you do, no matter what job you've got. Your school taught you discipline and gave you the core skills and connections you needed to get started. But you won't necessarily make more money because of your education. The truth is something that you mostly have to learn the hard way, and that goes above and beyond what they teach you at school."

"Brooke, I'm just trying to figure out what happened to you," Doc said, taking another mouthful of food from the Styrofoam container. "You're way ahead of me and we grew up together. I want to know how you got here. I missed all of it."

When Doc takes a bite out of the container, he loses sight of Brooke. I wonder if he missed something?

She gestured at the car and they started to climb back into it.

"Don't assume you know someone because you live with them," she said. "People change every day, and only a fool would think they knew everything about someone because they labeled them as their little sister."

Brooke's phone rang and she scooped it up, switching it to loudspeaker.

"Hey, dad," she said.

"Hey," Brian said, his voice distorted but clearly audible. "Did everything go okay with your brother? I haven't heard from him. Did he sleep at your house last night?"

"Yeah," Brooke said, starting the car. "We just ate and now we're heading back to the apartment."

"Alright," Brian said. "I've called him several times and he didn't answer. Is he okay?"

"Yeah," she said, looking over at Doc and watching him scramble as he tried to find his phone. "I'll call you back. I'm in the car. I love you, dad."

"Love you too, Brooke."

Brooke put the phone down and then turned to look at Doc.

"Did you have your phone on you when you left the house?" she asked.

"Yeah," Doc said. "The last time I remember having it was at the church."

He looked down at his wristband, which was flashing white. Brooke glanced over at him.

"What's that flashing on your wrist?" she asked.

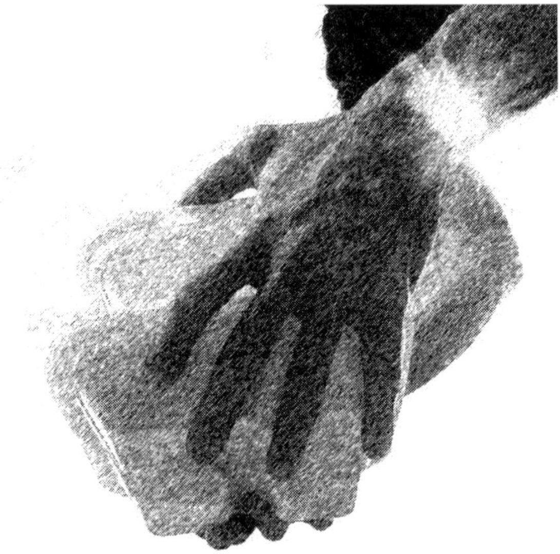

CHAPTER TWELVE: COMFORTABLE

BROOKE'S CAR PULLED AWAY from the ocean's edge and was soon barreling down the highway, skating onto the pavement as Doc's wrist flashed. She looked over at him.

"Seriously," she said. "I'm glad you're back to light up my life and all, but what are those lights on your wrist?"

"I made these glowing bracelets myself," Doc told her, his pulse racing as the panic mounted inside him.

"Cool!" Brooke said. "Can you make me one?"

"Uh…"

"Pretty please?"

"I can try," Doc replied, noncommittally. "Let me set

myself a reminder on my phone."

He patted his pockets but came up empty, then started looking around on the floor in front of his feet.

"Do you think you left it at the church?" she asked. "Talk me through it. When did you last have it?"

"Let me try and remember," Doc replied, stalling for time. "It was… oh, let me think."

A pressure on his forearm caught his attention, and he felt the bracelet growing into his hand, forming into the shape of his phone. While Brooke was concentrating on the road, Doc glanced down and saw that sure enough, his wristband had molded his phone into his hand out of the bracelets.

Doc glanced back down at his phone and directed Brooke to turn as they saw the church looming up in the distance. The car skidded into the parking lot and Doc got out, hiding his phone beneath the Styrofoam plates. The people inside were still serving food as though nothing had changed. Doc took a seat on the steps of the church and aimlessly looked around before glancing towards Brooke, who was sitting inside the parked car.

"What's the problem?" Soon asked over the earpiece.

"I've lost my phone twice now," Doc replied, adjusting himself on the concrete steps. "And it had an orb case on it. I'm worried."

"Remember," Soon said, "only you can see the orb in your Earth simulation. It's connected to your mind. When Jimmy brought it to you, he thought it was a snow globe. The orb will always reassemble itself for you just like you can always create new ideas."

I looked down and watched as the phone case absorbed the phone before shrinking back down around his wrist.

"Thanks, Soon," Doc said. "I was worried there, for a minute. I wish I'd thought to ask sooner about you losing part of the orb."

"Anytime, Kayden," Soon said. "Thankfully, you also have your phone. I'll keep you from flying into the glass as much as I can."

Soon's words reminded him of the story of the humble bumblebee.

Looking around at those who genuinely had less than he did, he realized that while he didn't have a home, at least he had a place to sleep. He touched his face and drifted away into his thoughts.

I'm grateful for learning where I can find a meal if needed, he thought. *I need to be mindful of all the small things in life, more like my sister Brooke. I'm grateful that I'll heal. It's time for me to buck up and be a man. I'll try to be more like Soon.*

As he rose from the steps, he decided to leave the church as a better person than he'd been when he arrived. He thought back to what his sister had told him.

My friendly gesture might be the only kindness that they have offered to them today. They matter to someone, so they should matter to me. I need to remember the circumstances that they're in, because I could be in them too at any point. I need to practice gratitude like Brooke practices being kind.

He glanced around and noticed the lady who'd helped him during his last visit. He walked up to her and smiled, then raised his eyebrows.

"Well, hello, stranger!" she said.

"Hi," Doc said. "I wanted to thank you again for what you're doing. I'm grateful for your kindness."

"You're quite welcome," she replied.

Doc smiled at her again and then walked back towards the car, an idea forming in his head. He could just tell his sister that he found his phone and thank her for putting up with him.

He was deep in thought as he crossed the church, and he didn't notice that a young woman was on a collision course with him until it was too late and she'd bumped into him, unbalancing his trays. They both made a grab for them and stopped them from hitting the floor.

"I'm so sorry," she said, blushing deeply. Doc noticed that she had burn scars on her face, and her embarrassment had turned them even darker. He could tell that the burns were new and still healing.

"No, no, it's alright," Doc replied. "I've got them, thank you."

"Woah, what happened to you?" she asked, looking at my drooping head and my bruised and bandaged face. "You look like you must be in a lot of pain."

"I was in a car accident two days ago," Doc said, smiling sheepishly as I rubbed at the bandage above my eye. "Thankfully, I'm just badly bruised. The airbag pushed my glasses up, and they cut me above my eyebrow. But that's enough about me. What happened to you?"

"I was caught up in a fire a couple of months ago," she explained, laughing awkwardly before continuing. "I get to see people as they are."

She paused, and then tears started to form in her eyes.

"Thank you for treating me like I'm a human," she said. "Accidents happen, but it's hard to watch people's reactions all the time. The burns are still healing, and I'm scarred for life."

They were silent for a moment as she wiped her eyes and brought her breathing back under control. Doc couldn't tell whether it was just the grief or whether her wounds were still physically hurting her.

"People call me Doc," he told her, looking into her eyes. "What's your name?"

"Willow," she replied, smiling innocently back at him. "You're the first person to ask me my name since this happened. Have a nice day, my friend."

"It was nothing," Doc insisted. "Thank you for becoming my friend, Willow. Can I get your number? Perhaps we can have lunch at a restaurant someday."

His phone ejected abruptly from his wristband, and Doc unlocked it and offered it to her. Willow's smile lit up her face, and Doc could tell that she was thrilled as she timidly took the phone and started tapping away at it.

"Keep smiling," Doc said. "It's good to see you happy. Last night, my sister told me that life is all about the step we're taking right now."

Doc, like a bumblebee, brought a smile to "Willow". The willow tree was covered in flowers because of the bees. Everyone teaches the world through their living example, regardless

Willow handed back the phone and Doc took it with a smile. He was still smiling as he left the building.

Waving his phone in the air, he walked back towards Brooke, who was waiting for him in the car.

"I got it, Brooke," Doc told her as they pulled out of the church parking lot and headed back down the highway towards the ocean.

"Soon was right," Brooke said, looking over at her brother as she was pulling out. "You have a lot going for you."

Doc's face remained as motionless as stone as Brooke looked down. There were bands on her wrists, and they were flashing. Doc looked over at her, squinting his eyes and studying her more closely.

"Aurora?" he exclaimed, softly.

"You're sharp, Doc," she said, whipping the car sideways and skidding back off the highway before driving onto the sandy beach. Doc braced himself in his seat as best as he could, holding on to his plates of food.

Aurora stepped into Doc's Earth Simulation to learn more about being human.

"What happened to my sister?" he asked, struggling to maintain the plates as the car accelerated.

"Well, the first thing I told you was not to assume you know someone just because you live with them," she said. "Getting in the car, calling your dad and losing your phone were all just a part of the adventure."

"You mean you've been Brooke all this time?"

"Yes," Aurora said, simply.

She smirked and tugged at the wheel, sand spinning wildly through the air as she steered the car aggressively across the beach and towards the ocean. It seemed to move in slow motion as they turned sideways and slid parallel to the water. A wave slid up onto the shore as the water kicked up beneath the tires.

"Are you ready?" she asked, as Doc watched her hair slowly start to lengthen and turn red as she rolled the window down.

"Ready for what?" Doc asked.

"Hold on," she said, slamming her foot against the gas pedal before gunning the engine and throwing me back against my seat.

Doc glanced out to sea just in time to spot a giant wave approaching them. He leaned towards it to get a better view, and then Aurora's hand pressed against his chest and pushed him back into the seat. Her shoulder slowly sprouted a flower through the lavender shirt that his sister had been wearing, and Doc watched as Brooke's outfit melted into the driver's seat, revealing that beneath the façade, Aurora was wearing a black survival outfit that was highlighted with vivid orange and pink flowers.

She reached down and pulled the stick shift as Doc looked over the hood and saw the massive wave crashing against the beach. Dropping the plates into his lap, Doc held his hands up in front of his face as the car collided with the wall of water. Its roof was ripped viciously away, and Doc felt a rush of air and water across his face. His glasses had fallen from his face, and he had no idea when it had happened.

He opened his eyes and saw that the hood of the convertible was black. At some point during the wave, the car had transformed from a red sports car into a futuristic black supercar. Doc glanced into the rearview mirror and saw pink and orange flower petals collecting together along the side of the vehicle. The engine had moved from the front to the rear of the convertible, and he could see that the grill was wreathed in orange blossom.

"You dressed like your car today," Doc observed as he reached over to grab at the metal roll bar that had formed inside the door.

"It was nice getting to know you for a little while," Aurora replied, as her bright red hair kicked up in the wind. "I'll see you again soon."

The car door slowly started to open, and Doc let go of the roll bar as Aurora whipped the car to the side, flinging him out into a tornado of sand. The plates of food caught some air time and crashed away from him as he tumbled and slid across the shore. A rush of water from the ocean caught hold of him and washed him up on to the beach. He sat up and looked for the car, but it was nowhere in sight. Instead, he watched the curtain of sand and water as it slowly faded from the air that the vehicle had left behind.

Dripping with saltwater, Doc stood up and brushed the excess sand away. He scanned the environment and watched the Styrofoam containers dissolved into the sand and washed out to sea.

In a world that memories can be relived what memory would you travel back to?

"I hope my sister's going to be alright," Doc murmured.

"I'm heading your way," Soon said.

Doc jumped and looked around frantically, not seeing him anywhere on the deserted beach.

"I'm communicating with you over the earpiece," Soon added. "I'll be there in a second. Aurora took you for quite the ride."

The sand next to Doc built itself up into a tower. He watched it solidify itself as a dark shadow condensed from within the sandy pillar. A gust of wind took away the excess sand, revealing Soon standing inside it. He reached up and dusted the last grains of sand off the top of his shoulder.

"How'd you do that?" Doc asked.

"Be the sandman? Kind of like a train of thought but in this case a grain of thought," Soon wryly smiled. "Everything is based on thought here, Kayden," Soon said. "You can do it too, anytime you like. Can I teach you a few things about life?"

It was a rhetorical question, and he didn't pause for long enough for Doc to answer.

"We can never learn what to do correctly by looking at what not to do. Focusing on what not to do to learn is like showering to dry off," Soon said. "That's why I love seeing you follow Aurora's lead, knowing that she's doing so much good. Your Earth simulation will pick up from where you left off."

"I'm still adjusting to how thoughts work here," Doc admitted.

"Aurora's understanding of how to mold her surroundings was keeping you safe when you were with her," Soon explained. "It's all about knowing how to make your thoughts become real."

"You were in a car wreck two days ago," Soon said, putting an arm around Doc. "We're aware that you're still in pain. Even after the talk you had with Brooke, you seem to be ignoring the fact that you're still injured. The throw from the car just now was intense. If Aurora hadn't been keeping you safe, you'd be in an even worse condition. Remember, Kayden, you can create anything with your thoughts and develop an amazing life."

They both looked out at the waves.

"This morning," Doc said, "when Brooke was trying to get me up, I was negatively thinking about how full of energy she was."

"Yes," Soon replied. "Unfortunately, the downside to our world is that if you would have wanted her to go away, she would have. That small moment would have been entirely different. But she does love you, and that's what I want you to remember. Over time, you can learn how to stay positive and how to avoid some things altogether. We're all open to you being you because we see greatness in your future. You already understand that we can get better, so we are all supporting your journey."

There was a pause as Soon took a deep breath and Doc waited for him to say something else.

"Instead of going over what not to do," Soon said, "let's focus on what you should do. That way, you can start growing. Luckily, you're starting over without distractions. Most people are too distracted to see that they're stuck. If we don't examine how we spend our time, we never learn how to make better use of it. Think of a bee stuck behind a window. If it just took a moment to take a look around, it could see that the window is open. Distractions hide in plain sight like a glass window. If only we'd stop for long enough to see them for what they are."

Doc thought about what Soon had told him and took a moment or two so that he could decide upon an answer.

"I'm willing to take steps to be better," he said, watching the light flicker off the rolling waves. "I'm also willing to listen to others with opposing views, but I'll only act on the guidance of those who are doing what I want to be doing."

"That's great wisdom. Otherwise, your guidance turns into blindly following the blind. You're going to do amazing things in your life, Kayden," Soon replied. "Let's go check on your sister."

Doc thought back to when they'd watched his memory of the car accident. The gears started turning in his head as he raised his hand in the air and rotated it backwards, like Soon had done to revisit the crash. Doc's wristband started pulsing in different colors as he looked out towards the water and watched a bird in the sky come to a stop before flying backwards.

Doc is beginning to understand that he can control his Earth simulation

The sand pillar that Soon had appeared from reformed itself and sank into the beach. As he looked down at the shore, a faint cloud formed and started floating towards them. The Styrofoam container condensed back out of the sand as the waves started washing backwards in a mesmerizing rhythm.

The sand and water sped up and collected into a dense cloud as Doc watched the wave that had sent him crashing into the shore. He thought about when he was flying through the air and watched the beach slide beneath their feet as his history floated across the landscape.

The dripping saltwater vanished from his body as they continued to travel back in time. The shadowy figure of his former self formed in his place as a profound sense of wonder passed through him. He watched Aurora's car splash back out of the ocean, and then the passenger door opened up. Doc watched the shadowy figure as it solidified and turned into his former self in mid-air before sliding back into Aurora's passenger seat.

Soon kept his hand on Doc's shoulder and guided them up the shoreline to witness the scene from a better perspective. Doc went into a trance, flicking his wrist as the world shuddered rapidly by, reversing his actual life. He watched the collision unfolding as they walked along the beach. The tide pulled at the vehicle as red paint smeared across it, turning it back into the sports car.

They watched the sand seem to force the tires around in reverse as it refilled the trenches that they'd dug into the beach. Inside the car, Aurora let go of the wheel and put her hands against Doc's chest. With another snap, they flew through the church scene and back to when Brooke and Doc were eating. Doc's eyes widened as he noticed that, from this new perspective, he could see Aurora.

"Here," he said firmly, thrusting his palm into the air as the world stopped. He looked over at his own unsuspecting face, which was hovering over a plate as he got a bite to eat.

"A little further," Soon said. "Let's see what happens."

"At that moment, you remembered seeing Aurora on the dolphins and she stepped through a ripple in your Earth simulation," Soon explained. "You were eating when Brooke stepped toward the ocean. Aurora stepped into your box and ended up driving off with you. Since Aurora was in your Earth simulation and you believed you were still talking to Brooke, Aurora became your sister. Even though she noticed your wristband, it didn't dawn on you that everyone in your Earth simulation couldn't but you figured her out when you both left the church."

Soon raised his hand into the air. Everything began to disappear as a white box began to grow around them. Doc walked over and rested his hand on a wall that had materialized within the landscape. As the white wall hid the ocean scene, his head started to hurt. He couldn't wrap his mind around how complex the artificial world was.

"I'm still adjusting to the idea that what I think becomes real," Doc said. "I'm living in a dreamland. So, is this place just made out of boxes?"

"No, we're not so 'boxed' in. Not entirely," Soon replied, smiling at him. Would you like to see the planet as a whole?"

"Yes," Doc said. "I'd like to know what this place looks like from a distance. Does everyone have a room that just creates their imagination inside it?"

"Mostly."

"Does everyone live in their own boxes here?" Doc asked, thinking about a timeless world. "It seems crazy to stay in a box your whole life."

"Have you ever noticed how birds stay close to home?" Soon asked. "The entire world is free to them, and yet most birds stay in the place they call home. Home is a big world, Kayden. I can see you're ready."

"Ready?"

"Yes, we all want to welcome you to our planet."

CHAPTER THIRTEEN: BELIEFS

IT FELT AS THOUGH Doc was standing in a room made of movie screens. As he watched the ocean completely disappear within white walls surrounded them.

Doc looked down at the sand and felt himself being lowered down onto the solid white surface. The ocean breeze and the smell of saltwater slowly faded away.

"Do you feel ready to see what's outside these walls, Kayden?" Soon asked, looking over at him.

Doc glanced down at his hands and thought about his childhood, and then he was interrupted by the sound of a barking dog. He looked around at the white walls and then made eye contact with Soon. Then he reached further back into his mind and heard the sound of tiny footsteps running down a hallway and getting closer. A small hole appeared next to him, and his heart was filled with warmth as he recognized the bark.

"Bobo?"

His eyes filled with tears as his childhood friend leapt into the room and slid across the floor towards him. Bobo ran over to him and started rubbing his head and his ears against Doc.

"Hey, buddy," Doc said, as Bobo rolled upside down. "Sorry, I don't have any treats.

Bobo sat up and turned his head to the side. A squirrel ran across the room and Bobo whirled and took off, leaping through another hole in the wall.

"A squirrel?" Doc asked, as the hole shrank back and disappeared.

"Bobo must have thought he saw a squirrel," Soon said, stifling a laugh. "And because he thought about it, one appeared for him."

They shared a laugh together as Doc thought about all of the adventures he'd shared with Bobo when he was a kid.

"The world outside of here isn't like anything you've ever known," Soon said, sitting down beside him. "No one here is like anyone you've ever met, Kayden. Everything in your mind comes alive, and that goes for negative thoughts and your beliefs in yourself, too. It's not about what happens to you here. It's about how you react to what happens. Would you be okay with me healing you, Kayden? It bothers us all here to know that you're in pain"

"That depends," Doc said. "What does it involve?"

"Our technology will temporarily merge with you to guide you into reducing inflammation while it heals you," Soon said. "It hurts to see you in bandages and in pain, my friend."

"I'd be so grateful for that."

Soon leaned forward and touched his shoulder, sending a feeling of relaxation through Doc's body. Doc could feel the aches and pains melting away. It was as though the floor was fading out from beneath him, sending a weightless feeling through every cell in his body.

"Take a deep breath and then relax," Soon said. "But don't force any additional air out of your lunges."

Doc did as he was told, closing his eyes, and filling up his lungs before softly letting it go. As he exhaled, it felt like toxic air was leaving his body. He then proceeded to take in another deep breath and noticed he was breathing through his nose and mouth at the same time.

"I want you to realize how calm this place is," Soon said. "Close your eyes and just listen to my voice. Breathe all the way in your belly, chest and head and let it go. Just keep on breathing this way and listen. When we cry our body does a double inhale and shutters our breath in order to calm ourselves down. Anytime you want to calm yourself down, a few deep double inhales followed by a sigh and internally your body will relax."

As he breathed fully in again, the room felt off, and he noticed his shirt loosening over his body. Softly he begins to rest after another deep inhale. He wondered what the bots were about to do.

"Your blood isn't as strong of an alkaline as it should be," Soon said. "Your body isn't used to being full of oxygen. Breathing deeply will bring your oxygen levels higher for a short time to bring you natural healing. Sit down in a chair or lie down and take six deep breaths. It'll do your body good. You can breathe until you feel tingling, and that feeling is your body removing inflammation."

Doc continued to breathe, allowing Soon's voice to wash over him.

"If you're feeling a tingling sensation or differences in your body temperature, that's okay," Soon continued. These sudden differences will appear throughout your body because your blood cells are getting more oxygen in them, which they can carry naturally. Now, take the deepest breath you can and simply let it out and relax without breathing for a couple of moments."

Doc did so.

"Because your lunges are relaxed your heart has more room to move and will begin to beat slower. Your brain doesn't know you have a lot of extra oxygen in your blood so it will send out natural adrenaline and activate your immune system," Soon said. "You have extra oxygen in your body so you will naturally hold your breath for longer than you normally can. When you feel the urge to breathe, take a deep breath and then hold it for a few seconds, slowly squeezing your core. Your blood and spinal fluid should move up in your body and bring healing oxygen up into your spine."

A few seconds passed and then Doc inhaled,

realizing as he did so that he'd gone for longer without breathing than he'd expected. He slowly constricted his abs, feeling blood rush up past his spine and back into his brain, which sent a calming feeling over his body.

"Let your breathing return to normal," Soon said. "Then, when you're ready, open your eyes."

A cold air drifted from Soon's hand and Doc sensed the swelling above his eye starting to fade away. The liquid bots that made up his clothing felt like water across his face as they soaked up the bandage that was over his eye. The feeling reminded him of when the bots had built a glass shield over his face to protect him from the fire. He felt a cool layer of them gliding across the cut above his eye, removing all tension and pain.

Doc opened his eyes, vividly bringing the world back into focus. The world was clear, and all of his pain was gone.

"Thanks, Soon," Doc said. "I've never done that before, and I feel better than I've ever felt.

"Deep breathing is a practice that, when done correctly, can be very beneficial to your mind and body," Soon replied. "Aurora suggests looking up guided breathing on your phone and learning more about how you can practice it. The larger your lungs are the longer you can live. You may not find someone that teaches you all of these steps together but deep breathing and deeply breathing through your nose gives you 20% more oxygen and many other benefits. When you're by yourself at home make sure that you're lying down or sitting comfortably and breathe when you feel the urge to, this is not a competition.

Remember, if your life is about just being happy to breathe, you need bigger aspirations," Soon joked.

"More inspiration and aspiration. Got it."

"There's a natural process that happens all the time in your body," Soon continued, moving his hand from Doc's shoulder and up to the base of his head. "Cerebrospinal fluid runs up your spine to your brain. This fluid passes through four chambers called cerebral aqueducts or ventricles at the bottom of your skull. Your body completes a full circulation of your brain fluids two times every day."

Soon dropped his hand back down again.

"Keep breathing," Soon said. "We're sitting down, so don't worry about the tingling you'll feel as you breathe. I'm going to tell you a secret, and I want you to keep on breathing while I explain it to you. By oxygenating your blood through deep breathing, you teach your cells to get better at carrying oxygen. Hold your breath for a moment, then take a deep inhalation and slowly tighten your midsection. By tightening your lower and upper abdomen muscles, you'll push all of the fluids in your body upwards, including the regular circulation of spinal fluid."

Doc nodded silently but said nothing, a burst of life flowing through his body.

"This cycle of your body's refreshing and newly oxygenated chemistry is healthy for your body and brain," Soon continued. "Your thoughts will be clearer and crisper, and the oxygen in your blood will revive your entire body. I encourage you to remember this and to repeat it to yourself. When you finish, simply let your breathing return to normal. Remember that when you're feeling down, you probably haven't been breathing deeply enough."

As his breathing returned to normal, Doc's mental fog started to lift, and he felt a lot better.

"Wow, Soon," Doc said. "There's so much that I don't know. I have a lot to learn. This place is so advanced. I just healed fully from a car accident in just a couple of minutes. That's incredible."

"What's incredible is your willingness to try," Soon said.

Doc looked down at his clothes and admired the way that they changed in accordance with his thoughts.

"So, is this the oldest settlement anywhere?" Doc asked.

"It's much older than you think, Kayden," Soon said. "I watched the creation of your reality, 13.7 billion years ago. I saw the moment that time and space formed simultaneously for you. It was a spectacular moment and I'll never forget it. I was bringing clarity to Aurora and the other students about how something came from nothing and their interest in finding the truth."

"Soon," Doc said, as the gears started turning in his head. "Considering how old you are, I'd love to know. What are your thoughts on religion?"

"What an interesting question," Soon replied, settling into the conversation. "Life here is different because we don't ever think about death and we don't seem to miscommunicate when we feel and hear each other's thoughts, so let's say this does happen one day though. I see much conflict happen when people are not connected. What actions would I live by? Simply thinking about losing someone here can remove them from our life entirely. The truth always reveals itself over time. Those who truly seek the truth must be open to using precise language, because we're all more complex than we fully understand. It's hard enough that we're all trying to figure out who we are without our ancestors talking to us. We have to take ownership of ourselves and what happens around us, for what do we all believe with more certainty than the nature of our own bodies? When people feel things, such as pain, it's unlikely for them to not accept and believe in what their body is telling them."

They both stood up.

"What you believe is very important," Soon continued, "and faith is what fills our need to be grateful for our existence. Your ancestors dressed the beauty of their night skies with life and gave clusters of stars names and stories of adventure. Naming stars like Polaris, the North Star, gave them the courage they needed to voyage to sea in their ships. These trips often resulted in death, but their discoveries forged a future, and those who survived never forgot who they lost. I've studied all of your world's cultures and know all about the deaths and conflict that have resulted. I've studied worlds without these things, and religion has always been necessary for the development of life. When we listen to one another and learn from other generations, it brings us together. It's when we lose that togetherness and history that we create the grief of war in the first place. Otherwise, war is just necessary survival."

Soon paused for a moment before continuing.

"Some birds can only fly south for the winter, even if there's a storm," he said. "People are more complicated. You can think and rethink and develop your understanding. Your religion and philosophy will determine the focus of your life. Your future depends on your beliefs, habits and actions, and the same goes for the people around you. That's why, in the life that you lived, a weekly or daily study was beneficial to the randomness of your limited existence. The word 'food' is just a word, and it doesn't keep you from going hungry. You don't need to know the name of a flower to know that it's beautiful."

Soon and Doc made eye contact, and Soon leaned in a little closer.

"When you know that the belief that you have means something different to someone else," Soon said, "it can take away from the value that your beliefs can give you. Attaching labels to each other prevents us from seeing that we all just follow what we grew up with and around. Labels alienate people from each other, rather than bringing them together. They create war. It's better to know each other than to not know each other. I'm grateful to be experiencing this moment at all and I believe that discovering the truth will bring us together. I religiously believe that we should all be grateful to achieve what brings us together. In a world like this, your beliefs become real. Do you remember when your suit protected you from the fire?"

"Yeah," Doc said, his head swimming with thoughts.

"Well, it feels like you've finally recovered from your journey," Soon said. "Are you ready to step outside of this room?"

He looked at Doc, who nodded in agreement, his anticipation building.

"Let's go!" Soon said.

The seam that ran between the floor and the wall burst, sending steam out into the room. The cloud spilled over Doc's feet while a clear panel climbed across his face, forming a solid surface. He looked down at his clothes and felt them developing into the next generation of spacewear.

"Remember," Soon said, "your focus is your reality, so be careful what you focus on."

Doc's face felt like it was underwater, so he reached up to touch the hard glass surface that covered it.

"The geo-carbon crystalline structure that moves with your face is as hard as diamonds," Soon explained. "But it moves like an extension of your skin. I love geo-carbon."

The joint where the wall met the floor separated, and the wall slid up and faded to a clear glass. The white ceiling lifted up and away, losing all its color and unveiling the gorgeous beyond. Doc got lost in it, staring at the dancing rays of light that streamed across the deep black sky.

"Woah," he murmured, unbelievingly. "Man, I've never seen anything quite like this."

He followed the amber and purple hues towards a gorgeous sun that was surrounded by a fog of light. They were standing on a flat platform as it slowly dimmed below his feet.

"The room that you've been in is an orbital pod that we brought down and placed on this tower for you," Soon explained. "We wanted to give you the best possible view of our evergreen community. You're so far from your home planet that we wanted to give you a place away from our own civilization that you could call your own. You can travel to whenever you like."

Doc looked towards the edge of the platform, eagerly anticipating the view below.

"Experience doesn't make you ready for anything," Soon said. "Comfort does."

"Why is the platform getting dim?" Doc asked.

"Your face shield is tinting to protect your eyes from what's above us," Soon said.

"Why can't I see your mouth moving?"

"Well, I don't like just mouthing off," Soon joked. "You can hear my thoughts through your headset. Until your biology has merged fully with our technology, you'll have to talk into your headset, but I'll hear you, Kayden."

"I'm just going to run with that," Doc said. "I'm asking a lot of dumb questions."

"It's more intelligent to get smarter," Soon replied. "So, your questions are the answer. Positive thoughts will keep you safe here, and nothing can hurt you. Remember, Kayden, this entire planet is like the room that you've been in."

Then he turned and fell over the edge of the platform.

CHAPTER FOURTEEN: FREEFALL

AS SOON DISAPPEARED from view over the edge of the platform, Doc eased over and looked down, seeing what appeared to be an endless green forest. Lakes and trees danced together beneath the light of the sun, alive with musical energy. The glowing tower that he was on was a seamless block of glass that extended upwards from the lush jungle below. He watched while a cloud of glowing white dust collected around Soon as he fell through the air. His cloak billowed in the wind as the sun flickered across the deep black fabric, highlighting the hidden metallic symbols as he soared through the air.

A cloud of macro bots swarmed magnetically from

the pillar around Soon as he fell towards the treetops. The fog tornado merged with his cloak and grew into a set of wings that carried him over the trees. Feeling inspired, Doc knelt and watched as Soon sailed towards the sun, his new wings carrying him through the air. Doc tilted his head to the side and watched Soon dive into a lake, leaving a mist of colorful waves that formed a decorative mist in the air.

Doc stepped back from the edge and looked out at the horizon. The swaying rays of the sun brought the sky to life. Birds peppered the air and sang to each other like old friends.

Experience doesn't entirely remove our doubts, Doc thought. *Our doubts are traitors for taking the good we would have won by making us too scared to begin. Comfort is the key, and comfort comes from our willingness to try.*

Doc locked his eyes on the edge of the platform and then bent his knees. The platform crawled mechanically up around his feet. He felt his back take on some extra weight and reached around to rub at his new set of wings. Closing his hands into a fist, he felt his wings folding back against him as he leaned forward and broke away from the platform, driving his feet forward as hard as he could and leaping off into the air.

He opened his hands and his body jerked upwards out of freefall while his wings extended into the wind. He saw the different shades of the forest, from the dark evergreens to the lighter weeping willows. The rivers, streams, lakes and ponds added notes of blue, and the sun played across the water and over the landscape as he soared through the air.

He dropped lower and was tempted to touch the tips of the trees as he flew by them. Reaching out, he grazed a few pine needles and smelled the pungent smell of the sap within. A light rainbow hung in the sky. The majesty of the moment compelled him to keep discovering and he flew up into the rainbow. The air tickled around his wings as he dove down and smelled the sweet honeysuckle. He recognized a flock of geese on the lake, which was exploding with life. A few bear cubs were splashing on the edge of a river in the distance. Turning, he spotted a bright blue hummingbird on the skyline. He got curious and decided to follow it into the forest below.

As he touched down in a clearing amongst the trees, the hummingbird flew up close to him and tilted its head. The sunlight on his chest captured Doc's attention as the bird flew closer. He could feel the wind from the hummingbird's wings on his face. The bird circled abruptly behind a tree and the sound of its wings faded away. Curiosity compelled him to follow his new friend.

Doc looked around and saw a beautiful blue flower that was out of place on the tree, but he couldn't see the hummingbird. As he reached for the flower, he realized that the tree's trunk was moving, almost as though it was full of breathing creatures that were running up and down behind the bark.

Prompted by his learning experience with the weeping willow that had changed into a haunted maple, he stepped back from it. Now understanding that the tree was alive, he looked at the flower and then gently slipped his fingers beneath it.

"You're so pretty," he said, feeling movement in his hand as the flower let go of the tree and came away with his fingers. To his surprise, the flower closed and then wings sprouted from two of its petals.

Doc watched it as it stretched into a blushing hummingbird in the palm of his hand. He was lost in amazement to be holding something so tiny, so delicate, seeing its vibrant colors up close. It wasn't just royal blue, because there were elegant iridescences and a hint of green that gave it a beautiful glow.

"Thank you for allowing me to see all your beauty," Doc said. "Come sit with me anytime you like."

The bird lifted its head and hopped a few times before flying away. Doc felt light as he realized how freeing it was to be in a world of pure imagination. The atmosphere in the forest was thick with joy, and it made him realize how happy he could become.

I don't think I'll ever forget this… he thought, briefly.

His wrist flashed back and buzzed into life, interrupting his thoughts as the tip of a handwritten note slipped into view. He pulled it out of the bracelet and picked it up.

I see so many people lose the best moments of their lives, it read, *waiting for a specific feeling to be gone so that they can enjoy the moment they're having right now.*

"You wrote it down so I'd remember," he whispered, a tear forming in his eye. "Thank you, Soon."

As he slipped the note back into his wristband, he felt grateful to be there at all. He realized that there were probably many beautiful things around him that he hadn't yet noticed, and so he let go of the idea of being alone and embraced the idea of how far he could go.

Feeling full of joy, he laid his hand on the tree and heard the deep, rumbling purr of a big cat.

"There's no danger," Soon said, his voice echoing in Doc's head. "And there's nothing to fear."

The tree breathed softly under his hand as the bark became soft and dark around his palm. He looked up at the tree and a black, silky fur grew up around it. There were slow, swelling areas moving below the bark. He couldn't tell if it was the tree itself or a multitude of smaller creatures that had been blended into a single entity.

I wonder if that could be a mink or a ferret, he thought.

There was a crack from the top of the tree, and he pulled back his hand. A chunk of the tree, was growing feathers and forming into a bald eagle, which shuffled to the end of a limb and inspected what he was doing.

"Where I'm from, you're a protected creature," Doc said. "Eagles are the symbol of beauty and strength, liberty and bravery."

I'd love to see you like I saw the hummingbird, he thought, as the eagle dived off the limb and opened its large, feathered wings. *It needs a perch to land on.*

A branch sprouted right in front of him. The eagle flapped its mighty wings and then settled down on it.

"Oh my," Doc said, "you're larger than I thought you'd be."

He slowly and gently reached out with his fingers to touch the eagle's soft feathers.

"May I call you Freedom?" he asked.

The eagle lowered its head and gently rubbed the side of its face against his hand, and Doc took that to be a yes. He sat up and looked into Freedom's bright yellow eyes, and for the first time in his life, he saw the gentleness that he'd always expected to see when he'd looked at photos of eagles. The fear of death that wild animals have seemed to no longer exist.

"Freedom," he said, as he gently ran his hands down the bird's wings, "I hope that when I come back, you'll come to visit me. Thank you so much for allowing me to meet you in person."

Another eagle called to Freedom from overhead, and Doc encouraged his new friend to take to the sky.

"I'll see you again soon," he said. "Farewell, Freedom!"

As Freedom soared into the air, Doc heard the barking of a dog and then Bobo burst through the undergrowth. Freedom's perch turned to mist and faded away.

"Hey, buddy!" Doc said, hugging his beloved dog before rolling around on the ground with Bobo. When he stood back up, he noticed Bobo's tail wagging, and then the dog bounced forward so that his front legs were flat on the ground as his rear end wiggled in the air. He felt a cool air by his hand and looked down to see a bright yellow mist forming into a tennis ball.

"Oh, that's what you had in mind, huh?"

Doc grabbed the ball and threw it into the air, and Bobo immediately took off after it. As the ball flew out of sight, there was a strange noise and then a muffled voice from the fog before Bobo came back.

"Good boy!" Doc said, hugging Bobo before throwing another ball through the air. Curiously, instead of chasing after it, Bobo set the first ball down and barked at a bright pink and orange butterfly that caught his attention, causing him to bound off into the woods.

Pink and orange made him think of the way that Aurora had decorated her car, and so he guessed that she had to be nearby.

He started to walk towards the muffled voice, and then his wristband vibrated. His phone appeared in his hand as he stepped over the roots and watched as the trees thinned out. The tree line opened up abruptly into a gorgeous beach, and his black wings closed up around his face. The feathery cocoon startled him until the dawn fell away like the tower of sand that had encircled Soon. The geo-carbon mask darkened over one of his eyes and he noticed that a bandage had appeared. Glancing around, he saw Brooke, and the tree line sank away into the sand as the

Doc remembers the last time he saw Brooke & travels back into that memory.

scene reset itself.

The sound of the ocean waves lapping on the sand brought his attention towards Brooke, who was sitting on the beach and looking out at the water.

"You're only right if you don't know of any other way," she said, staring out at the sea. The sand rose between her and her brother and left behind a bench. Two plates of food were sitting on one end of the bench, still half full of the free food that the church had been giving away.

"We all learn the right way more than we create it, brother," Brooke said.

He glanced down at the black feathers all over the ground and watched them evaporate into thin air. His phone started ringing and he answered the call as he continued to walk towards his sister.

"Hello?"

"Hi," Ms. Rain said. "Are you free to come and clean the museum tonight? I could use your help."

"Sure," Doc replied.

"Thank you so much," she said. "You did such a great job last time. I'll see you tonight!"

Doc smiled to himself and cut the call, then smiled up at his sister as he returned his phone to his pocket.

"That was Ms. Rain," he said. "I told her that I'd work tonight."

"That's positively promising. You're progressing, and I'm proud of you," Brooke said laughing. "Wow. That came out so pleasingly full of 'Ps'. Maybe because we're all so full of perpetual possibility. Okay. I'll stop now. I promise," she said as he sat down next to her on the beach. "Oh, just one more...can you promise me something?"

"Sure."

"Promise not to quit your job until I tell you that you can," she said. "It's just that I see so many people quitting their job too early. You're taking your first steps on a path to abundance, but you'll need to commit to something if you're to be successful. Motivation comes and goes like any other emotion. You're not always bored or always laughing. Lacking motivation is just a garbage excuse to rest when you're not tired."

"I'm not sure what I need to do to get started," Doc admitted. "I'm lost."

"I'll teach you a few things," Brooke replied, as the two of them stood up. "Go and figure out how to help someone. That's all you need to do. You're focused on your situation right now, but that's what I would have been doing. I've learned that when you ask what people need, you'll start making friends and earning money. If you don't decide on something and see it through, you'll never learn and grow. Instead, you'll just shift around in the sands of time. With the internet, you can look up how to get better, but taking hints for an easier path is a fool's game."

Doc walked past the bench and grabbed the plates of food before getting into the passenger side of the sports car.

"Brooke, did I ask what happened to you?" Doc said. "You're so far ahead, and we grew up together."

She shook her head and pulled away from the bench.

"No, you didn't ask me," Brooke replied. "Mom and dad treated me differently because I was their little girl. One of my great friends is a gold medalist, and she's only in her early twenties. Her parents did something to her that was a lot like what ours did to me. When I played soccer, mom wouldn't let me quit on a bad day. Even when I was frustrated, mom used to tell me that I had to practice anyway. Then, when I was having a good day, she'd ask me if I still wanted to quit, and I'd always say no."

"Yeah, dad was in my life some more after the divorce," Doc said. "It felt like I just did whatever I wanted to."

"The other thing was the strategy," Brooke continued. "Mom used to sit down and help me to figure things out. She'd pick apart my weaknesses, my team and even my opponents. She taught me that success in life all comes down to discipline. I kept trying to figure out ways to make myself better in my life."

She paused for a moment while she pulled into the apartment complex and parked the car.

"For instance," she continued, "all of these individuals need a place to stay, and I'm helping them by providing accommodation cheaper than anywhere else."

"How did you get started?" Doc asked. "What's the first step forward I need to take?"

"Bro, grab a pen and paper," Brooke said, giggling at him as they walked towards the door of her apartment. He stashed the food he'd got from the church inside the fridge, then sat down at Brooke's desk in the living room.

"What did you do today?" she asked.

Umm, well, I got food," he said. "I'm still processing the crazy thoughts about what happened today."

He thought about his flight, the hummingbird, Freedom and playing with Bobo. His eyes glazed over as Aurora's adventure – along with her wild driving – replayed itself in his head.

"I need you to focus," she said. "What are some skills you have? What are all the jobs you've worked over the years?"

"You know about most of the jobs I've worked," Doc said. "I was a scientist, a clerk at a gas station, a server, and a few others."

"Write down ten tasks you were good at when you were working," she instructed. "Then you can figure out which one you can start to make money from. Don't forget crash test dummy, you have this chance right now to make something of yourself. You did just miraculously survive that accident," she teased.

Brooke took out her phone and snapped a photo of her brother.

If there's something on your mind a lot, your mind may be trying to tell you what you should start working towards. Priorities are everything

***

Jessica was looking into an ice chamber with a mouse in it, describing the ice crystals on the mouse's fur as she took down notes. Her phone vibrated and lit up with the picture that Brooke had sent her. She held the end of her pen in her teeth.

Why can't I get this little guy down to a low enough temperature without ice crystals forming? she thought.

Her white, unbuttoned lab coat glowed under the fluorescent lights as she walked out into the hall. Her soft green blouse and charcoal gray slacks framed a petite body. She thought about Dr. Ti, the head of the lab, who she had to report her findings to. Their chances of successfully getting the mouse into suspended animation weren't promising.

She knocked on Dr. Ti's door.

"Jessica!" Dr. Ti exclaimed, swinging the door open from the inside. Come on in. I'm going over your findings."

"Hey, Dr. Ti," Jessica said. "What do you think?"

"You did a fantastic job," Dr. Ti replied. "But I wanted to talk to you about something. When someone's in an ambulance, there isn't much the paramedics can do but drive. Someone I knew died on the way to the hospital, Jessica, and I don't want anyone to ever go through the same thing that I did. I'm open to doing whatever it takes to figure out our next step. Progress is key. Do you have any new ideas?"

"Not when it comes to freezing them," Jessica replied, shaking her head. "Maybe an outside perspective?"

"What's your idea?" Dr. Ti asked.

"Well, my friend's brother is a scientist," Jessica said, holding up the phone to show him the photo. "He might have some new ideas."

CHAPTER FIFTEEN: VISION SEEKING

JESSICA RAN HER FINGERS up the back of her head and fluffed up her curls. She subtly readjusted her lab coat, walked over to the coffee machine and picked up a mug, then read it to herself.

"Clarity comes when our inner voice isn't talking," she read. "Not bad for a coffee mug. I always tell myself negative things in the morning, but I still need to get up anyway."

She heard footsteps from behind her and then Dr. Ti joined her at the coffee machine. His stark white lab coat stood out against his skin. He reached into his shirt pocket for his notepad, made a quick note and then replaced it. His stonewashed blue jeans seemed almost out of place in the lab, but they had the strength he required for a pair of work pants.

"How have you liked being in the lab this week?" Dr. Ti asked as he walked over towards her.

"It's been fun," Jessica said. "I've enjoyed it. But I was wondering, what's the purpose of the cryo research I'm working on? It feels like more than just reverse engineering people back to a living state."

Dr. Ti paused and leaned against the counter.

"Did you know that preventable medical errors are the third leading cause of death in the United States?" he asked. "If we can successfully pause a patient in time, the majority of those errors should go away."

"What do you mean by medical errors?" Jessica asked, selecting a coffee.

"Mostly mistakes by doctors or hospitals," Dr. Ti said. "Or an incorrect prescription. Even unnecessary medical procedures. It ranks just under cancer and heart disease when it comes to the death tolls."

Dr. Ti paused again and then grabbed a mug, reading it aloud to Jessica.

"'I'm probably going to spill this,'" he said. "Seems like a good message for a mug. Anyway, that's why I want to do the best that I can in this lab, every single day that I'm here. I want to save people's lives. One day, our technology will be used during surgery and to transport patients who need immediate attention. It will even take care of the people on waiting lists who just can't wait anymore. Imagine how powerful surgery could be if you could pause a patient in time."

While he was talking, Jessica had been filling her mug with an extra shot of expresso. She slid over towards the creamers.

"Is that why so many people who need help are afraid to go to the doctors?" Jessica asked. "What's this preventable medical problem called?"

Dr. Ti tapped the black coffee button and went for a double espresso.

"Iatrogenic death," he said. "But it doesn't serve a medical institution's interests to put it in plain language so that everyone can understand it. Most don't even know that the medical industry needs help. I'm hoping to get the research from this lab into ambulances and to have patients moved into these tanks."

He gestured to the room behind them, which held a couple of vertical tanks and a small desk.

"One of the goals is to merge these tanks with surgical robotics," Dr. Ti continued. "Once a patient is inside, a new organ or bone will be printed for them and surgically added while they're in suspended animation. One day, people will be suspended in a hospital until the proper procedure is complete in one of these chambers. That's the ultimate goal, anyway. To give people a fighting chance. When patients are given our atomized oxygen, it could deliver oxygen to their brains despite blood clots. It makes large blood cells look like rocks and passes through clots like water."

"I'm excited to be here at the lab," Jessica said, following Dr. Ti towards the tanks.

"So," he replied, laying a hand on the tank, "how do you know the scientist in the photo that Brooke sent you?"

"He's Brooke's brother," Jessica said. "He was working in the lab where my boyfriend works and where the orb is being held."

"Oh, in that case, bring him by tomorrow," Dr. Ti said. "Their research mirrors our own goals."

***

Brooke was fixing her hair in the bathroom while her brother sat at the desk, finishing up the list of old jobs, skills, and hobbies that she'd told him to write out by hand. He turned over the page and made a couple more notes, recognizing as he did so how much he already knew and could do.

His bracelet turned black, and he looked down at his wrist.

"Kayden," Soon said over the headset. "I wanted to let you know that you can send me things when the bracelet turns black. You can add stuff to your bracelet and I'll receive it. Likewise, if you need me to send anything to you, just let me know."

Doc looked up as he heard the sound of his sister washing her hands in the bathroom.

"How does this bracelet work again?" he asked.

"Thousands of bots work together using swarm technology," Soon explained. "The bots are our hope for the future because they can construct and destruct most materials using various building techniques. One of the ways that the bots create is by using electrical currents and welding materials, but there are many others. The bots on your wrist can construct materials with organic and atomic precision as fast as you can articulate it in your mind. Now that's what you call sharp thinking."

"Cool," Doc said. "So the world I'm in right now is fake?"

"It's as real as it gets in the material sense," Soon replied. "You just can't control anything cognitively, only physically. Everything around you is indistinguishable from the real thing when you touch and interact with it, so be mindful of that. Since you're still asleep, we can't risk your dreams coming alive. When you begin to reminisce, you'll have to go back to that created world as well. It's a safety feature to allow your mind to stay healthy and stop any accidentally harmful thoughts from hurting you."

"I'm learning," Doc whispered, looking back at his black wristband. "Thanks, Soon. Is my sister real?"

"Brooke is biologically an actual person," Soon replied. "And all of her cells are functioning. You're living a real life, Kayden. It's more real than you understand."

The black wristband faded away, taking Soon's voice along with it. Doc leaned back in the chair and tapped his fingers on the desk.

"How could something so realistic be created from scratch?" Doc murmured.

Then he sighed and looked towards the door, where his sister was entering the room. He slouched back over the paper and called across to his sister.

"So why am I writing things down, Brooke?" he asked. "It seems like a waste of time. I haven't forgotten any of these things."

Brooke walked over to him and picked up the sheet of paper.

"What was your third skill?" she asked.

"I didn't memorize it, but I know what I wrote down, sis," Doc mumbled, feeling like an elementary school student.

"The greatest inventors, artists, mathematicians, dreamers, authors and minds started by creating," Brooke said, rolling her eyes at him. "The greatest geniuses of history just got their ideas out of their heads. They became famous by remembering their ideas and making their thoughts become real. They assembled their thoughts through the tip of their writing tools. Don't call them unique, because that gives you the excuse to not give back to the world. This pen and paper is your first step to creating anything. I want you to learn that all of their scrapped ideas and crumpled designs are the reason why they became geniuses in the first place. You'll only become as good as what you write down. So, jot those thoughts!"

She slapped the paper down on the desk in front of him.

"It's the act of creating something that makes you into something, brother," she said. "People turn themselves into geniuses by being willing to make a rough draft. You just need to get started immediately and then make your rough draft better."

"I'll do my best," Doc said. "So what do I need to

know?"

"Okay," Brooke said. "First off, be a teacher only when someone asks you, because there's no point teaching someone who doesn't want to learn. Otherwise, just be interested in other people. Never simply do your best. Always do what's necessary."

Brooke paused for a moment and grabbed herself a stool from the kitchen before continuing.

"You're beginning to take control of your life and to remove the feeling of being stuck from yourself," Jessica continued, picking up the page with his ideas on it. "Nothing is worse than learned helplessness. Eventually, we get beat down so much that we give up on our dreams. We learn that we won't ever have the money or the time to pursue them, and that leaves us feeling stuck. By learning there are more options out there, it can teach you that where there's a will, there's a way."

Brooke licked her finger and turned the page, then took a deep breath before continuing.

"Don't do what other people do and just stay feeling lost because you think someone will help you," she continued. "The truth is, half of this is stuff I didn't even know about you. Most people never try to figure life out and they just stay stuck, building their own stockade and confining themselves with one wrong idea built on another. You have to make plans and act on them, otherwise you're just hoping that things will change. Most people never think of using what they already know to make progress, but that's the irony about why our brain remembers. The greatest 'new' ideas in history were just combinations and refinements to existing ideas. True genius is taking two things that already work and making something new. Can you imagine how easy that is? It's like the brookie. Brilliant. The brownie as a cookie."

She laughed and shifted position on the stool.

"Dad's going to get you to stay with him tomorrow," she said. "The next thing you need to figure out is where you want to live out your life."

"I've just got a job," Doc replied. "You're putting a lot of pressure on me. Don't worry, I'm trying."

"I love you, brother," she said. "It hurts to see you like this and I'm suffering because of it, but I'm working through my pain. Help me to figure out why you want to be a better version of yourself so that we can get you there. Why do you want somewhere to live? You were living out of your car!"

"So I'm not a burden to the family..."

"I'm going to keep asking you deeper questions to guide you to a greater understanding," Brooke said. "I learned this from my therapist friend Mike. You should talk to him. We're going to figure out the thing that drives you so we can figure out how to accomplish your vision. Okay, so why don't you want to be a burden to the family?"

"I don't want to see my family in pain because I'm a part of their lives," Doc said, his voice weakening.

"And why don't you want your family to be in pain?"

"Because it feels like I was born by accident," he said. Brooke stood up from her stool and then sat down on the floor beside him.

"Why do you feel like you were born by accident?" she asked.

"Because I don't feel like I'm able to give back to you guys," he said, as tears started forming in the corner of his eyes. "And I feel like I can't help any of you."

"Why do you feel like you can't help?"

"Because I want to help the ones I love," he said, dropping his head. "And I want to help the ones who can't help themselves, like how you're helping me. I don't want to feel like I'll die as nothing more than an accident."

"Brother, look at me," Brooke said, softly. The tears had spread to her eyes, too. "That's your root reason. Most people with kids try to give them a better life than they had, and it's the same with family and the same with me.

The purpose of life is to be happy and to responsibly lead the ones we love towards happiness. You can't build lasting happiness through others or on the unhappiness of others. That would be like trying to build a sandcastle on top of the ocean. And luck has nothing to do with success. Being prepared for an opportunity does. New opportunities will come. You've just got to be ready the next time they do."

"So, how do I feel happy again?" he begged. It felt like he had a watermelon stuck in his throat.

"Start moving forward and building discipline," she insisted. "Let's both make sure that you're growing, brother. I'll have you living at the top in no time."

She reached over to him and hugged him.

"You can do this, big brother," she said. "*We* can do this. I'll be your helper, and I'll kick your butt, sideways, backwards, whatever, when you need it."

***

Cyrus was sitting in his cabin and thinking about nothing in particular when his mobile phone rang. He checked the name on the screen and then answered the call."

"Hey Cyrus," Jessica said. "I just got off work. What's the plan tonight?"

"Seeing you," he replied.

"I'm on my way," Jessica said. "See you in a few. Love you."

"Mmhmm, love you too."

He put his phone back down and closed his laptop, then walked into the large dining room. There were photos of his successes and framed newspaper articles all over the wall. He walked over to one of them and took a closer look.

The photo showed one of his proudest moments as he wore his impressive lab coat and inspected the crystal sphere that was glowing because of the star map inside it. He looked at the orb in the photo.

"I'm going to figure out where you're from," he murmured. "Mark my words."

Then he went into the kitchen cabinet and pulled out a couple of wine glasses.

CHAPTER SIXTEEN: CONSCIOUSNESS

A DING ECHOED through the room and Brooke pulled the phone from her pocket. She took one look at it and then broke into a smile.

"Woohoo!" she shouted. "They're on their way over, brother. I've got to get ready!"

"Who's on their way?" Doc asked, watching his sister's back as she walked away from him and into her bedroom. She closed the door behind him, and silence drifted through the apartment.

"Guess I'll find out soon enough," he whispered to himself.

He looked over at his notes and cautiously tapped

his invisible wristband, looking around as it started to glow.

"Soon," he whispered. "I've got a delivery, if you're available."

"Sure thing, Kayden," Soon said, speaking to him through the headset. "How can I help?"

"My sister got me to write out a list of skills and talents," Doc said. "I wondered if you could take a quick look at it."

Doc folded the paper and placed it on his wrist, watching it get absorbed into his wristband as though he'd dropped it into a cup.

"Thanks for sharing it, Kayden," Soon said. "Let's discuss it when we meet up again. You'd be surprised by how many skills and talents we'd like to learn from you."

Soon slipped the paper back to him and it fell out of the wristband and onto the desk as the wristband faded back into his skin.

Doc tried to process what Soon had told him, replaying it over and over in his mind. An unsettling feeling fell over him.

Did Soon really read the paper that quickly? he wondered. *The paper looked as though it fell through my wrist as quickly as it went in. Did he share it with everyone else as well?*

Brooke's door opened up and she walked back into the room, adjusting her soft blue blouse as she did so. A subtle silver thread ran down her stretch pants. She looked over at her brother.

"Go and take a shower," she said. "When my friends

get here, you need to be ready to meet them."

Doc stood up and walked over to the bathroom, closing the door behind him. He looked in the mirror at his perfectly white bandage and peeled it off his eye, then dropped it on to his wristband, which absorbed it. He stared at himself in the mirror and then looked over at the shower.

Sighing, he turned on the water, which started filling the room with steam. After a quick shower, he dried off and then looked at himself again in the mirror, which was completely clear.

"Hey, Brooke?" he called

"Yeah, broski," she replied, her voice muffled by the door.

"Do you have a magic mirror?" he asked. "Or am I going crazy? Why is the mirror fog-free?"

"No, I don't," Brooke said. "Looks like you're crazy, brother."

"That doesn't answer my question at all."

"Get in here, you goofball," Brooke shouted. "I cleaned the mirror with shaving cream. It makes it fog-resistant. I learned that online!"

Doc tapped his wristband and took the towel away from his waist. Almost instantly, a gray fabric spiraled its way around his body as a new bandage coiled around his head. A pair of comfortable faded jeans closed in around him. While he was admiring the precision of his outfit, he heard the towel hit the floor. He quickly pulled himself together and then scrambled through the bathroom door.

"I see you're healing up nicely," Brooke said,

smirking.

"So who's coming over?" Doc asked uncertainly, sitting down on the couch.

"I got involved with this marketing team a year ago," Brooke said. "And we all make money together. We meet each week for a think tank."

"That's different."

"It's quite common," Brooke replied. "It's the fastest way to grow financially. The more seasoned, the more ambitious and the more tenacious the people in the group are, the better. When you get a group together and they all actively help each other by sharing life experience and ideas, they all grow faster financially."

"I've never heard of people getting together to make money," he said. "Are you guys in one of those network marketing things?"

"That's how we all first met," Brooke said. "We shared the same direct sales company. I made hundreds of new connections with seasoned entrepreneurs practically overnight. I was shocked by how much I learned from everyone. That led me to discover a ton of fun people, and I made a lot of money outside of network marketing."

There was a knocking at the door and Brooke chuckled. Then she walked over to the door and opened it, letting in the four visitors who'd arrived together.

"Hey, everyone!" Brooke exclaimed, exchanging hugs with them while Doc watched on uncertainly. They filed into the room and grabbed chairs or beanbags as though they were already at home. Brooke introduced them to her brother using his old lab nickname, Doc.

Sora was a skinny and soft-spoken girl in a red and white printed t-shirt and all-white yoga pants. She plopped down next to him on the couch and said, "So tell me, what personality type are you?"

Unsure how to respond, Doc shrugged his shoulders.

"I read a book today which said that when we face trials in life, we snap back to our old characters if we haven't grown ourselves first," Sora said. "All that we've created and built could go away in hard times if our character doesn't allow that life to continue. If we don't know who we are, we don't know where we're going. I tell you what, as you're Brooke's brother, I'll get you a copy of the book. It was great!"

"Thanks," Doc replied. "That's kind of you. It sounds interesting, I'd love to read it."

Brooke stepped into the center of the room and gestured for everyone to settle down as they finished gathering in a circle.

"So, I'm super excited my brother is here. This is the guy that I tried all my pranks on, like short sheeting his bed or filling the saltshaker with sugar. And honestly, he's always been a good sport about it," Brooke said. "I want to start this week with a fun speed round. Can everyone share a few helpful tips before my brother goes to work? Let's imagine ourselves starting again at ground zero and share some of the things we've learned. I want us to all toss out ideas to kick the night off."

She paused and looked over at her brother, who was still sitting on the couch.

"So, bro," she said. "As you're the newbie, why don't you get us started? What's something you've learned that could get us going?"

Doc cleared his throat, feeling out of place and uncomfortable from the several pairs of eyes that were fixed upon him. He looked out at the four new faces and cleared his throat again.

"Well, uh…" he said. "A wise friend told me to make notes, not because I'll forget but so that I'll remember."

He glanced over at Sora who was still sitting next to him, then his face turned red, and he stood up abruptly and approached Brooke's desk.

"Would you guys mind if I take notes to look back at after work?" he asked. Without waiting for an answer, he took a pen and pad from Brooke's desk and sat back down on the sofa. He smiled sheepishly.

"Good idea," someone said.

"Maybe he's not at ground zero after all," someone else added. "He wants to take notes. Most never learn that that's the first step towards understanding."

The art of copying doesn't turn information into memory as effectively as using different words to describe the same thing.

"Mmhmm," Sora replied. "I used to remember about ten percent of everything I read. Once I started taking notes, I started to remember over half of everything I wanted to learn."

Doc looked up from his notebook and glanced around the room. They were tastefully – but not expensively – dressed, with kind, open faces and welcoming expressions. He made eye contact with a middle-aged gentleman in a golf hat, who perked up immediately.

"Hey," he said. "My name is Cap. Your sister Brooke told me that you've been called Doc ever since you worked in the lab. Is it alright for me to call you Doc?"

"Sounds great, Cap," Doc replied. "Nice to meet you. So what do you do?"

"I've been in real estate for a while," Cap said. "Doc, let me give you some advice. You have about six seconds to grab someone's attention, so dress in a suit as much as you can. Stay away from the idea of selling an investment and only borrow against that purchase, never sell something that is going up in value because it's working to make you rich. Buy something going up in value until you find something better. A professional is simply someone who's always ready to make progress."

Doc noticed that Cap's orange polo shirt had a real estate logo over the chest pocket.

I have six seconds to grab people's attention, Doc thought, as he scribbled away in his notepad. *Wear a suit and stay prepared.*

"People are everything," Cap continued, "so join some country clubs and attend some seminars because the people in the audience are just as valuable as the speaker. Hang out with people that have deep pockets, because your peers rub off on you. When you're getting started with real estate, be picky about your roommate but rent out an extra room rather than filling it with junk. A room costs you money you could be earning each month and making more money is usually the problem and not where can one save more money."

"Thanks," Doc said, making a mental note to join the local country club as he continued to scribble away in his notebook.

A light round of applause echoed out around the room, and Brooke plopped herself down on a beanbag.

"Thanks for making it this week, Cap," she said. She turned slightly to look towards a dark-haired man with a clean-shaven face. His salt and pepper hair made him look distinguished. "Mike, what do you have for us?"

Mike stood up and introduced himself, then turned to look around the group. His blue and white checked shirt and jeans made him look dapper and approachable.

"I'm a therapist," he said. "This week, in our group lesson, we talked about how identifying our feelings can help to calm them. We've found that being able to identify emotions helps us to understand them and to resolve them internally. Otherwise, our unknown feelings control us. Emotional intelligence is far more important than IQ. The goal is to listen to other people and to get answers from them. Most of us are so eager to interrupt that we don't listen."

Doc wrote down that understanding someone's emotions, listening and getting answers was more intelligent than revealing how much he knew.

"There isn't a cut or bruise that's shaped the same," Mike said. "So when it comes to experiences with life, it's impossible to predict what someone's going to say or what they're going through. The greatest art is recognizing that pain is unique and that emotions affect everyone differently. Every challenge is unique, and listening with fresh ears and seeing with fresh eyes will allow us to better understand things. And remember that just listening to someone allows them to trust you."

My sister and I need to talk, Doc thought, as the pencil flashed across his notepad. *Pain is unique to everyone. Taking time to learn about people helps you to gain trust. Knowledge and understanding comes from being interested in others.*

"Sora," Brooke said, looking toward the couch. "Any thoughts?"

"Sure," Sora said, tilting her head as she responded. "Well, create a venue to advertise so you can entice people to come and talk to you. Busy people always enjoy free publicity, like podcasts. When it comes to maintaining success, I'd say to never share your doubts with anyone. Doubts are for others to give out, but you should never say them yourself. Criticism helps people to improve, but doubts are invisible viruses that grow over time and destroy integrity and ambition. Solve problems and work on issues, but never share doubts."

I need to create a venue to get publicity, Doc wrote. *Never share doubts about anything because the wings of birds are made of ambition and doubts cause the wings to hesitate. Uncertainty can cause a bird to fall from the sky, but a guided descent gives it a chance to fly again.*

There was a murmuring around the room as people agreed and reinforced what Sora had said.

"Kai, homie, what do you have for us tonight?" Brooke asked.

Kai was a skinny man in a dressy, soft yellow shirt and charcoal grey dress pants. He'd been sitting in the corner, but he quickly perked up when Brooke mentioned his name.

"Success is built over time," Kai said. "Losers never smile and don't know happiness is a practice, so take something from failure so you can win the next time. Gifts are only temporary and giving lasts forever. Always act like you're just practicing, and keep your chin up even through hardship. Teach yourself that the past is something you learn from but not a place to live. Never lightly lie to yourself but always talk like you've already succeeded, so you shine your positive vibes throughout your day and stay focused. Failure and criticism are the first signs that you're working towards success. Remember why you got started and practice walking every day until you just naturally start running."

Doc looked at his sister with admiration and then read his notes to himself. *Keep your chin up and act like you're succeeding and success will find you. Happiness is a skill we get better at giving, any that we receive is only temporary. Talk as though you've already accomplished your goals and that will lead you to success, because actions follow beliefs and understanding. Stay focused on your one outcome and know that failure and criticism are the first signs of taking the road to success that many never travel.*

"Thanks for sharing, everyone!" Brooke said, smiling gleefully. "I'd just like to add my own advice, which is to always look for ways to make moments more magical. That's why I made everyone these buttons."

She climbed up from the beanbag chair, reached into her desk drawer and pulled out a handful of golden lightning bolt pins. She started handing them out to everyone and was just making her way towards her brother when an alarm went off on her phone.

I need to always look for ways to make the moment more magical, Doc thought, glancing down at the paper and scribbling some more notes onto it.

"Is it that time already?" Brooke asked, laughing and silencing her phone as she did so. "It's time for you to go to work, bro."

Doc nodded and then looked around the room.

"I wish I had more time to get to know you all," he said, glancing down at his invisible wristband. "Thanks so much for sharing your knowledge. I hope I remember it."

Doc folded up his notepaper and waved goodbye to his new friends before exiting the apartment and secretly tapping the folded paper against his wristband, watching as it dissolved and disappeared. He took a second to admire the lightning bolt pin and then he dropped that into the wristband, too.

The sun was slowly dipping down in the sky as he weaved his way through the cars that were parked outside Brooke's apartment. The museum was on the other side of the street, and it only took him a couple of minutes to walk there, admiring the night sky and spotting a few stars as he did so.

"First impressions are key," he whispered to himself, when he reached the museum and knocked on the door. "Those people are on a whole different level.

If I hang around them enough, I'll become as smart as they are. After all, we all started out as babies."

Ms. Rain opened the door and led him out into the museum. A cool breeze flowed down the hall as he walked over to the broom cabinet and pulled out the equipment that he needed. While he was cleaning, Ms. Rain bustled around him, reorganizing some of the exhibits. The ambient silence was broken only by the swishing of the broom throughout the museum.

When they were done, she called him into her office, circling her desk and pulling out a drawer before handing him an envelope.

"You've done another excellent job," she said. "I've got something for you. How far away is your dad's place?"

"I'm living with my sister now," Doc replied. "In the apartments across the street."

"Oh, that's convenient," she said, walking him to the door and pointing out a few of her new exhibits as she did so. "I'll see you tomorrow night."

Ms. Rain locked the door behind him, and he took a couple of steps away from it before opening the envelope to find a handful of dollar bills. He sighed with relief as he crossed the road and walked into the apartment. Once inside, he sat down on the couch, exhausted. Then he grabbed a blanket that was lying on the couch and tossed it towards his feet as he relaxed into the cushions. Lying down in a cocoon of warmth, he closed his eyes.

***

DOC'S PERSPECTIVE

I felt a soft surface cover my face as I curiously opened my eyes, but I couldn't make anything out in the blackness. I felt worry sweep through me as I struggled to move.

"Brooke, what are you doing?" I gasped, confused.

A deep rumble shook its way through me as I jerked and fought to sit up.

"Brooke, this isn't funny," I urged, finally pulling my hand up and pushing the dark material away from my face.

My hand forced a dark, feathery cocoon to open up. I realized I was lying on a beach, trying to map out where the rumbling sound was coming from as it continued to grow louder. In the distance, I could see palm trees falling over along the seashore as something massive crept along towards me.

CHAPTER SEVENTEEN: NEON

MY EYES WIDENED as the blanket from Brooke's apartment turned into a pair of black wings. I remembered where I was, but I still didn't know what was in the trees and coming after me.

"Kayden," Soon said via the earpiece. "It looks like you've got company."

I looked back at the shoreline and saw that the trees were being ripped from the ground and flung through the air. I leapt to my feet and started sprinting down the beach under a crisp twilight sky. Reassessing what was going on in my head, I felt the tug of my black wings. I was having trouble figuring out an answer to an important question, which was,

"What's going on?"

Behind me, I heard the snapping of timber intensifying as I turned and watched clusters of giant palm trees being thrown into the air. Their leaves scattered in the wind as the palms created geysers of water far off in the ocean. Light flickered within the tree-line, outlining the trees as embers snapped through the forest.

A massive metal hand sparked and clicked as it moved smoothly over the ground, folding the trees over onto the beach. Standing there, motionless, I could only imagine the rest of the giant being. I watched as the hand reached out of the darkness and drove its fingers into the sand, scooping up the area I'd just been lying on. Trails of sand ran between the mechanical hand's fingers as it disappeared back into the forest, leaving a thick silence in the air.

"Monty didn't scare you, did he?" Soon asked over the headset. My head replayed the giant iron hand knocking over the trees.

"I, uh–" I began, still stunned. "I was getting out of the way. I didn't know what was happening. Trees were flying through the air. Look, there's a lot of damage."

Then I remembered the rich experiences I'd had with the hummingbird and Freedom. I had to trust that they were safe.

"Monty is an inventor," Soon said. "He enjoys creating larger-than-life structures to push the limits of the materials we have so that we can challenge what's possible. Monty was going to move you away from the rain that was headed your way. Around here you never know what can happen with foul weather. It could start raining chickens," Soon chuckled. "None of us knew how long you were going to be there."

A rustle in the tree-line sent a few bright lights into the sky. I watched a flock of glowing white birds as they took to the air. Listening to the birds as they talked to each other, I heard a deep rolling thunder in the distance.

A bright white fog crept through the trees as neon lights zipped down from the pale gray clouds above. The rain brightened up the twilight air with flashing threads of color as it fell like a stringed symphony. The luminous fog thickened across the ground and covered the jungle floor, slowly approaching me from the heart of the grove. I watched the splintered fibers of the broken trees as they reorganized themselves and lifted the fallen timber back upright. I realized that the fog was healing everything it touched, and I admired the care that the forest was getting from mother nature.

I started jogging down the tropical seashore as the fog poured out over the coast from the tree-line beside me. As I picked up speed, my wings curled tightly against my back, motivating me to run. I looked out across the shore and memorized the shape of the waves as they climbed out of the ocean and up onto the sand. Leaning into my stride, I watched the landscape whisper past in a blur as a supernatural rush of air riffled through my wings. The trees vanished beside me as the landscape became a grassy plain. I slowed my pace, taking in the stars as they flickered over the ocean.

A few mounds of sand slid out from under the waves and across the shore in front of me. I slowed as the small lumps in the sand moved next to me and held my attention. The egg-sized balls of sand curved and started circling as I stopped and knelt to inspect them.

I found myself looking at a few small fish made out of sand, wriggling along the beach as though it was a pond. They started jumping off the surface of the beach and then returning as though the shoreline was a fluid.

I held out my hand and a sandfish jumped into it, disintegrating back into the sand that it had once been. My dark, feathered wings extended out and lifted me to my feet with a gust of air as I tapped my wrist, turning it black.

"Soon," I said over the headset, as I watched the fish swim back into the ocean across the sand's surface. "Am I going crazy, or are there some fish made out of sand swimming around?"

"There's much to discover in a world of pure imagination, Kayden," Soon replied.

I turned around and could see how far I'd come from the storm, which seemed to be miles away.

"So is everything connected here?" I asked, continuing my jog.

"Back where you were from," Soon said, "it took thousands of people to create a world around a person. Here, however, thoughts form instantly around us and allow our remarkable differences to shine through. We each shape our surroundings individually, rather than our surroundings shaping us. It's like donut theory. You can't see anything on the inside, but it's the inside that creates and shapes the outside. You could say we live in a very wholesome way."

"So what are the limits of this world?" I smirked, as I continued to advance along the shore.

"That's a great question," Soon replied. "What are the limits to this world? Well, you've heard of a date with destiny. It's one you can't miss. And it's your turn. It's your destiny to discover limitations."

As I looked out over the ocean waves beneath the starry sky, a giant blue whale leapt out of the water. My wristband faded away, but I was too spellbound by my surroundings to notice.

A splash filled the air as the whale fell back into the surf. The water faded and took on every color imaginable. I noticed a glowing rainbow ripple its way across the ocean surface. Overwhelmed by wonder, I stopped and plopped down in the sand, whispering to myself, "What a marvelous world."

I studied the water and realized that the speed and direction of the waves determined their various colors. The waves slid up on the shore with a twinkling effect before turning blue again and fading away in the ocean.

That was the most beautiful thing I've ever seen, I thought.

Another whale leapt into the air, a dance of sparkling color decorating the starry sky as my eyes drifted down the coast. I noticed a white baby turtle looking up at me. The turtle had a black ring on the top of its shell and it seemed to be investigating me, curiously.

I looked over at the water and saw the whale leap up and fall back into the ocean. My heart rate shot up as I looked to my left and saw myself. I was standing there and watching the whale leaping out of the water. I couldn't believe my eyes.

I look so tall, he thought. Am I having an out-of-body experience?

Cold chills raced across my skin as I watched myself lumbering across the beach towards me. The other me plopped down right next to me and I saw that I was almost ten feet tall, even though I was only sitting down. My vision switched so that I was looking back at the turtle and I paused, just staring at it. Then my vision switched again and I was looking up at myself from across the sand.

It was only then that I realized that I was looking out through the turtle's eyes. I saw the colorful ocean and then gazed back upwards at myself. Then I looked back down at the turtle's head and watched the little guy looking across at the sand.

I'm swapping vision with a turtle, I thought.

Then I looked out at the water and whispered, "Everything truly is connected here."

I was unable to contain myself, so I tapped continuously at my wrist and shouted, "Soon! Soon! I just looked through a turtle's eyes!"

"You just looked through a turtle's eyes?" Soon repeated. "Tell me more about your experience."

"I was running across the beach," I explained, "and

a whale jumped up and crashed into the water. The stars don't feel out of reach. The blue whale was dressed in wonder and the blue sunset sky framed the spell I was under. There was a healing fog in the trees behind me, and then I randomly found this turtle, just looking out at sea. My imagination is on fire because I'm connecting with all this on my own. I'm at a loss for words. This world transcends everything I've ever known."

I looked out at the stars, staring at the rainbow as it hung above the ocean.

"Very poetic, Kayden," Soon said. "Your suit is giving you a taste for what it's like to be connected to this world from inside your helmet. Here, you can be a part of all the life that there is, using another pair of eyes like a virtual-reality headset. Everything is connected at a level that goes far beyond sight. However, you're limited by the connection in your suit. Your brain is very different to a turtle's brain, but through our technology, we can experience life through animals and others as well, far beyond just sight."

If you could feel and see the world through an animal, which animal would you want to become? Are the people here meeting him through the animals?

"Thanks for listening, Soon," I replied. "I wanted to know I was thinking clearly."

I watched the wristband fade away as I dropped my hands and rested on the sand. I couldn't see the turtle anywhere, so I reset my gaze over the ocean. Lying back in the sand, I took a deep breath and

started to sing as the emotions poured out of me...

"Mist at my fingertips, sending me round and round, just wow.
Looking at these stars tonight, I wonder where you are right now.

I'm surrounded by sand with my mind only interested in the past.
Looking up from right here, I see the stars through my face of glass.

You've got me entranced and you're miles and miles away tonight.
I'm alive with pain right now so I don't forget what I want in time.

I may just be as alone as a star in the sky.
However, being alone is good, so I'm wondering why.

Why do I insist the company of the stars isn't enough?
Their beauty so majestic, their beauty so untouched.

The cool air blows the sand right here in front of me.
I feel peace and calm in all the colors that I see.

My heart has blown wide open, my past has led the way.
To a future that I love far more than the gone of yesterday.

Do I need to seek shelter out of the neon rain?
Or do I need somebody to hold through the suffering?

The feeling I have, I now see isn't loneliness.
No, I'm missing you for not seeing all of this."

I'd stood up during the song, and once it was over, I let out a groan and fell to my knees, starting to weep. Overhead, lightning rumbled through the cloudy sky. I fell on to my side and started to sink into the sand.

As I stared at the waves, I saw a large object flying towards me. It pummeled into me and formed a blob around my entire upper body.

CHAPTER EIGHTEEN: BILLIONAIRE SECRETS

THE OBJECT came down again with a boom.

"Get up, brother!" Brooke blared, lifting the beanbag off Doc and hitting him again as he waved his hands in the air in surrender. *Wham!*

"I'm up," Doc muttered, scrambling to put some words together. "I'm up!"

"You're lucky I had a plan for you today, so you're not just stuck here at the apartment living your life like a lost breakfast, just waffling around doing no one any good," Brooke said, giggling at him as he swatted at the air. She tossed the beanbag next to the couch. "Let me get you some water. You'll be ready to go in no time."

"I was having an amazing dream," Doc murmured, his voice trailing off as he had an epiphany.

Dreaming and daydreaming could be the way I switch between worlds, he realized, smiling gratefully as he received the glass of water that Brooke had brought for him.

"Do you remember Cap from yesterday?" she asked.

Doc pictured the people he'd met the night before, but he drew a blank. He looked down at his wrist and tapped it a couple of times, eventually saying, "I remember the guy in a golf cap and an orange shirt."

"Yeah, that's him," Brooke replied, moving over to the blender and opening it up. "He wants to meet you this morning."

What did Cap teach me yesterday? Doc thought, and then a slip of paper slid out of his wrist. He read it to himself while Brooke added some fruit to the blender and then secretly returned the paper to his wristband.

"Cap was the real estate guy who talked about first impressions being important," Doc said. "He also mentioned that we tend to act like the people we spend the most time around."

"That's right," Brooke replied. "Your memory is better trained than I thought. I'm proud of you."

She turned the blender on, and Doc waited for the blades to stop whirring before he continued.

"What's a trained memory?" he asked.

"Everyone could have a photographic memory if they just learned how to use it," Brooke said, pouring her smoothie into a glass.

"Go on," Doc said, perking up a little as she tasted her smoothie.

"Be patient!" Brooke said, holding her finger in the air and taking a swig from her smoothie. "Cap will be at the golf course. Let's get you ready to go right now. Since you asked, when I drive you over to your meeting with Cap, I'll teach you how to start developing a photographic memory."

Doc pulled himself to his feet and went through to the bathroom, leaving the door open as he looked at himself in the mirror. The oil across the lenses of his glasses was frustrating, and so he pulled them off and cleaned them on his shirt. Then he glanced down at the taped hinge and called out to Brooke, saying, "It doesn't feel like I got enough sleep. I feel so groggy."

"You slept for ten hours," Brooke reminded him, walking over to the open door of the bathroom. "You have to get up at some point today. You're probably just struggling with your new schedule. The good news is that those groggy feelings will go away in time if you get on a healthy schedule."

"Well, hey," Doc said, turning towards his sister. "Do you know any ways to feel less sluggish in the morning? You always seem to wake up faster than I do."

"You're changing your schedule and adjusting," she said. "It's okay to feel slow to begin with. Change and struggle are an important part of growing. But since you asked, I'm going to tell you, though your nervous system is about to hate me. A simple trick is to leap out of bed. Just by rushing yourself to get ready, you'll wake yourself up in a couple of minutes."

She reached over to the faucet and let the cold water run over her hands for a while before lightly flicking some into her brother's face.

"Ah, Brooke, come on!" Doc protested. "What was that about?"

"A cold shower is wake up power! You're awake now, aren't you?" she said, cutting off the water and tossing him a towel.

"Yeah," Doc admitted, burying his face in the towel to stop himself from starting an argument. "Now I'm awake."

"I told you that you'd hate me," she said. "I just used the shock of the cold water to activate your fight or flight system. If you're feeling tense, it's because your body thinks it's under attack. And as your sister I claim my right to gently attack to keep you on track. And you can use the attack any time you need to trick your body into being more awake. Being dehydrated and having low oxygen levels is partly why you're groggy."

"I've heard something like that before," Doc said, taking several deep breaths. He shook his head and closed the bathroom door before looking back at himself in the mirror. He glanced first at his wrinkled shirt and then at his wristband. Extending his right hand across his body, he grabbed his left wrist and a thick vapor flowed between his fingers. The mist ran up his arm and solidified into an aqua blue fabric. It wrapped itself around his body and formed into a shirt with a button-up collar.

Doc gasped and took off his glasses, then raised an eyebrow as he tapped the taped hinge of his glasses against the wristband. The tape dissolved away and when he looked at them again, his glasses were as good as new.

He put them back on and tucked in his new shirt. Then he leaned into the shower and added a dab of conditioner into the palm of his hand. He ran his fingers through the water in the sink before pushing them through his hair to slick it back.

"I have to do the best I can to make a good first impression," he said, before exiting the bathroom.

***

The morning light shone through the stained glass on the wall next to Jessica. She rolled over and felt a warm spot where Cyrus had been. Shocked, she realized that she must have fallen asleep while the movie was playing. She was glad to see she was still dressed.

Cyrus was cooking up breakfast in the kitchen when Jessica snuck past him and into the bathroom. The cottage wasn't far from town, but it was tucked far enough away that it avoided the worst of the traffic. The birds outside were zooming through the yard and the smell of breakfast was floating through the house.

Jessica had just returned to the bedroom when Cyrus abruptly leaned his head through the door to check on her. He was holding a pan out of view and teasing Jessica by asking, "Where do you think you're going?"

"What are you doing?" she said, replying with a question of her own.

"I'm making breakfast for you to eat in bed," he said, leaning back into the kitchen and out of view. "But you can't have breakfast in bed if you're standing up, so get back under the covers."

Jessica smiled mischievously at him before crawling back into bed while Cyrus clinked and clanked in the kitchen. Before long, he was bringing a steaming tray of eggs and toasted bread into the room and presenting it to her. She didn't know what to say, but she felt blessed and frustrated at the same time.

How did I get so lucky? she thought, looking at the tray and the plates that he'd put on the bedside table. Cyrus scooched down beside her and the two of them started to eat.

"Hey," Cyrus said. "Do you remember last Halloween, when we met each other at my lab?"

"Yeah," Jessica replied, playfully. "I remember. You were acting like a bigshot, telling me how the lab's funding came from donations from people who wanted to see the orb that fell from the sky."

"To be fair, it was my job," Cyrus protested. "Remember? We were doing a Hallowe'en tour, letting people see it from the viewing hallway. I got the chance to hang around all day, mingling with people and checking out their costumes. I'll never forget that outfit you were wearing."

"I remember it too," Jessica replied. "I was finishing my last semester of college and interning at another biotech lab. I didn't know who you were beneath your mask."

"Just goes to show that you're with me for my brains

and not my beauty," Cyrus said.

They were teasing each other, but they were also happy. It was the first time they'd officially spent the night together, and they laughed over the rubber eggs that Cyrus had cooked for them. It was a trial run of spending a full day together.

So far, so good.

***

"Good morning, Kayden," Soon said, after Doc tapped his wristband. "What's happening?"

"I'm heading off to meet Cap, a real estate billionaire, at the golf course," Doc said, pulling the Styrofoam plates out of the fridge. "I've never played golf before, so I was wondering what my options are."

"Let the master be the master," Soon replied, "the less you speak, the more you learn. The best way to boost your communication skills is to use their language, rather than to understand with your own. You can improve rapport by asking people questions using two or three the words they just used, because it shows you're listening."

"It does show I'm listening. Thanks, Soon," Doc said, cutting the communication and leaving the apartment before getting into his sister's car.

"So, Brooke," he said, as he settled into the car. He clicked his seatbelt in and laid the plates of food on the floorboard between his feet. "A photographic memory can be a learned skill?"

"You'll shutter at how easy it is to learn," she

replied, as she drove them towards the highway. "Most of us just don't know it. We have problems remembering names, but for some reason, faces are easy. That's because we're wired to remember images and patterns, not letters and numbers. They're just the tools we use to communicate. Our brains weren't built for letters and numbers. We've evolved to learn through images and interactions, not books and numbers. Once you turn those numbers and letters into a movie that plays in your mind, you'll be able to remember ten times as much information instantly."

She paused for a moment as she reached the highway and the car merged with the other traffic.

"Having a photographic memory is easy. It's all about focus," Brooke chuckled. "It's as simple as that," she continued. "For example, instead of a list of three things like eggs, socks and coffee, imagine those items as body parts. You'll never forget your grocery list again. If you imagine that your head is made from eggs and you have socks on your hands while holding cups full of coffee, you can dramatically improve your chances of remembering it."

"How come?" Doc asked.

"I'm getting there," she replied. "All of a sudden, you have that wild image with you as you walk around the store, and you can instantly remember everything on your list. The key is to imagine strange things, though. Wearing socks and holding coffee is something you've seen before, so you're more likely to forget that. The funny thing is that your body has an almost unlimited amount of potential. Thinking in pictures and not in words is the first step towards creating a photographic memory. I'll teach you more some other time."

She clicked her signals on and pulled off the highway, then navigated along a winding driveway through some trees. They parked up and walked onto the green.

Glancing around as they saw the other golfers, Doc realized that his sister looked very professional. Her crisp yellow blouse, navy slacks and tennis shoes made her look like a businesswoman. She wasn't his little sister anymore. Cap was on the green and lining up a shot.

"Fore!" echoed through the air as a whipping sound zipped across the golf course.

"Looks like it's cutting to the left," Brooke called, watching the ball sail through the air. "I got Doc up earlier than he's used to, but he's here in one piece. I've got places to be, though. I'm going to leave you two alone."

She hugged her brother and added, "Love you. Call me later."

They turned to watch her as she left them on the links, waving with enthusiasm as she disappeared.

"So, Doc," Cap said, looking over at him. "It looks like I've got you as my caddie for the day."

Doc was still holding his food trays, and so Cap waved for a man in a suit to come over and take the plates from him.

"Would it be too much trouble for you to take my friend's dinner containers to the fridge in the country club kitchen for him?" he asked.

"Not at all, sir. I'm all for keeping things cool and chill," the butler replied, taking the plates from Doc and setting off towards the building. Cap watched him go before sliding his club back into his golf bag.

"I'm so proud of Brooke," he said. "I taught her how to get the apartment complex, and now she's making $50,000 a month. I guess you're here because you want to do the same, right?"

"That would be nice," Doc agreed, looking out over the golf course. Cap gestured for Doc to take the clubs and then led him over to a waiting golf cart.

"Kayden," Doc heard, as Soon's voice filtered in over the headset. "I wanted to let you know that you can record audio with your wristband and that it can also take notes for you.

"You're the best, Soon," Doc muttered, as he tossed the golf bag over his shoulder. "That sounds like a great idea."

Doc pressed a thumb against his wristband until a glowing green dot appeared on it. The rustling of the trees and the whisper of the wind seemed to fade away, and when Doc lifted the golf clubs into the back of the cart, he barely heard them clink as they settled. The wristband had silenced all of the distractions in the world and Cap's voice was the only thing that Doc could hear, loud and clear, as he twisted the key in the golf cart's ignition.

"If you just want to make $50,000 a month, I can teach you to do that," Cap said, as they pulled away from the driving range. "But you can make that in a day by taking a company public. Have you ever thought about taking a company public before?"

"I don't really know what that means," Doc admitted, shaking his head and thinking about what he'd just heard.

"Taking a reputable company public will allow people to invest in it," Cap explained. "That then gives you the opportunity to further invest that money and grow your net worth even more. That's the big money world you won't hear about in school. They don't teach kids how the markets work. This world is run by big money people. But people like you and me know all about them."

Cap nudged Doc with his elbow and slowed the golf buggy to a stop.

"The first step towards greatness is recognizing you're at the starting line," Cap explained. "I'll teach you how to get going, but we also need people to run our companies. Leaders lead by example, so your first step is to become a leader that others will be willing to follow."

He gestured around them at the golf course.

"This is more than I deserve," he said. "I've worked hard for what I have, but many people do. So I want to ask you, why don't more people have golf courses and vacation homes?"

Doc shook his head, unable to come up with an answer.

"Sacrificing the present and understanding that it will lead to a brighter future is too much of a challenge for most," Brooke said. "Doc, I want you to remain skeptical of things you learn the easy way. If you're going to learn something, commit to it until you understand it. We all forget the things we don't follow through with and it can lead to nothing but a wasted life. Sacrifice rewards you because it cements what you learn into your mind and teaches you the truth. Be present in the moment but make sure that your time doesn't get taken away from you."

Cap and Doc got out of the golf buggy and paused to look out gratefully at the morning dew as it sparkled in the fields.

"The problem is that most people don't study their lives to understand how to improve them," Cap continued. "Everyone expects to retire by giving people like us their life savings in retirement plans. We can invest that almost free capital into our companies and grow them even bigger. But if you're trading time for money, you're living life on a wheel and you'll eventually burn out. The key is to grow your passive income stream or to have multiple checks each week going straight into your pocket. Be honest because integrity and ambition are what pay off in the end."

Dog nodded and unloaded the bag of clubs from the cart while Cap continued to talk.

"The harder I work, the more money I make," Cap said. "But the best managers can train crews that barely need them. Stick with me and you'll create a Fortune 500 company that your family can benefit from in the generations to come. Your products and services can help millions of people, and if you get the right people in the right seats, you can take the company public.

You'll make more than you'll ever need if you do that. That's how you make more than you can ever hope to spend."

Cap reached into the bag and selected a club, then got down on the ball and eased into his stance. He was silent for a moment as he lined up his shot and hit the ball, before handing his club to Doc.

"Brooke's not going to be around forever to make sure you get your life together," Cap said. "And she's 100% the reason why you're standing here right now. You're blessed to have her. So what's your reason for being out here today?"

"Because I want to help the ones I love," Doc said. "And to help the ones who can't help themselves, like Brooke is helping me. So I don't feel like I'll die as an accident."

"That's a noble answer," Cap replied, stifling a laugh. "And one that your mom will kill you for."

They both climbed back into the buggy and set off after the ball again.

"So," Cap said, "no girlfriend, because you're sleeping on a couch. You're lucky you're not comfortable. If you were living comfortably in a home, you wouldn't be fighting for a way out of your situation and losing sleep while trying to improve yourself. Unfortunately, pressure and pain often push us to do difficult things. Are you grateful that you're out of your dad's trailer?"

"Yeah," Doc said.

"Good," Cap replied, as the buggy puttered to a stop again. "Count your blessings every day and you'll be counting the reasons why you shouldn't give up. If you forget to think about the things that you're grateful for, you'll forget why you started this journey. So fight to remember every day to be grateful for what's happening in your life. Now, I'll send you a few contracts in an email that you can use to double close a home if the opportunity presents itself."

"You've got my email address?"

"Of course," Cap said. "Brooke gave it to me. Now where was I? Oh yeah. Double closing homes is the easiest side hustle there is. You'll make thousands of dollars from a couple of hours of paperwork. You're basically going to be the middle man. You'll find someone here at the country club or in a business magazine who'll buy a home that you find that's for sale."

"Don't I need a real estate license to do that?"

"Not necessarily," Cap replied. "As long as you stay within the law. I want you to genuinely look for a home for yourself so you can get off your sister's couch. If you happen to find a home that you can't afford, get it under contract for you to buy over the next thirty days. During that time, you can present it to people and try to sell it at a markup. You're just pocketing the difference. If you can't find a buyer then the contract becomes void after thirty days and you can just walk away."

Cap paused for a moment as they got out of the buggy. Doc carried the clubs over and he inspected them briefly before selecting one of the irons. He lined up his shot and took his swing, sending the ball sailing along the fairway and bouncing on to the putting green.

"Nice shot!" Doc said.

"Thanks," Cap replied, handing him the club. "Remember to check out the business magazines. Most of the people in there have got extra money on hand for investment projects."

He reached into his pocket and handed Doc one of his business cards.

"Here," he said. "You can email me whenever you want. I'm sure you'll still have a bunch of questions once we're finished here. I've only got time to play the first few holes. Then I'll take you back to the clubhouse."

***

Cap and Doc stayed on the links for an hour or so and then headed back to the clubhouse, where a uniformed butler was waiting to greet them. Doc thought that the butler in his suit and tails looked out of place on the golf course, but Cap seemed unfazed and greeted the man by name.

"Henry," he said. "Doc is ready."

"Very well, Doc," Henry said, nodding at him. "Follow me."

They started to walk towards the clubhouse together with synchronized strides.

"So, Doc," Henry said. "Have you enjoyed your visit with Cap today?"

"Yeah," Doc said, "but I'm still trying to figure some things out."

"Anything I might be able to help you with?"

"Making first impressions in six seconds," Doc said.

"I'm trying to figure out what to do."

"Well, the first thing to do is to beat someone to the greet," Henry said, leading them across a marble bridge, over a stream and towards the clubhouse. "Get there first and shake their hand. It's that simple. If you use their name and show genuine interest, you'll be fine. The best handshakes are when you drive your hand deeper into the shake. Occasionally, you get a fun pop sound that happens when both hands come together. Other than that, you're off to the races with a smile."

"Thanks for being so helpful," Doc said. "So tell me about yourself and what it's like working for Cap."

"Well, I used to be a monk," Henry said. "But now I'm running the butler service business that I founded."

"You were a monk?" Doc asked. "What was that like?"

"I challenge people all the time to be nicer and more caring to themselves than they are to me," Henry replied, as they approached the door of the clubhouse. He beat Doc to the door and held it open for him to walk inside. "I have a great day if I'm better to others."

Henry led the way as the two of them walked down a black corridor that was lit with candles and which had armed mannequins along the walls. The cobblestones echoed beneath their feet as they headed deeper underground.

The corridor eventually opened up into an old, western saloon themed bar. The curved wooden beams behind the bar were lined with endless bottles. Doc's eyes roamed up the walls as he admired the tall, vaulted ceilings and the large, curved rafters above him. As his eyes continued to take in the room, he noticed the bartender. His back was turned, but his dark blond hair captured the light.

"Cap said he was ready," Henry said.

The bartender turned around slowly, still drying a tall glass with a towel. He was wearing what looked like a pair of old mining goggles on his forehead and was dressed in centuries-old leather wrapped over unbleached cotton. His suspenders were tucked under his long jacket.

"Kayden," he said. "I've heard a lot about you."

The bartender set down the glass, and Doc noticed as he did so that one of his arms was made of metal. A glow shone out from his arm and across the bar. The bartender leaned over and started to tap the counter with his metallic fingers. A familiar spark flew from his mechanical hand and Doc felt a cold shiver run down his spine.

Something inside was screaming at him that he needed to run.

CHAPTER NINETEEN: PUZZLE

AS DOC REACHED THE BAR, the bartender looked at Henry and bowed, adding, "Thank you, Soon."

The old rickety wooden floor cracked and splintered open. Doc spun around and watched the boards separating like curved fingers. He glanced quickly over at the butler and saw him wink before becoming a whirling mist that flowed down through the gaps between the floorboards. As the floor weaved back together, he stood there silently, studying the old wooden floor.

"My name's Monty," the bartender said. "I'm the creator of the Emprium. Welcome back, Kayden."

Empire + Stadium = Emprium

A strange look passed across Doc's face as he stared at the bartender. He cleared his throat and said, "I like your floor."

"Thank you," Monty replied. "What's on your mind?

"What's the Emprium?" Doc asked.

"When you see it for the first time, you'll know," Monty replied. "I'll let you experience the discovery for yourself and with your own eyes. But the name comes from a cross between 'empire' and 'stadium', and the goal is edutainment. We've found that huge performances and competitions are the best ways to inspire us and to bring us all closer together."

In the background, a couple of bottles floated silently on and off the shelves, switching places in the flicker of the candlelight.

"I appreciate the amount of detail you've invested in yourself," Monty said. "You've changed so much. I'm proud of you."

Monty's metal fingers slid off the bar and he grabbed the tall glass he'd been drying. As he returned the glass to the shelf behind him, his long, leather jacket gave Doc a glimpse of his mechanical body.

"I've wanted to meet you in person for a long time," Monty said.

The entire bar abruptly divided itself like a pair of large bay doors swinging open. Monty stepped quickly towards him with his hand extended and they shook hands.

"Is your arm actually mechanical?" Doc asked, motioning towards his other hand.

"Yeah, it is!" Monty confirmed, loaded with enthusiasm. "Now come on, everyone is waiting to meet you."

Doc's eyes widened as he felt his clothes shifting around his skin as though he was sliding into bed. He reached up and touched the clear glass film as it crawled over his face. He took in a frantic breath of air and looked down at the spacesuit that his clothes had turned into.

"Who do you mean by everyone?" Doc asked.

Monty walked towards the wall of the saloon and the boards slowly broke open to unveil a view of deep space. In the distance, a bright explosion of light was being held back by a blue ocean planet with vibrantly green land in a large section at the top. The swirling water world had a hole that went all the way through it, and a dense city was thriving in the middle of it.

This is the Cover of this Book. The Planet is called: "The Origin"

"That's where we all live," Monty explained, pointing towards the planet's interior. Then he gestured to the lush forest on the top of the hollow planet. "And that's where you were on the beach when I saw you for the first time."

"When my sister hit me with a beanbag?"

"Yes," Monty said. "When your song ended, I surrounded you with a memory room and you reentered your Earth simulation. The beanbag was the transition you experienced going back into the real world."

A blank look crossed Doc's face as he confessed, "I

don't know what's real and what's a dream anymore."

Monty held out his mechanical hand and a flat disk started forming above it. A small but strikingly realistic beach appeared on the disk and rain clouds floated into view. A lightning storm erupted onto the scene as Doc watched a miniature version of himself getting lost in his memories as he sang.

As the three-dimensional replay of his past unfolded in front of him like a movie, all of the sensations from the beach flooded back to him.

Monty slowly lowered the living moment down onto the counter and reached into the pocket of his jacket with his mechanical hand. He pulled out a small, glistening cube that seemed to be made from black crystal. Doc watched him as he reached into the micro-replay with the cube and plopped it over the simulation like a cup. He tapped his metal finger against the cube and it softly faded into a solid black as he lifted the mysterious object back into the air. The miniature Doc inside the living memory was no longer on the beach at all. Instead, he seemed to somehow be captured in the blackness of Monty's metal claw.

"This room is essentially inside the cube," Monty said, pointing around at the walls.

"What are the sounds in the background?" Doc asked, looking around and listening to the clocks in the walls.

"Feel free to visit the others," Monty said. "Soon is with Aurora in the cube below."

Doc's eyes were drawn back towards the glowing city on the planet outside the opening at the end of the saloon. He was entranced by the wood as it slowly weaved itself back together in front of the mysterious planet.

"Where are we all going if that's home?" Doc asked.

Smoke filled the bar as Doc watched the miniature beach scene evaporate off Monty's white disk. He waved his hand over the disk and it stretched up and reemerged inside his palm, reigniting its internal glow.

"The Emprium awaits," Monty said, walking over to an old grandfather clock. He rotated the hands until they showed that it was just before midnight, and a faint click echoed out as he swung the door of the clock open.

"The Emprium brings me joy because it's in the service of others," Monty said. "We'll be arriving soon. I'll see you there."

He stepped through the mysterious door inside the tower of the grandfather clock and Doc watched him disappear as the door closed.

A knock at a far door echoed across the bar, and Doc noticed that the bottles had stopped shuffling around and the ticking clocks reminded him of funeral bells. He heard another thump at the far door and crossed the wooden floor, curious about everything around him.

It's getting hard to breathe, he thought, as another wooden thud sent a shooting panic through his body. The candles flickered out and he was surrounded by darkness. He reached for his wristband but stopped as a further thought occurred to him. *Nothing can hurt me, right?*

A beam of light flickered beneath the crack of the wooden door, sending an eerie yellow-green glow swirling through the room.

I should've made a run for it when I had the chance.

Doc gasped and watched a dripping cloud curling in on itself across the bar. He stood stock still and watched without moving. The cloud lit up the entire saloon and rose towards the curved ceiling. A deep burst rippled across the room and splintered some of the floorboards, tipping bottles off the shelves. Smoke from the candles was drifting upwards towards the swirling mass.

"What's happening?" Doc whispered.

The air suddenly felt heavy and wet as the clock chimed on the wall. The glow moved towards him as he tried to figure out what to do. He heard a bottle shattering, and it compelled him to close his eyes. He felt an intense heat burning in front of him and opened his eyes again to see a face and a pair of glowing red eyes holding him in place.

"Can I wake up now?" Doc muttered.

"You're not dreaming," the man replied, his raspy voice dripping from his lips. "Don't you know who I am?"

"No," Doc replied. "I'm new here."

"I'm the Halter," he said. "The games are about to begin."

"Huh?"

"I'm the Halter," he repeated. "I'm auditioning for the games."

"Woah," Doc said, raising both of his hands. "Auditioning?"

"I'm ready to compete in the games this time," the

floating mass said, as he raised his skeletal finger.

"I don't know how to help you," Doc replied, pointing towards the clock. "Monty left just before you got here. That's a secret door."

The Halter sighed as his eyes sank back into their sockets.

"You're not Monty?" he said. "My bad. I see. I have to show Monty my new being to see if I can compete in the games with it."

"What are these games?" Doc asked, as the Halter floated over to the clock door. "What is this Emprium?"

"Your time is coming, great seeker," he replied, before disappearing through the clock's door.

"I just met someone who called himself the Halter," Doc said in disbelief, standing up in the dark and tapping at his wrist.

"The Halter?" Soon asked, the candles relighting themselves around the room.

"He said he's been preparing himself for the games," Doc said.

"That will be exciting to see," Soon said. "I've never witnessed the Halter performing. Sometimes our friends disconnect and they're free to redefine themselves in secret. These games are going to be incredible."

"Monty showed me your planet before I ran into the Halter," Doc said. "Where are we going?

"To the Emprium," Soon replied, chuckling. "All of the animals get to freely enjoy the world while we get together at the Emprium. We only can visit home but our animal friends are able and noble one enough to always be at home. Come down and join us, Kayden. We'd enjoy your company."

The floorboards next to Doc cracked open and a white light beamed up from below.

Peering into the light through the gaps in the floorboards, he remembered the butler winking at him before turning into smoke and flowing down through the boards.

"Soon," Doc said, "how do I vaporize myself?"

"This world is built from your imagination," Soon reminded him. "You can even grow wings."

Doc imagined himself shrinking and the room seemed to grow around him. He fell through the cracks of the boards as the wood and everything else closed up behind him. He stumbled through the air, his suit sprouting wings while he tried to figure out where he was. He landed inside a white room that looked just like the one that had started it all.

Soon was there in his black cloak, sitting in a chair across from Aurora, who was dressed in a bright, form-fitting suit. Her legs were crossed, showing off her knee-high boots. Doc looked around and locked his eyes on a black-painted body lying on top of a table. As he walked over towards it, he remembered taking a sip from the glass that was sitting at the end of the bed.

"Is this a replay of me?" Doc asked.

"Yes," Aurora replied. "You called me Jessica when we first met."

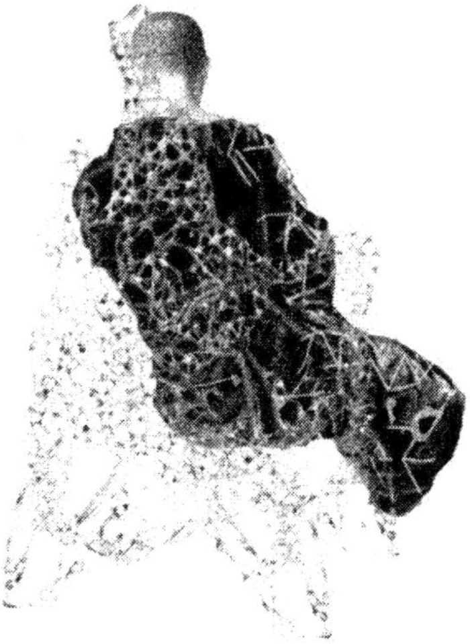

CHAPTER TWENTY: HENRY

DOC LOOKED OUT at the memory of his body covered in paint. He was starting to see the bigger picture.

"Wow," Soon said. "You really have been through a lot, haven't you?"

"Catch you later, Kayden," Aurora said, waving at him as she faded away from the chair.

Doc walked over to the now-empty chair and sat down next to Soon.

"So here we go," Soon said. "Flying through space. It almost seems like we're nervous, but most of us are just unable to contain our excitement. If your performance in the Emprium is anything like that song you teased us with on the beach, it's going to be a magical moment."

"I'm confused," Doc replied, hesitantly. "What kind of place is this Emprium? Where are we going?"

"It's a school that we use to teach each other about ourselves, Kayden," Soon replied. "Even though you're not fully integrated into our society, you're leaving a positive impact on the people around you, just like a monk would."

That's a big compliment, Doc thought. *I wish my dad would do that. But he'd rather assume I'm using drugs instead of listening to me. He won't even listen to the doctors.*

"There's just one more thing you need to learn," Soon said, smiling at Doc. "But it's a lesson you need to teach yourself, Kayden. The nickname Doc suits you well."

Doc looked down as his spacesuit evaporated away from him, leaving behind the clothes that his sister had bought for him. Soon stood up and held out a hand for Doc to join him. A door in the wall opened up and they walked into the unknown.

As they entered the country club where Cap had been playing golf, a swirl surrounded Soon and he turned back into the butler. Doc peered backwards and watched the door to the white room as it closed behind them. The butler led Doc into the kitchen and opened the fridge to reveal his Styrofoam plates. Doc reached into the refrigerator and felt a suspicious vibration from his invisible wristband. Secretively, he pulled his phone from his wrist while he was hidden inside the fridge.

"Hello?" he said.

"Hey brother," Brooke replied, her voice bursting through the phone and hurting his eardrums. "I've got Jessica here and we're on our way to you. How far along are you and Cap on the golf course?"

"I'm not on the golf course," Doc replied. "We only played a couple of holes. Cap said something about me being ready."

"I'll let Cap know that we're on our way," she said. "He told me he mainly just wanted to give you his contact information. There's some exciting news headed your way. I love you and I'll see you soon!"

Doc closed the fridge and scrolled through his phone, then tapped on a text that his dad had sent the night before and started reading it to himself.

Your sister told me you got the job at the museum, it said. *Come give me a hug sometime, son. Love dad.*

"Thanks for putting these in the fridge for me," Doc said, glancing across at the butler. "What's your name?"

"Henry Alger," the butler replied, as a flicker of green light from his wrist caught Doc's attention. He made eye contact with Henry, and he realized that he hadn't seen the flash from the wristband.

"Mr. Liang," Henry said, reaching up to his headset and transmitting to his staff. "Could you make sure that Cap knows that Brooke is on her way to pick her brother up from the front entrance? Thanks so much."

Then he motioned for Doc to follow him from the kitchen, adding, "Just this way, Doc."

They left the kitchen and walked along a glass hallway and out into the garden. Then they sat down on a bench that overlooked an aged copper statue of a bald eagle in full flight. Its majestic talons overshadowed a small pond that teemed with coy carp. A stone path led back from the pond to the bench, which was next to a small copper statue of a hummingbird feeding from a flower blossom. He caught his breath and smiled as he remembered the adventure of flying for the first time.

"So tell me, Henry Alger," Doc said. "What does your name mean?"

"Thanks for asking," Henry replied. "My name means 'strong home warrior'. It makes me feel like I was always meant to be a father. I admire everyone in Cap's circle of friends, they're all interested in people. It's inspiring to see that he only keeps people around him if they're good. He's on another level."

"Cap is still human," Doc said, looking across at Henry. "I've learned that if we all did the things that he does, we'd all be at his level, given time. When I was growing up, my dad taught me to do a little each day. Even being a hard worker is a skill that takes practice. Anyone can tackle a big project a little at a time if they just stay consistent each day."

Silence descended, and they spent a moment or two listening to the running water and the birdsong.

"I have questions about that," Henry said.

"Maybe I can help," Doc replied, as his wristband flashed green again.

"When it comes to tackling big projects," Henry said, "what would you say was the greatest lesson that your dad taught you?"

Another pause filled the air as Doc leaned back in the bench, thinking about his life.

"Well," he said. "Are you up for a long but true story?"

Henry nodded and leaned quietly back on the bench.

"Okay," Doc said. "Well, my biggest failure came after my parents got divorced. My dad never wanted to marry again after that. He lost his job, which was difficult for him, and started doing carpentry. I think he felt like he needed to be harder on me to make me understand, which led to him beating me senseless. Throughout the years, a bitterness grew up between us, because I never forgave him for hurting me."

Doc paused for a moment, blinking back tears.

"One day," he continued, "my dad got hurt at work. He came and picked me up from school, hunched over in the driver's seat. My life changed that day. I didn't allow myself to see him in any other light than the label that I gave him back then. I shut down and ended up running away, which didn't change anything. I didn't think about how my actions would hurt the ones I loved. My father came after me and lost his cane, then put his back out."

He paused again and glanced at Henry, who nodded encouragingly at him for him to continue.

"Sorry if I get emotional," Doc said, taking a firm, deep breath. "A month later, I held my dad's arm and we walked out into the woods. We rounded a tree and I saw his cane, so I knelt down to get it. That moment showed me my purpose in life: to help the ones I love and those who can't help

Everyone's purpose in life, involves someone else

themselves. It was easy to forgive my dad for doing everything he could to keep me from learning the hard way, because it was all he knew to do. But forgiving myself? I failed my father by assuming that there was an easy way and I suffered even more trying to prove that I knew better."

If you are not the same person you were 5-10 years ago, why is it so hard for us to forgive and change?

Doc sighed and looked down as an orange and turquoise butterfly landed on his knee.

"I still don't know how long he was out in the woods," he said. "I've learned that taking responsibility for what happens in our lives gives us the chance to change things. I might not be perfect or be able to change someone else, but if I'm strong enough to keep bettering myself, that will be enough to encourage others to want to do the same."

"That's deep, Doc," Henry said. "Thanks for sharing. I've never heard that before, but it reminds me of when I go to the gym. I'm far more inspired by the insecure individuals who struggle with small weights than I am by the people who are at the gym all the time. I can't imagine what you're going through with your dad. As a father myself, I know I could do better."

"Can I ask you about something I'm struggling with?" Doc asked.

"Sure," Henry replied. "If I can help, I will."

He pointed at the butterfly on Doc's knee and added, "Looks like you've made a friend."

Doc nodded, and they watched as the butterfly fluttered towards the pond.

"I'm looking back at a few of the different points in my life that I'd like to learn from," Doc said. "As a monk and a dad, when someone lies to you, what do you do, and what's the best way to handle it?"

The silence returned as Henry thought for a moment before responding.

"I could initially feel disappointed when someone lies," he said. "But I know that truth is eventually learned in time. I also occasionally discover that their reason for lying to me isn't ill will or bad intentions. They could simply lack confidence in me because of what's happened to them in a similar situation. I do briefly feel disappointed, so I find it's best to step back and to take a look at them with fresh eyes. Someone might decide that I can't keep their secrets because someone else betrayed them."

Henry paused again and looked peacefully out at the tranquil waters of the pond.

"As I monk, I try to look for a positive angle with a person," he continued. "But I can occasionally still come up short. For instance, if I'm angry at someone, I can only see negativity. Since I meditate so much, it's easy for me to not let myself get angry, but it can still happen if I'm not careful. When I'm strongly attracted to someone, I might only see their positive qualities. The reality is, though, that no one is fully aware of everything, and nobody is completely perfect or entirely bad."

"I see."

"Everyone has good qualities," Henry said. "We just have to search for them. If you see someone in a completely negative light, it's probably due to your perception and your own outlook at the time. If you still can't find any positive angles or perspectives, it's best to simply weaken that memory. Every time a bad memory pops into my head, I let it remind me of something different or I picture it playing on a screen and then focus on something else. Eventually, you'll teach your mind that you're ready to stop suffering with that memory and that you want to focus on something else."

They both looked silently across at the statue again.

"I agree with you," Henry said. "It might be difficult, but anyone can tackle a big project a little bit at a time, if only they stay consistent each day. I think that a monk's outlook is just being human. A conversation is never time wasted, Doc, so tell me. Who, aside from your family, has had the most influence in your life? You're very enlightening, and I admire your outlook."

"There have been so many," Doc said. "Especially recently. But I'd probably say Soon."

"Okay, you can tell me soon," Henry said. "Besides, your sister is here."

CHAPTER TWENTY ONE: THE ROOTS

DOC AND HENRY shared a laugh as they walked up to Brooke's red sports car. The butterfly fluttered in front of Doc and he smiled.

"It was good seeing you, Aurora," he whispered, as Henry opened the car's back door.

Doc climbed into the car and he, Brooke and Jessica turned to wave to Henry before Brooke pulled out of the golf course.

"Henry is a nice guy," she said. "I'm glad I met him. He started a butler service a few years ago. Before that, he had a mobile car washing business and occasionally did yard maintenance for the neighborhood. Henry

Alger is a great person. No doubt about it, brother."

"I had my head in a fridge when you called me," he said, leaning forward to pop his head between Brooke and Jessica. "What's this news that you have to tell me?"

"Well, how do you like it over there at the museum?" Brooke asked.

Doc shrugged and sank bank into his seat.

"The museum is okay," he said, "but I don't want to clean it forever. Is there a job opportunity that you wanted to talk to me about or something?"

"Dr. Ti wants to meet you," Brooke said, glancing at him in the mirror. "Our lab has been partnered with the lab you worked at for a long time now. Dr. Ti wants to ask you to work with us, so we're heading there now. Looks like your college degree might get paid off after all. Jessica, could you get him ahead of the curve and let him fill out the application on your phone before we get there?"

Doc accepted Jessica's phone when she offered it to him, and he browsed through to the lab's website before downloading the application form and starting to fill it out.

"Ah!" he said. "What's your password? I accidentally locked it."

"It's 0204," Jessica said, chuckling and glancing over her shoulder at him.

"Thanks, Jessica," Doc said. Then he stuck his head through the gap again and looked at his sister. "Do you think I'll do a good job, sis?"

"I don't know everything," Brooke replied, laughing softly at him. "And that means I'm not smart enough to be a pessimist."

Doc handed Jessica her phone back and the sports car pulled into the lab's parking lot. Brooke parked and they all got out of the car, then walked into the building together. Dr. Ti was standing at the front desk and waiting to greet them.

"Hello, Jess and Brooke," Dr. Ti said. "And this must be Doc. I just printed off your application. Brookes told me a lot about you. Are you ready?"

"Sounds good to me, Dr. Ti," Doc said. He was already imagining his life getting back on track at last. He smiled and strode towards Dr. Ti with his hand extended, and the two exchanged a sincere handshake.

"Excellent," Dr. Ti said. "I'd like to show you what we're working on."

Doc followed Dr. Ti as he led the way down a corridor, with Jessica tagging along behind them. Brooke waved goodbye at him and then sat down on the couch in the reception area to wait for him.

They walked into a white room and a standing submersion tank came into view behind bulletproof glass.

"I'm ready to make a positive difference in the world," Doc said, an overwhelming feeling of wonder bubbling up inside him.

"That's exactly what I wanted to hear," Dr. Ti said. "We're currently working on animal trials which consist of mice being frozen. Our goal is to revive them back to full health from their frozen state. This process is the only thing we currently know of that can pause the ticking biological clock of life. The only problem is that we don't know how to unthaw them without them dying. We're open to other solutions if they're worth pursuing."

Doc glanced down at his invisible wristband and had a sudden epiphany.

"I've got an idea involving robotics," Doc said, looking back at Dr. Ti. "It's a stretch, but we could repair the damage from the ice crystals by reprinting or reassembling them as they thaw. I'm not sure how consciousness plays into all of that, though. If we built a brain from scratch, I wonder if it would create the same consciousness or jumpstart a new one. I don't think we can restart the same consciousness, unfortunately. However, I'm willing to start working on any solution that could conceivably pause the clock of life."

"That's why we need you, Doc," Jessica said. "You're a genius, and your fresh ideas are unique. I've already done a significant amount of work, and I'm the registered doctor here at the lab. We're looking to use surgical robots to allow sterilized operating rooms to be taken anywhere. The idea of using robotics to reprint or revive cells that have been destroyed by ice crystals hasn't come up yet, but I see what you're getting at. We might be able to help the damaged cells to heal during the thawing process. It's madly brilliant. I also need someone to go into the suspended animation tank so that we can do some more testing on how the digestive tract reacts to being frozen, since we got approval for isolated human testing."

"So what's this big chamber being used for now if freezing mice is the main focus?" Doc asked.

"Our last full-bodied trial ended with a large portion of the patient's digestive system needing recovery," Dr. Ti said. "When someone is put into hibernation in the large tank, they're basically just unconscious. We need to study the effects inside the gut. We need someone who's willing to let us finish the studies we were doing so we can take our findings into hospitals and save lives."

"A few ideas spring to mind," Doc said. "I look forward to figuring the future out and getting into the tank. I'd love to be a guinea pig for the clinical trials."

"Good," Dr. Ti said. "I'll see you tomorrow morning."

Doc and Dr. Ti shook hands again and Jessica began to lead Doc out of the lab. He followed her into the waiting area, still brimming with excitement.

"Brooke has an incredible umwelt," Jessica said, her eyes widening.

"Umwelt?" Doc repeated, looking confused.

"Her circle," Jessica clarified. "All of her contacts are amazing."

"Yeah, I know what you mean," Doc replied. "Brookes like Cap in that she's careful about who she's friends with.

But his mind was already drifting, and a different thought had pushed itself to the forefront.

I wonder if I can get Soon to help me in the lab.

***

Cyrus was in his cabin, wearing a red plaid shirt and jean cutoffs as he looked through his old photos. The lake behind his house had always been an attraction for his friends, but that had all changed when he'd met Jessica.

He'd been dressed up as a pirate, and Jessica had walked in wearing a clown outfit. His world had lit up with wonder when they started talking. Two scientists in two local labs were only the beginning.

Cyrus picked up his phone and called his old friend Karla, who he hadn't seen since meeting Jessica. They exchanged pleasantries and chatted for a while before Cyrus steered the conversation towards the subject that he wanted to talk about.

"So," he said, "I've been looking at the old lake photos. Do you remember when everyone used to come out to the cabin and we used to go on the lake? Can you believe that it was a year and a half ago?"

"Time flies," Karla said.

"It sure does," Cyrus replied, walking over to the old cabinet in his bedroom and opening it before looking inside. "So, I have a question, Karla. If your guy took you down to the lake, would a picnic be a nice touch?"

As he listened to her response, he reached into the cabinet and pulled out a small black box, which he opened up to reveal a glistening ring. He glanced at his hiking gear and then out of the window at the branch of a tree.

"I want tonight to be perfect," Cyrus said. "I wonder if it would be romantic for Jessica to find the ring on a tree branch. I'll let you know how everything goes. Jessica is coming back over later and I'm excited about it."

"Good luck," Karla said, her joy bursting through the phone line. "I'll let you get on with it."

Cyrus hung up the phone and stared out of the window for a minute or two before cleaning and sweeping the house. He felt himself getting carried away, pulling out the drawers in the bedroom and cleaning out the random garbage behind them. He found a stack of magazines in his wardrobe and paused for a moment.

They're in the way, he thought. *Do I want to keep these magazines more than I want us to be comfortable?*

He shook his head and tossed the magazines in the trash before getting back to the cleaning. Almost as an afterthought, he grabbed the ring and slipped it into the pocket of his jeans.

***

Doc climbed out of the car and waved goodbye to Jessica and Brooke after they dropped him off at the apartment complex.

You become the people you spend the most time around, he thought. *Jessica's onto something. The information my sister surrounds herself with every day is directly connected to her progress. The more she learns the more she ends up accomplishing.*

He let himself into Brooke's apartment and locked the door behind him, then pulled out his phone and navigated down to his dad's name in the address book. He hit the call button and started talking as soon as his father picked it up.

"Hey, dad," Doc said. "Brooke took me over to the cryogenic lab to meet Dr. Ti. It went really well and he wants me to go in and help out. I start working there in the morning."

"It's about time you got yourself a decent job," his dad replied. "I need to get this place cleaned up. A little bit every day is enough to move mountains, as long as you stay consistent."

"I understand," Doc said, sitting down on Brooke's couch. "There's a lot I need to learn."

"Son, anxiety hits us all," his father replied. "Let me give you an example I learned about when I was in therapy. I feel anxious right now because I need to clean the house up. I have two options. I can either suppress my anxiety and relax into depression, or I can recognize that my body is using my nervous system to make me uncomfortable and use that energy to start cleaning and being productive."

Doc realized that he was unconsciously nodding along with what his father was saying.

"If I start cleaning," his father continued, "my body will feel better. If I decide to eat a candy bar or go online to watch some funny videos, my body will trick itself into thinking I was productive. I can actually make it worse by suppressing my anxiety now, only to feel it later when I realize that it's still not done. The best cure for depression is to do something productive. Most people fail because they try to do everything and then give up when it gets hard. I kept going so that my son wouldn't end up in a trailer park. When the going gets tough, make sure that your reason for getting up is stronger than your anxiety. It will go away in time if your reason is good enough."

"I'll remember that," Doc said. "Thanks, dad. I still have to go to the museum tonight to clean."

"Are you going to need a ride in the morning?"

"I'm not sure where the girls went," Doc said, vaguely. "I was planning on riding with Jessica in the morning."

"You've slipped back into expecting other people to take care of you," his father said.

"You're right," Doc replied. "I should have asked Jessica if she'd be able to give me a lift to work."

"I can pick you up if you don't have a ride."

"Thanks, dad," Doc replied. "I guess we should make those plans solid. Would you mind if I call you when I get off work at the museum to let you know if I need a ride in the morning? I think the girls will be home by then."

"That's probably going to be pretty late," Brian said. "If you hear from them sometime sooner, give me a call."

"Oh, by the way," Doc added. "I was learning about real estate today, and I wanted to talk to you about getting into it. Didn't you think about investing in real estate when you were younger? I remember you telling me about it."

"Son," Brian replied, "a person can only teach you from where they are in life. I'm going to shoot straight. A dilettante is someone who knows enough to teach but not enough to actually accomplish things on their own.

People don't learn by almost doing. Just because I should have done real estate, it doesn't mean I can teach you."

***

The evening sun shone down on the sports car as Jessica slammed the door and pulled away from the cabin in the woods. Jessica knocked on the door and a burst of music from inside interrupted the air as Cyrus opened it.

"Hey babe," he said, wrapping her up in a firm hug. "Come inside. What did you and Brooke do today?"

"Not much," she replied. As she entered the house, she saw an old picnic basket on the kitchen table. She knelt down and hid behind it. "What's this?"

"I just got it for us," Cyrus explained, smiling at her from the other side of the kitchen. Only his face was visible over the top of the basket. "I thought we could go down to the lake. I've already packed some lunch if you're hungry."

"I'm excited," Jessica said, popping up from behind the basket and running over into his arms. "Let me get changed really quickly. I've got my bathing suit out in the car."

Jessica rushed out to the car to grab her bags and then carried them into his room, closing the door behind her. She looked around at how clean it was and made a mental note to keep the place tidy as she started rooting through her bag for her swimsuit. As she tossed it on to the bed, there was a knock at the door.

"Time's up!"

"Not yet," she shouted. "Can you give me five minutes?"

"You've already had five minutes!"

"Well how about five minutes more?"

"Well, okay then," Cyrus said, sighing theatrically. She could hear him chuckling to himself as he walked away.

Jessica walked over to the bed and sat down on it. She took off her shoes and her earrings, then walked over to his dresser to set them down.

A pair of underwear caught her attention.

CHAPTER TWENTY TWO: THE HEIRARCHY

JESSICA GRABBED her earrings and put on her shoes.

I really thought he cared, she thought. *He's been seeing other people, just like my ex.*

She felt a stabbing pain in her heart and grabbed her swimsuit, the betrayal burning inside her as she stormed out of the house. Cyrus followed her with a look of bemusement on his face.

"What's wrong?" he asked.

"Don't talk to me!" Jessica yelled.

"I don't understand," Cyrus said, upping his pace to catch up with her. "What happened?"

"I said don't talk to me!"

Jessica had reached her car and unlocked it, but Cyrus placed his hand against the door.

"Jessica," he said. "Please, tell me what's going on."

"I found your other girlfriend's lace underwear on your dresser," Jessica said. "How many of us are there?"

"I don't know what you're talking about," Cyrus insisted. "If you found some lace underwear here, it must be yours."

"Does it look like it's mine?" Jessica growled, shoving him away from her so that she could climb into her vehicle.

"Where are you going, babe?" Cyrus asked.

But she'd already gunned the engine and pulled away, sending rocks spewing into the air.

***

Cyrus had a lump in his throat.

"No," he murmured, shaking his head as he tried to process everything. He watched the dust blowing down the driveway for a moment before running back inside, knocking the picnic basket from the table in his haste. "No!"

He reached his room and looked across at his dresser, then picked up the black lace underwear before balling them up and letting them fall onto the floor.

He thought for a moment, then opened up his phone and scrolled down to Karla's number. He hit dial and started pacing back and forth. When she answered, he cut straight to the point, his voice cracking with emotion.

"Karla, hey," he said. "Listen, did you ever leave any underwear here?"

"Uh, okay," she replied. "Kind of a weird question…"

"Just answer it," Cyrus said, wearily. "Jessica just found some silk underwear on my dresser and then stormed off."

"Oh, jeez," Karla said. "Yeah, I think I did. Are you–"

But Cyrus had already cut the call. A bitter silence accompanied him as he fell back on to the bed. He started bashing the phone against his head.

Everything was perfect, he thought. *Why did this happen? I have to call her.*

And so he started calling Jessica over and over again, but her phone only went to voicemail. Then he went online and found out that she'd blocked him from her social media profiles.

"What did I do to deserve this?" he murmured, pulling the ring back out of his pocket. As he sat up in his bed, he allowed it to slip slowly from his fingers as the sky darkened. It felt as though his whole life was over.

How do I make this right?

***

Doc heard the thunder rolling in as he looked out of the window of Brooke's apartment.

"Brooke," he said, tapping his wrist to start recording so he could listen back to the conversation later. "How do I figure out what my anxiety is telling me?"

"Your schedule hasn't been very consistent, has it?" Brooke asked, sliding off the couch onto the floor. "Have you tried to burn a candle from both ends? Well, it doesn't make scents…just smoke. The truth is, no one needs to burn themselves out. Depression occurs when you're caught up in the past, and anxiety occurs when you're worried about the future. People think that it takes weeks to make new habits, but the truth is that it only takes a strong emotional experience. Where you place your attention is where you place your energy, brother."

She patted the ground and Doc sat down beside her.

"Whenever I overcome the past, I feel better," Brooke said. "By keeping the promises that I make for myself, I feel great and can see a brighter future for myself. You're doing so well, brother. You're going to be great. I can see you learning and growing every day, and I'm proud of you. Close your eyes for a second."

"Meditation, again?" Doc said. "I don't get what it's supposed to teach me."

"Well you had a good interview, but now you need to take time for some inner view, if you know what I mean," Brooke replied. "Feel for a second and listen to your thoughts and cravings. Meditation means to become familiar with and you need to understand what is causing your anxiety. This is war, and the distractions from life will all hit you like they always do, but don't move or let them move you. I want you to practice letting go of distractions with me. We're just practicing staying focused and calm, instead of being worried. What are you feeling right now?"

"I'm thinking that my butt's getting sore," Doc said.

"You asked me to help your bony butt," Brooke reminded him. "Now be honest with yourself, what do you feel strongly about? The little thoughts that you're noticing right now are actually there all day. They affect your energy and how you feel."

"Lately, I've been thinking about what I can do to be helpful," Doc said. He sighed, and his eyes closed. "I'm so far behind everyone else. I feel like I'm not good enough. It feels like it'll take me forever to figure this out and I can't help wondering if I can do it."

"When you feel low, sad or dull, I want you to ask yourself something," Brooke replied. "Ask yourself if that feeling is how you've always felt."

There was a pause as they both breathed in and out.

"I haven't always felt like this, no," Doc said.

"Now ask yourself if you know for sure that you'll always stay that way," Brooke said.

"I get what you mean by not being smart enough to be a pessimist now," Doc said. "Because no, I don't know what the future holds. And since I can't actually predict the future, assuming the worst doesn't bring me any hope at all. I'm just always down and hoping that something good will eventually happen."

"How do you treat other people or feel when you think that you're not good enough?" Brooke asked.

"I don't like myself," Doc replied. "And I don't do my best because I don't care. I slow down because I don't see any point in what I'm doing. Just about anything that happens can bring me down."

"And how would you feel if you didn't think that?"

"I'd feel better," Doc said, opening his eyes. "And I'd probably be more driven to do other things. If I was comfortable enough to practice, then I'd try harder for sure."

"If we don't challenge our thoughts, we just believe them," Brooke explained. "Ideas and memories are both true inside our minds. The final challenge is to seek the truth from the other end. Are there any instances in which you're ahead of others?"

"Well, I'm working a new job now," Doc said. "And I seem to be learning, even though I might need to relearn things, so they stick better."

"Don't beat yourself up for trying," Brooke said, as they both stood up. "That can make you too unmotivated to do anything. In time, I'm sure you'll come up with more examples. Don't believe everything you think, brother. Realize that we all have ideas that form in the shape of life, sometimes. If you have an idea in your head that's upsetting you, challenge it just like I taught you. If things get terrible, you can talk to Mike, my therapist friend. Speaking to someone knowledgeable can straighten you out if you want to let something go or to escape from a feeling."

"Why do people get so consumed with negative thoughts?" Doc asked. "I can see how thinking about negative thoughts all day could lead to bitterness."

"The first step is recognizing where you are," Brooke said. "The opposite of bitterness is being grateful. We all get consumed by negative thoughts because our brain is designed to keep us from suffering right now. The bad news is that it doesn't think about suffering later in life. A happy life comes from committing to an achievable goal and overcoming any obstacles that are in the way as quickly as possible. You have to work through the difficult things for the completion of the big picture. Failure comes from abandoning the goals you promised yourself you'd reach because it was harder than you were expecting."

"So what does staying positive look like?" Doc asked.

"Follow the first rule," Brooke replied. "Keep your head high and smile, because winners do just that. Speaking of posture, here's something interesting. Did you know that there's a success level amongst chickens?"

Doc shook his head and Brooke laughed, leaning on the kitchen counter.

"The healthiest and strongest chickens are at the top of the pecking order," Brooke explained. "They always get the first pick of the food. The weakest chickens, the ones with their feathers falling out, only get the leftover crumbs. This success ladder occurs naturally throughout life. Lobsters fight aggressively over the best and most secure spots for shelter, and they don't share because they're so shellfish," Brooke said peevishly. "And the winners and the losers have different chemical balances in their brains, which affects their posture and leads to the winners being more agile and upright while the losers stay tense and curled up."

Doc nodded, and Brooke paused to pour herself a

glass of water before she continued.

"That difference factors into further contrasts," she explained. "The upright lobsters appear bigger and more intimidating, causing the tense ones to stay submissive. Humans are the same. They begin from the foundations that their parents provide for them, but how successful they become is based on their control of themselves and their emotions. If you're in the grip of alcoholism or depression, you're less likely to enter a competitive situation. On the other hand, if you're on a winning streak, it often leads to more confident body language. That can then help you to keep the streak alive."

"I see," Doc said.

"Humans are just like lobsters, sometimes we're just crabby crustaceans," Brooke continued. "They're constantly measuring themselves up against each other. Give yourself a winning advantage and allow yourself a smile and good posture. Don't compare yourself to others. Sit up and make yourself better than you were yesterday. That's what you should aim for, brother."

"That sounds too easy to be true," Doc said.

"Can I give you some advice, brother?" Brooke asked. Doc nodded, and she continued. "Act like you're always practicing and be willing to mess things up. That's how you get better. Focus on getting things done while remembering that they don't have to be perfect as long as you get better each day. Criticism and failure are the first signs that you're headed for success. They'll teach you what you need to work on and help you to identify when a better opportunity comes around. But when you're feeling down, staring at your shoes, it's the only time you really want to know defeat. Get it? Okay that was pushing it. But know you're not a loser unless you act like one."

With that, she walked back to her bedroom and shut the door.

Doc looked down at his wrist and tapped the green dot, replaying the conversation to himself. He sat at Brooke's desk and started to scribble down notes on how to challenge his feelings. Before long, Brooke's desk was covered with notes and drawings of strange clocks and a robotic hand. He scribbled down a few last lines and then folded up the paper and shoved it into his pocket. Then he stood up from the desk and went to knock on his sister's bedroom door.

"I'm starving," he said. "Can I grab something to eat before I go to work?"

"Sure," she replied, without opening the door. "Go ahead and fill that belly, silly. Feel happy!"

"Thanks, sis," Doc replied, before wandering into the kitchen and grabbing a microwave meal from the freezer. He took it out of the box and put it in the microwave, then pressed the start button.

He felt a sharp zap shooting through him as Brooke pinched his sides.

"Bang!" she exclaimed, laughing playfully at him. "All happy!"

He frantically jerked and watched her duck down the hall towards her bedroom and then closed the door behind her. Shaking his head, he sifted through the drawers for a fork, his heart still pounding. He looked down the hall as he waited for the ding of the microwave, before pulling the meal out on to the counter. He ate it quickly and then yelled goodbye to his sister before leaving the apartment and crossing the road.

He knocked on the museum door and Ms. Rain let him inside. Doc started cleaning as usual, and after a while, Ms. Rain came to join him. Before long, they'd struck up a conversation.

"I've got an opportunity to work with Dr. Ti," Doc said. "I'll get to work first-hand on something that's going to help millions of lives."

"That's fantastic news," Ms. Rain replied. "I'm proud of you. Have you always been good at science?"

"It's a subject I enjoy, yes," Doc said.

"Did you know that we learn to write because it teaches us how to think?" Ms. Rain asked. "Never get into an argument with a writer. They spend their lives figuring things out. That's also why it's so rare to find a bestselling author under 30 years old. They need the life experience and just keep getting better and better over time."

"My sister told me that we can only become as good as what we write down," Doc said.

"Yes, exactly," Ms. Rain agreed. "Your sister sounds like a smart woman. Schools don't teach us how to take notes properly or how to learn. It's ridiculous. They teach us to bring up failing grades rather than to pursue what we're good at. That's why most gifted kids like you end up cheating themselves out of success and achievement outside of academics. Instead of getting better at what we're good at in school, we're being told to work harder at the things we're not good at, and that just brings us down. Schools should give us a baseline of knowledge and then let us narrow in on our strengths. Once we do, we should only grow the weaknesses we need to be good at team building. Let kids build passion over time and enjoy doing the things they're good at."

"I need to learn team building and delegating," Doc said.

"It'll come with time," Ms. Rain replied. "I've taught many bright kids over the years."

"Where did you teach?" Doc asked, as a roll of thunder boomed outside. His voice echoed through the museum without getting a response. The power cut out and the lights turned off, plunging the museum into darkness.

"Ms. Rain?" Doc asked, as the front door of the museum rattled and shattered. "Ms. Rain?"

CHAPTER TWENTY THREE: THE CHASE

DOC'S PERSPECTIVE

I WALKED THROUGH the museum and passed the front doors, seeing shattered glass all over the floor. I could hear the eerie noise of light thunder and sprinkling rain from outside as the wind picked up and blew through the front door.

As I rounded back into the hallway, I paused and listened to a rustling sound that was echoing around the museum behind me. I followed the sound to Ms. Rain's office and found Bobo sitting on top of her desk and panting as though he'd just finished a long run. Ms. Rain's desk papers were scattered everywhere.

"Hey, buddy," I said, as Bobo jumped down and

started barking at me. I noticed muddy paw prints all over the desk. "You had me worried there for a second. Do you realize that now I have to clean up the mess you made?"

As if on cue, Bobo shook himself, sending mud flying all over the museum.

"Wow, I spoke too soon," I said.

I looked around the museum again and noticed a light under the bathroom door as Bobo took off, running down the hall. I turned and watched him jump through the broken front door, and then he turned around and barked at me. I realized that he wanted me to follow him.

"Don't worry, Ms. Rain," I yelled. "I'll clean everything up for you!"

I jogged up to the front door, then pressed and held my wristband as it spiraled with color. Outside, beyond the shattered glass of the front door, it sounded as though the rain was settling down.

My shoes crackled and shifted while I tiptoed carefully across the broken glass. I wondered how long everything would stay frozen for. As I stared at my wristband, I became aware that I'd stepped into a magical world. The floating rain amplified the glow of the streetlights. I paused for a moment to admire the rainbow of light that was shining within the endless frozen droplets of suspended rain.

"What are you trying to do to me?" I asked, shrugging and looking over at Bobo. "That mud is going to take me forever to clean up."

I shook my head and reached out to touch the

raindrops, feeling them melting around my hand and noticing that the drops were leaving spots of water on my clothes as I walked through them. Bobo sprinted playfully away from the museum, and I chased after him towards the highway.

When we got there, I stopped and looked both ways and then laughed at myself as I remembered that everything was frozen. We backtracked to Brooke's apartment and Bobo barked at the apartment door while I turned the knob and rushed inside.

Bobo took off running towards the blank wall, and I shrugged as I ran after him. We both passed through the wall and a shield grew over my face as everything seemed to slow down. I looked out at a landscape of sand, which spiraled up around my feet. I immediately felt weightless and realized that I was underwater.

For a moment, I worried that I was going to drown, but then I realized that my suit was somehow giving me air as I looked out at the vast, flourishing coral reef. Bobo's waving hair and long tongue stretched out as we floated underwater. I turned my head to get a better look at him as his slow-motion smile captured my attention. He turned and bounded swiftly through the water as though he was flying. I looked down at my hands and realized that we were in a sea of liquid-bots.

I jumped up from the sandy sea floor and imagined myself moving as the ocean began pressing me forward. I felt the water itself tugging me along. Plumes of sand formed every time Bobo leaped over the coral reef as he playfully pursued the colorful fish.

Gliding through the water like I was flying again, I breathed in the fresh air through my helmet.

Bobo jumped up through the surface of the ocean into the unknown. I followed him, looking down and watching my feet sail from a whirlwind of sand. I felt myself break the surface of the water, and a wooden floor closed around me as I flopped into the bottom of a ship. Sitting up inside its hull, I watched as Bobo shook off the water and ran up the steps towards deck. I stood up and chased after him.

When I reached the deck, I looked around but couldn't see any sails or a crew. We were sailing on an open wooden platform that was crashing through the wild waves of the ocean. Bobo ran up to the bow and I felt a rush of air across the front of the ship. The water seemed to be pushing us along as we approached a few islands and rocks.

Our strange vessel started surfing between giant mossy pillars as waves splashed across the deck. The ship seemed to be guiding us wherever Bobo pointed his nose. As we narrowly missed a boulder, I watched the landscape passing by faster than a typical ship should be able to sail.

We rounded an island and Bobo aimed us towards a cliff. My eyes widened as he jumped abruptly into the surface of the rock. Splintering beams and twisting boards lifted me into the air and threw me towards Bobo and the cliff's surface. All of a sudden, the sounds dissipated as I passed through the cliff face, landing softly inside the cliff and rolling across the ground. I lay there and listened to the waves and the ocean outside the new room. Bobo padded over and started licking my face.

"Hey, buddy," I protested. "I'm getting up."

I looked around the white room and noticed a small home in the distance. It looked to be just a couple of bedrooms in size and had a front porch and an aged shingle roof. As Bobo slowly strolled towards it, I began to follow him. A doggy door appeared in the front door and he walked through it.

I followed him, reaching for the doorknob as the doggy door swung back and forth. Suddenly, the knob slid away from my hand and towards the other side of the door. As my hand closed around nothing but air, I clumsily bumped into the door before taking a step backwards, disoriented and confused.

The window slid down the side of the house and the door soon followed, returning the doorknob to where it was supposed to be. As I took another step backwards, I heard the siding and the wooden boards beginning to creak. I sprinted away from the porch and watched the roof rotate around atop the walls. The brick chimney disappeared out of view and a few shingles slid off the room.

The Puzzle House represents life, and our mind shifting between a painful past & uncertain future. The house is Doc's life, visually changing before him. The house is the wrestle between what we finally understand and what we will never know.

As I tried to take in the house, it moved and turned like a shifting puzzle. I took a deep breath and stepped up to the porch, then watched as the door circled down around the side of the house. Then the windows slid across as the roof rotated like a spinning top. The siding scrolled around like a conveyor belt as the door flipped back into view.

I reached out for the doorknob as it passed and watched it plop down onto the porch as it fell from my fingers. I followed it off the porch and picked up the runaway doorknob. Bobo's barks caught my attention and I turned to see him sitting on the porch and wagging his tail. The front door caught my eye as it fell off the side of the house. Confusion and frustration overwhelmed me as I dropped the doorknob again.

Bobo turned and effortlessly walked through the passing doggy door as it circled the house. His timing was impressive. I picked the doorknob back up and walked over to the door, which was lying on the ground. The knob attached magnetically to the door and I turned it.

I lifted the door open and saw Bobo wagging his tail and barking. He looked like he was sitting on a wall below me. I took a deep breath. Space and gravity seemed to have their own rules there. It was a madhouse.

I panicked as I fell softly through the door that was lying on the ground. To my surprise, I swiftly came to a stop as I found myself kneeling on the floor that had once been a wall. I paused and took a seat in the doorway, letting my feet dangle out of the room. Then I leaned forwards and looked down at the mixing house, wondering if I was really there. I stood up and reached around to pull the door closed. Still holding the doorknob, my curiosity compelled me to reopen it. When I did, I saw that it had returned to the front of the house.

I closed the door and locked it, then looked around to see an old cabin with a roaring fire and a portrait of a snowy mountain above the mantelpiece. Bobo was sitting on the rug in the middle of the room, and he started barking at me before jumping up and passing through the snowy picture as though it was an open window.

I shrugged and dived after him, landing in a blanket of snow. Bobo barked and bounced through another floating picture frame.

"Bobo, give me a moment," I said, shaking my head. "This is amazing!"

I laughed and looked out at the mountains. A gentle breeze kicked up a soft white powder as I took it all in. Then I looked up towards the starlit sky, catching the sun as it dipped below the glowing mountain range and plunged me into a twinkling twilight. The snowy peaks began to sparkle under the stars and I felt like a kid again, growing attached to the view. I sat down, smiled and traced the cliffs in my mind, wondering if I could make an echo.

"Hello!" I shouted, grinning to myself as I heard the echoes return. I hummed and started hearing music in my head, so I reached into my pocket and pulled out the crumpled piece of paper that I'd been scribbling on when I was sitting at Brooke's desk. I looked back at the fragments of lyrics that were

scribbled all over it and thought back to the weather the night before.

I hear the music in my head pound
***Boom**, the night transformed*

I yell, hearing the echoing around,
***Boom**, I'm out of the storm.*

I feel lost in this sound.
***BOOM**! The light is formed.*

***BOOM**! A star is born.*

"Time to make this moment last," **I sang in a whisper as I cast away the feelings of my past. A bassy echo rumbled through the peaks as snow slid down from the mountaintops in silky sheets. I stood and listened to the wind and began to sing from within...**

You can't even imagine what's happened
Like a cannon, you've lit up the skies
A passion, for action, guides me because again,
I'm looking into your eyes!

You bring out a universe of color!
My worlds on fire because I love her!
I can see a future burst of wonder!
The focus of my mind is my lover!

Boom, boom, boom,
the night transformed

Boom, boom, boom,
I'm out of the storm

Boom, boom, boom,
the light is formed

Boom, boom, boom,
a star is born

Love is the answer, forged in the flames of the stars
Truth is the ember that claims this moment as ours

I watch the snow swirl into the mountain peaks
The world is alive with the glowing streaks
down through the meadows to the echoes glow
fountains from the mountains made of snow

You and I have created... everything
There's a cosmic wonder... just happening
I don't know why... you selected me
You lit up the sky... so that I could be

As I listened to the echoes from the mountain continuing the melody, I found myself wishing that I could share the energy, this happiness. I looked out at the peaks, drifting away into thought, and then noticed a flickering pair of pink and orange butterfly wings.

"Aurora?" I said, looking up and watching the stars flicker. I looked around and noticed that people were holding the stars, and they started cheering as I whispered, "The Emprium!"

CHAPTER TWENTY FOUR: DIMENSIONAL

DOC'S PERSPECTIVE

THE STARS IN THE SKY divided themselves along organized ribbons of blackness as a flickering face slowly appeared behind the starry silhouette. As I took in the scene, I realized that the mountains I was in were within Monty's mechanical palm, and that his fingers were gloved with the cosmos. Monty opened his fist and peered down at me in his hand, making me feel smaller than a grain of sand.

"Welcome to the Emprium!" I heard, as his voice echoed through the mountains. He smiled and his face disappeared behind the stars as he closed his fist back around me. The mountain range descended into a white floor in Monty's massive palm, revealing a flat field inside the night sky's galactic dome. A door appeared in the distance where the starry edge met the floor.

A massive wall of smoke appeared from a doorway. A few characters emerged from the smoke in the distance and zipped across the stadium grounds towards me. It was easy to spot Soon's black cloak as it shivered, showing off the hidden symbols in its fabric. Monty was wearing a long, black jacket and strange goggles on top of his head. His long, red scarf flickered in the wind. Aurora's tight, black cargo outfit and boots were splashed with orange and pink, which matched the flower on her shoulder.

They all hovered effortlessly across the white field, extending a familiar greeting and congratulating me for chasing Boba and for my caring performance.

"So, Monty," I said, my curiosity forcing me to ask him. "Did I just see you holding this entire area in your hand?"

"Yeah, you did," Monty replied, his features lighting up. "I like looking at the whole picture. It's how I see things better."

"So was everyone watching me run with Bobo?" I asked. "I saw Aurora fluttering by on the mountain."

"Everyone was watching you through Bobo," Aurora explained. A mesmerizing breeze was blowing small strands of her hair around. A few of the tendrils entangled themselves around the flower on her shoulder and a pleasant scent drifted over us.

Aurora's indescribable, I thought. She's just wow.

Then I wondered whether Monty was still holding the place in his hand.

Bobo started barking again, interrupting my thoughts as he raced across the open arena. Aurora smiled and waved at me, a small butterfly lifting off her shoulder from the flower. It fluttered into the air and Bobo jumped up, trying to grasp it in his jaws. The butterfly divided into two and Bobo caught one as the other fluttered away. Aurora dropped through the floor so swiftly and seamlessly that it was almost as though she'd vanished into thin air.

"Those two have been our eyes and ears," Soon explained. "Just like you in the turtle."

"Oh," I replied. "That's why everyone knows so much about me. I still haven't grasped everything yet. I'm learning, but it feels like there's so much more."

"I'm proud of you for making it this far, Kayden," Soon said. "Everyone loved being part of your exploration with Bobo. Here when we say you can reach for the stars, we mean it literally. Now let's all grab a star and carry on the adventure."

"Agreed," Monty said with a smile as his goggles slid down from his forehead. A metal shell formed from the goggles and expanded over his face. Several smoky white tornadoes span up from the ground in front of Monty as a white object the size of Bobo buzzed into the air like a drone. Monty whipped out a metallic strand of steel from his hand and lassoed the flying object as it hoisted into the air.

"Kayden, follow me," Soon said, turning to look at

me. "Let's see if you remember how to fly."

His cloak opened up and he launched into the air as his giant wings unfurled. I clenched my fists as a cloud formed around me and bonded to my back. I stretched out my own wings and flew off after Soon, soaring above the ground. The unsettling scale of the igloo stadium became apparent as I looked down.

Rising towards the stars, I watched the silvery shimmer of Soon's cloak in the darkness. As we neared one of the stars, it came into sharper focus and I watched Soon disappear through the wall of light. I followed him and appeared inside a circular room that appeared around me as I landed. My wings slid off my back like sand and settled on the floor.

I looked around at the familiar-feeling white room. Soon as walking behind a giant black orb that was covered in stars and which was hovering just off the floor.

"What is this place?" I asked.

"Look closely," Soon replied, smiling and pointing at one of the thousands of shimmering dots on the star globe. The star dimmed in brightness at the same time that the room did. "The stars that you can see are the rooms around the Emprium. This is where we are. Now, everyone has their own unique experiences and gifts to share with society, and this next-dimensional stadium is Monty's. This star map is no ordinary object because it allows us to be in two places at once."

"Monty figured out how to hold the object that he's inside?" I asked, looking too Soon for confirmation.

"Yes, exactly. It gives new meaning to the saying, 'Your future lays within the palm of your own hand'," Soon replied. "Each of these stars is a room like the one we're in now. They all have the potential to create adventures like the one you had with Bobo. All of us can live separately in our infinite personal worlds. Still, we can also experience together, thanks to Monty. The Emprium allows us to connect them all at the same time. Monty was looking down into the Emprium because the Emprium created a projected version of him for you. This digital creation allowed him to be in two places at once."

"My head just went blank," I admitted. "So correct me if I'm wrong, but it seems as though this floating, starry map takes the merging of liquid bots and people to the next level. This map allows people to interact directly with each other's worlds by arranging the rooms in a sphere."

I stepped back and saw that the room I was in was like any other blank room, except for the floating ball in the middle.

"So the outside of this white room is the inside of this star sphere in front of me?" I asked.

Soon nodded and my eyes widened as I thought about how no one could be in two places at once. I realized that the sphere was somehow giving us the freedom to be in multiple locations at the same time and decided that I'd have to talk to Monty about it. Then I broke the silence, spouting off an idea that I didn't yet fully understand.

"So life here is like a phone call while you're on

your way to a friend's house," I said. "But with our whole body, as opposed to just a voice?"

"You're on the right track, and I like the way you think," Soon said. "Keep going. Understand that this is more dimensional than a copy, though."

I looked over at the starry globe and one of the stars started flashing pink and orange. Soon reached over and tapped the glowing light as though it was an elevator button, and the white walls of our room lit up with a soft orange and pink.

"We're in Aurora's world right now, outside these walls," Soon said. Then he walked over to one of the walls and passed through it.

I shrugged and continued to think. I could almost understand, and I guessed that another way to put it would be to call it a spherical hotel. I decided that was how I was going to think about it until I learned more from Monty.

I shook my head and walked after Soon, excited to see Aurora's world. A single beam of light fell through the blackness surrounding me and a piece of music filled the air as I watched a flower rapidly start growing towards the light. As I approached it, I could hear Aurora singing.

Is there a more beautiful moment to be in right now?
Can you feel that? This moment feels alive somehow.

The giant flower opened up and Aurora floated into the air out of a plume of pink steam. She looked over at me as she opened her butterfly wings.

The bite of the sunset, on my neck
I'm lost in the clouds
Our colorful duet, when our eyes met
My heartbeat is so loud
I spread across paradise
looking into your eyes

Aurora slowly curled her colorful wings around her, creating a cocoon. The wings cracked and frosted over, opening up with a musical tune. Several smaller versions of herself flew out of the cocoon in an eruption of color. The group spiraled into the beam of light, their wings sparkling as they fluttered. Her music carried me to a new horizon.

Flying across the sky like a rainbow,
lighting up the air with a new glow
Progress made, a little every day,
makes every little thing seem worth the wait.

The bite of the sunset, on my neck
I'm lost in the clouds
Our colorful duet, when our eyes met
My heartbeat is so loud
I spread across paradise
looking into your eyes

Aurora waved at me and scooped up a handful of pink smoke before blowing it towards me. The heart-shaped smoke ring pushed me lightly back into the

room as Soon followed. I looked over at him and the room slowly faded back to white.

"Talented, isn't she?" Soon said.

"Um, that's one word for it," I replied. "So, Soon, where am I? I feel like I'm beside myself."

"You're at the Emprium," Soon explained. "A place designed for us to live in a world of infinite possibilities that can be shared instantly. Bobo is a fun new character that's exploring our system. Once you merge with our system, you can view the world through Bobo's eyes, just like Aurora with her butterflies."

"So the wild chase I went through with Bobo was just his everyday life?" I asked, excitement flooding through me.

"Oh yes," Soon said, looking towards the floating black star map. "Everyone on our planet lives in mirrored ways as Bobo does now. Monty's Emprium is brilliant. He figured out how to take our culture and to give us all the ability to teach each other onstage. It's truly remarkable."

"How did it all begin?" I asked. "What's a simple way to explain everything?"

"I could be wrong," Soon replied, "because we're not cognitively connected yet. I'd love to have a crack at your question. Can you ask it another way?"

"I get that space is vast," I replied. "And that through computers, you're able to connect everyone in infinite ways. You have a society that I'd call a singularity, but how did everything begin? What I don't get is what existed before everything existed?"

"I remember teaching Aurora and Monty this very thing," Soon said. "Many lives ago, before they decided to be connected. Since you're not connected cognitively to us, I have a few ideas on how I could explain it."

"I'd like that, yes," I replied. "I want to be connected to this world. It's beyond words."

Soon smiled and gestured at me to follow him as he stepped away from the sphere. Without selecting a star, he walked to the exterior of the room and through the wall. As I stepped through the wall, my hands brushed into a field of tall grass. The white room had disappeared entirely, and I found myself looking out an infinite rolling plain beneath a black, starless sky. The grass shifted lightly in the breeze.

"So, correct me if I'm wrong," I said, "but we're now inside our room in the black orb, right?"

"Exactly," Soon said. "All of the rooms are dark around us, and the grass glows because it's digital."

"Made out of miniature electronic objects holding onto each other?"

"Yes, precisely," Soon said. "You could also call them organic robots."

I ran my fingertips through the grass and shook my head in disbelief. Even though I knew that the grass was digital, it felt indistinguishable from the real thing. The green blades looked like they were lit up by the sun, but the grass was glowing all on its own.

"Truly remarkable, isn't it? So remarkable, that one could say the grass here truly is greener," Soon said. "The grass is creating the wind as well, instead of the wind blowing through the grass like you're used to."

A soft breeze caught his long, dark cloak, and the mysterious silver symbols shimmered across its fabric. Around us, the blades of grass waved back and forth, pushing the air around like water.

"Soon, your cloak has got to be the coolest one I've ever seen," I said.

"Thank you, Kayden," Soon replied. "The metal symbols have a secret of their own. But enough of that. 14 billion years ago, Aurora asked me how something came from nothing. It sounds like your question is another way of asking the same thing."

"Aurora asked that?" I replied, gasping at the thought of living for 14 billion years. "How did you explain it to her?"

"At the time," Soon said, "she was a few years old on your timescale."

"So, just a child?"

"Yes," Soon said. "Can you imagine that? We simply believe that until someone chooses to connect to our collective consciousness, we shouldn't connect them. Have you ever wondered what someone else was thinking?"

"I have," I replied. "If someone simply knew what their friend or partner was thinking, it could save a lot of pain. Knowing that that's how everyone here lives makes it an exciting thing to be a part of."

"How are you really creating thoughts, Kayden?" Soon asked. "And where do they come from?

He turned to face me, his expression uplifted and

radiating energy. I sensed that I was about to learn something that I'd never thought I would.

"I'm taking the information in front of me and connecting it to what I understand," I replied, grasping at straws.

"Our bots can easily build the neurons inside your brain," Soon explained. "As well as all of the chemicals and matter. Interestingly, that new brain doesn't create consciousness on its own without energy. Isn't it strange that a dream or even writing things down can teach us things that we didn't know before? Where does that new information really come from? Kayden, I want you to look up at the sky and to imagine being there. It's cold, settled and calm. Your brain creates thought in the same way that the universe was created."

As I looked towards the blackness above, I saw a white star appear and then erupt in a fiery explosion of energy.

CHAPTER TWENTY FIVE: THE LAW OF GROWTH

DOC'S PERSPECTIVE

"YOU'VE BECOME A DREAMER," Soon said. "I watched your origin burst begin and here you are, flying among the stars. You're now venturing out and discovering the truth along the way."

"Origin burst?"

"The origin burst, well that's just the beginning for you, but I could be wrong," Soon said. "But didn't I just watch you create a universe above us? Your mind is still processing that everything's changing. You can infinitely imagine and think to yourself, and the universe is infinitely full of mystery, isn't it? For example, is it hard to conceive that the mind can learn to create things over time?"

"No, not at all," I replied. "The mind can figure out a lot. People create all the time. Our world is full of things that other people have created, like books, stories and sentimental objects."

"The best way I can explain the creation of the universe is to say it's like you," Soon said. "Your imagination is as infinite as the universe. Still, your thoughts are only real when they're made real to others. You're taking nothing, just information, and turning into something else with just the power of your thoughts. So you yourself are demonstrating how something can come from nothing. And only something can come from nothing, but something can't make nothing. Ah, never mind, it's nothing...but wait. Isn't that something?" Soon said, lightly chuckling at his own humor.

Soon paused and raised his palm as the grass next to us parted and a smooth white dome grew up from beneath the field.

"We can only build on what we already understand," Soon said. "We learn in steps. I could be wrong because I'm not sure where you are with your understanding of the universe, so I can only teach you what you ask of me. Knowing that, we all tend to group together the things that we don't fully understand, thinking that they're somehow connected. When we're unsure or uncertain, we tend to stop looking for answers even though we might not actually know the truth. When we stop learning, we ultimately stop growing. Promise me that you won't be afraid to ask yourself difficult questions, Kayden. Until we're connected and our understanding continues, that's the best advice I can give, and it will lead you to your next question. Start by visualizing infinite expanding worlds being created from each other. Your consciousness and the material world go as far as you want them to. So what do they have in common?"

I followed Soon into the white room, plucking a blade of grass as I walked through the curved wall.

"Aurora created an origin burst," Soon continued, "and here you are as a result. I watched Aurora create your origin burst over 13 billion years ago, and in that time, she hasn't ceased to surprise me. Taking kids outside of the starscape, which is the name we use for the place beyond the stars, has been a fun yet simple way to show students how everything started. Time and space are infinite, but over time, light itself fades away. You might say that it's like a fallen empire. Our ancestors have gone, and so have the worlds they once built. But their stories carry on through you because without those events, you wouldn't be alive. You're a story that's older than the space dust from a lost star. Everything has the cosmic symmetry of existence itself, which is why your thoughts control so much of your life. Why isn't there much of a difference between where your thoughts come from and the origin of everything?"

I looked down and twirled the blade of grass in my fingers as we approached the Emprium, the star-covered sphere in the middle of the room.

"I still have a lot of questions," I said. "But one thing that I've learned is that you've got to be open to opposing ideas. The truth will form a solid foundation as I throw new ideas its way. I'm looking forward to finding out what's next."

I paused and watched the stars flash in different colors. I could smell the fresh blades of grass as they began to turn into dust. A tingling sensation swept over my sinuses as the grass turned into a thin wisp of cloud.

"You've always been a curious one," Soon observed, laughing as he looked over at the cloud around my hand.

I sneezed as a mist settled over the room and stuck to the globe. I began to worry about the mess of dust. The floating star-map rapidly swelled in scale and pressed up against me, pushing me out of the white room.

***

Doc stumbled backwards and landed in a spot of mud, pressing the wet clay into his hand. He looked around and saw that he was back in the museum.

"Yep," he murmured, looking down at his wristband. "I've got to clean this up as well. Is everything all right over there, Soon?"

"Oh yeah," Soon said, his voice echoing through the invisible headset tucked behind Doc's ears. "I believe you just thought about the mess at the museum, Kayden."

"Thanks, Soon," he replied, looking at the mud on

his hand. He tapped the wristband and it faded away.

He walked over to the front door and took in the scene.

"I see where I paused everything," he whispered to himself. "And I see the rain sitting still."

He took off his wristband and set it on the floor, then sat there, surrounded by the broken glass. He studied the web of metal on his wristband and examined how it aligned along the edges of the broken shards. Almost magnetically, the shattered glass skittered across the floor and started clicking back together. Like a puzzle being assembled, the glass grouped together into a single sheet that Doc carefully lifted before setting into the opening in the front door. The metal web reached out and pulled at the glass, and the broken seams slowly faded to leave a clear, solid window.

Doc's wristband reformed around his wrist as he examined the mud that Bobo had tracked around the museum. He took it off and tossed it into the air, where it spiraled into long, vibrating lines as it floated into the broom cupboard. A blanket of strings slowly extended from the closet, stretching out across the museum. The liquid machines that made up my wristband began funneling a cleaning solution through their new form from within the cupboard, cleaning up the mud and the dirt.

Doc watched as the lines of bots crawled across everything. Within moments, the whole museum was spotless. He plopped down in Ms. Rain's chair and allowed the bots to climb back onto his wrist. The glowing band faded softly away and he sighed.

This technology could free the world, he thought. *If everyone's ideas just happened in front of them, what would be the point of money? I need to remember to ask Soon if money is even a part of their world.*

He noticed a glow from under the bathroom door and stood up, tapping his wristband as the sound of the storm started up again, breaking the silence. The sound of running water caught his attention.

"Did I just hear a dog barking?" Ms. Rain asked, opening the door and walking into the office. "Bless his heart. The little thing must be trying to escape this weather."

"I'd recognize that bark anywhere," Doc said, laughing softly. "That crazy dog loves water and hates thunder. I guess his love is stronger than his hate. Anyway, I finished up the cleaning."

"I noticed," Ms. Rain replied. "I couldn't believe my eyes. This is the cleanest the museum has been for years. You did an amazing job. Let me drop you home so you don't get soaked in the rain."

She walked past Doc towards her desk, then reached into a drawer and withdrew an envelope with Doc's name written on it. He looked down and noticed that his wristband was glowing black.

"I know you want to thank her for the offer and turn her down," Soon said, his voice coming through Doc's headset. "But it will make her feel better and you'll build a stronger relationship with her. Welcoming kind gestures will help to bring more of them into your life. Remember that we're constantly teaching other people how to treat us."

Doc looked Ms. Rain in the eye and smiled.

"Thanks so much, Ms. Rain," he replied, taking the envelope from her when she offered it. "It's coming down pretty hard out there. I won't complain too much about you taking me across the road."

He followed her as she led him out of the museum and into a covered parking area, locking the back door behind them. They climbed into her car, then she pulled away and cruised along the road until Doc directed her to pull over.

"Thanks, Ms. Rain," Doc said.

"No problem," she replied. "And remember, if you do one good thing for someone every day, the world will be more magical."

Doc smiled at her, then stepped through the door and into Brooke's apartment. As he closed the door, he could hear Brooke talking into her cellphone. She sounded concerned.

"I'll drive him to work in the morning," she was saying. "Love you, bestie."

Doc walked into the room and Brooke beamed at him, cutting the call and returning her phone to her pocket.

"Brother!" she exclaimed. "How was work?"

"Good," Doc said, as he took off his shoes. "I've learned a lot lately. It's been an interesting day."

"Jessica is pulling an all-nighter at the lab," Brooke said, "so I'll be taking you to work in the morning. She's going to come back here to get some sleep once we get there. But enough about that. Who drove you here? I heard you thanking someone as you came in."

"Oh, that was Ms. Rain," Doc replied. "The nice lady over at the museum."

"Oh, right," Brooke said, sighing and leaning back against the couch. "I've been talking about relationships all day. And sometimes those ships are so loaded, they give me a sinking feeling."

"All day?" Doc asked, leaning curiously in and taking a seat at the desk near the door.

"Yeah," Brooke said. "But I don't want to unload on you about how I feel. I doubt you want that."

"I wouldn't want you to break anyone's confidence by revealing their conversations," Doc said. "I'm curious, though. How do you feel about relationships, Brooke?"

"It's not simple," she said, standing up and walking to the kitchen to grab her travel bottle from the cabinet. "But it's easy to understand the differences between people and how to stay in a lasting relationship. I'm not talking about harmful people but about peaceful relationships."

Brooke sighed, setting the bottle on the counter with a loud thump of frustration and grabbing a container of nutrition powder.

"Admiration isn't important in a relationship," she continued. "We all admire people throughout our lives. Connecting with someone's interests is important when building rapport and friendship, but a successful relationship needs more than just a connection. You've got to be compatible and to build towards something together."

Brooke reached into the fridge and grabbed a carton

of almond milk, then set it next to the bottle. While she was preoccupied, Doc tapped his wrist and the glowing green dot appeared.

"The little things are all a relationship ever is, in the end," Brooke continued. "It's nice to look forward to a vacation twice a year, but that's not a relationship. If you're not both ready, getting emotionally attached above being friends is immature. There's no such thing as finding 'the one'. Anyone can be the one."

"Kayden," Soon said, his soft voice coming through his earpiece. The almond milk that Brooke was pouring slowed to a stop before it reached the bottom of the open bottle. The raindrops stopped hitting the windowpane and the world came to a standstill.

"Brooke seems to be very stressed and needs someone to talk to," Soon said. "Remember, she's been a shoulder for people to cry on all day. In Brooke's case, she wants you to be interested in what she's saying because she wants to help you to learn from her pain. High emotional intelligence comes from calmness because emotions like anger are similar to muddy water. Our hands can't settle the dirt with force."

"Soon, that's profound," Doc replied. "I like that."

"I'm glad you like it, Kayden," Soon replied. "Remember, we're always teaching others how to treat us. One example that I've often overlooked is to be interested in what people want to tell me. The act of listening teaches people to return the favor and to be interested in what you say. I can't imagine what Brooke is going through, spending all day on the phone to people in pain. Your sister is a strong woman. She might just need someone to return the favor and to listen to her. She seems emotionally drained."

"Thank you so much, Soon," Doc replied, touching his wristband. "I'll be there for you when you want to talk to me, too."

The black band faded but the light green dot continued to glow, recording everything. Softly, slowly, the raindrops picked up in tempo and the almond milk hit the bottom of Brooke's bottle as time started back up again.

"When people talk about 'the one'," Brooke continued, "they mean the one who ends up building and growing with you, putting in as much time as you do, brother."

She shook the powder into the almond milk in her travel bottle.

"When tensions start getting high, you've got to learn what they need and let them have it," Brooke said., "Some people need space. Others need touch or loving words. The challenge is to understand that people are different, and sometimes you might be different to what they need. That's an important part of a couple's compatibility. You need to understand each other to grow a relationship, and you need to be willing to learn together."

Brooke grabbed her bottle and put the lid on, then shook it vigorously before taking the lid back off and tasting the mixture.

"We all have to be careful about who we take advice from," she said. "A single girl is the best company for another single girl. People can only give advice from where they are themselves. Always remember to ask if a person is living the advice they give, because times change. People only understand what they are themselves."

Brooke walked towards the hallway and approached her bedroom, then paused. She turned around and leaned against the wall.

"I know that you don't want me to preach at you, brother," she said. "But I want you to remember this stuff. The secret to a lasting relationship is to fall in love with someone all over again, because times change everyone and people learn things the hard way. Until we learn the hard way, most of us won't know things for sure. Maybe no one cared enough to teach them how to love, or maybe you need to see something progressing inside them."

"I understand," Doc said.

"When relationships don't last," Brooke said, "it's usually because they want to keep each other in the same, familiar box. It becomes a very closed relationship. That's why people feel nervous when their partners start something new or unexpected. The problems occur when people assume that their partners or friends will always stay the same. Everyone changes, and yet we worry about losing each other because of that change. When people stay together for over sixty years, it's because they're excited and constantly falling in love with their new beings."

Brooke was still leaning against the wall, and she paused for a moment to get more comfortable before she continued.

"If you don't learn this," she said, "you're going to hit the same roadblock over and over again with every new relationship. You need to be able to see that they're putting in as much effort as you are. When you're looking for someone, simply do a 30-day commitment challenge and only decide at the end. Don't jump ship early and be willing to work through things because even if you don't stay together, it'll give you practice for whoever you finally click with. Open up early because we might never have our story told anyway, in the end. Both sides could teach each other enough to become lifelong friends."

"Any more advice?" Doc asked.

"Couples should have a date night every week or as often as possible," Brooke said. "They should treat each other with as much excitement and anticipation as they did on their very first date. Give them flowers, even if they're just wildflowers. Enjoy the special dessert that she made. Make each other feel excited, not taken for granted. You know, that makes me think of when we used to live with grandma and grandpa."

"I don't remember that," Doc replied. "I was in college when grandma and grandpa moved in with you guys."

"Oh yeah," Brooke said. "Well, they'd dance together every evening, and the joy and the love that they showed when they were doing that made me want that when I get married."

"I remember a friend telling me that he had seven children with his wife," Doc said. "Sometimes they couldn't afford to go out for dinner or a movie, so they'd just take a ride and sit by the lake and talk. He told me that during those dates, they'd refuse to talk about the kids or work or anything else that wasn't centered around them reaffirming their love for one another. I thought it was special how they tried to make time every week to be a spouse. Not just a mom or a dad but a spouse, a lover and a friend. I've always wanted to see the look in the eyes of someone who loves me. I want it, Brooke. I really do."

"And one day, you'll have it," Brooke said. She looked down at her travel bottle and then took another swig from it. "Thanks for listening. It's been a long, wearying day. Goodnight, brother dear."

"Goodnight, sis."

"Oh," Brooke added. "One last helpful tip. The reason that so many people have heart attacks during the night is that they eat within three hours of bedtime. I'm not eating anyway, but I'm probably not going to sleep much tonight and so knock on my door if you need anything."

"Thanks, sis," Doc said, as Brooke went into her room. "Love you."

Then Doc returned to the living room.

I wonder how a billion-year-old feels about relationships, he thought.

His eyes settled on the envelope that Ms. Rain had given to him and he checked it out, smiling when he saw that there was a little more money in there than last time. Feeling accomplished, he grabbed the blanket and flipped the light off, then took a deep breath and settled down to sleep on the couch.

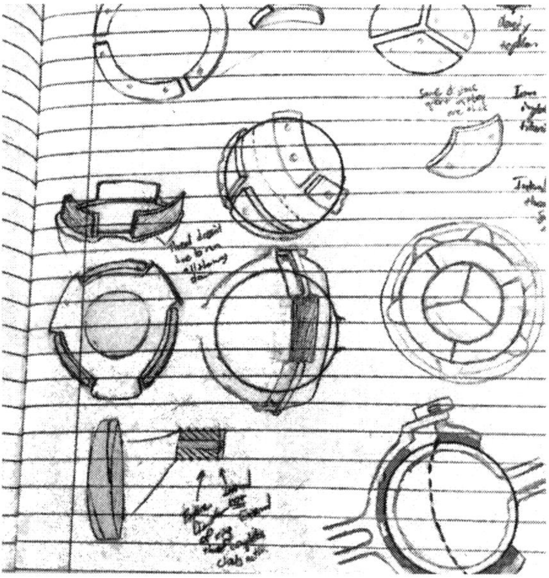

CHAPTER TWENTY SIX: IT'S B-DAY

DOC'S PERSPECTIVE

I ABRUPTLY SANK into a tank of water and the icy liquid threw me back and forth as though I'd jumped into the ocean. The temperature shock tensed my body and I gasped in panic, fighting for air as the saltwater bubbled into the inside of my mouth.

I saw a light in the distance and swam towards it. Each stroke took me closer to a familiar scene in the water. I could see the orb that had crashed into the ocean and realized that I was in my memories, on the night that my mom found me on the beach. I tapped my wrist but nothing happened, so I continued to swim frantically towards the orb on my quest for answers.

Each passing moment felt like an eternity as I swam towards the orb, just like I had as a child. As I drew closer and closer, time felt like it was standing still while I struggled with the current. I could see a familiar map of stars floating in the water.

The beams of light stretched through the saltwater, rippling across my face as I swam closer. I remembered that the crystal sphere's shell didn't exist and that the stars were just floating together in the water.

I reached out and grabbed one of the stars in my hand, bringing it closer to me and cupping both hands so that I could peer into the glow. My arm twitched as I looked over at the remaining stars. I noticed that the glass shell of the sphere was starting to take shape. The crystalline structure grew like molten glass around the other stars, solidifying them into a single object.

I immediately reached out and slid my hand across the cold glass surface. Looking back into my hand, I remembered this moment from long ago. I closed my hand around the star and the light escaped through the gaps in my fingers as I started to lose consciousness. I was running out of oxygen and I wondered what would happen next.

Inside my fist, the star's light reached out and wrapped around my fingers. Stunned, I let out a last few bubbles of air. Then the star shot up, lifting me towards the surface at an incredible speed. As I accelerated upwards, my head dropped under the flow of water. I briefly saw the orb below me sending out a wave of flickering symbols. It started to emit letters all over the seafloor that looked exactly like the ones on Soon's cloak.

I broke through the surface of the ocean and realized that this was that moment in my childhood and that I was reliving what happened that night.

I was dragged by my hand onto the shore, still gasping for air. My arm flopped down onto the beach and my fist opened, releasing the star as I caught my breath. I dropped the star onto the sand as I coughed and tried to gather myself.

The sunrise glowed over the beach, leaving an amber shine on the sand as I coughed on the floor. I lifted my head and looked down at the ocean's rolling waves, seeing the rut that I left as I was dragged from the sea. My eyes widened as the star zipped away and into the palm of a pale, outstretched hand that was reaching out of the water. Black fabric rose from the foamy waves as I shivered on the beach.

A hooded figure appeared, and Soon's familiar face appeared from within the dark hood. I saw a flickering, silvery light appearing around him as all of the symbols gathered up into his cloak and merged with the fabric. Soon's words were muffled by the rush of the waves as I turned and disappeared back into the ocean. I could only hear one of them: Soon.

"What do you mean, 'Soon'?" I yelled. "Soon!"

***

Doc jerked awake and sat up on the couch, gasping, "A star was missing."

"Someone was dreaming," Brooke said from the counter. Her orange shirt and yellow skinny jeans were hard to miss, and her ponytail reminded Doc of how she'd looked when she was little. "Morning, bro."

"I don't remember falling asleep," Doc muttered. He thought about the dream he'd been having and remembered going out on the beach before his parents woke up that morning. Then he cleared his throat. "When do you get up? You look like sunshine, by the way."

"Thanks. Now if I can just figure out how to bottle and sell that sunshine. I think you'd be my first customer, sleepy head," Brooke said. "And I was up at five, maybe earlier," Brooke replied, beaming across at him. "It's best to get up early while the world's asleep so that you have some time to yourself. I make my to-do list before bed, so I usually naturally wake up early, drink some water, do some writing and deep breathing and then brush my teeth. It can be a blessing to wake up a little early and to give yourself some time to write ideas and dreams down. I find that going to bed early and rising early helps me to be more productive and to feel more energized."

"The only thing I know I need to do today is to go to work at the lab," Doc said. "Do you or Jessica know which shift I'm working?"

"I told her I'll get you there at two," Brooke said, watching him make his way towards the bathroom. "So let's get the morning started, brother."

Doc closed the bathroom door behind him and looked over at the toilet seat, where there was a note on top of some folded clothes. He picked it up and read it to himself.

"Today is the day you change the world," he murmured. "Get it? Change? Love, Brooke."

He laughed and looked over at the new clothes, then changed into them before using the toilet, washing his hands and leaving the bathroom.

Back in the living room, Brooke was smiling to herself and scribbling away in her notebook at the desk.

"What are you doing?" Doc asked.

"I'm looking over my to-do list," Brooke replied. "I always ask myself what would make my day if I did it today. If you want to get a lot done or if you're juggling several things at once, you'll need to take notes and keep lists to stay organized. Without tracking, you can't run and operate properly."

"Cool!" Doc exclaimed, rolling up the soft blue sleeves of his dress shirt. "Thanks, Brooke. I really like it."

She clapped her hands excitedly and danced in her chair while Doc walked into the kitchen to pour a glass of water.

"It's good to see you in some fresh clothes," Brooke said. "I'm just going over my to-do list and trying to figure out what to do to add more magic into the day. My schedule isn't a prison, bar none, and it's allowed to change, but I'd love certain things to get done today and will do everything as soon as humanly possible. So I've got a serious question. What does your list say about you eating today?"

Doc's eyes widened as he set his glass down on the kitchen counter, facing away from Brooke. He tapped his bracelet and winced as the corner of a page slid out of his wrist. A sigh of relief flowed over him.

"B-Day is opening in 20 minutes," Doc said, looking down at the paper. "I have no idea where or what that is. So what's going on with you? What are you doing today?"

"You've got a few hours before work," Brooke reminded him. "Do you really want to spend a day in my life?"

"Yes, of course," Doc replied. "I'm genuinely curious about what you do with yourself as a young, retired millionaire."

"Then let's go to B-Day!" she exclaimed, jumping out of her seat with her hands in the air. She made her way out of the house and he swiftly followed her, slipping the folded paper back into his wristband. They got into the car and Brooke started the engine before pulling out into the road.

"So, bro," she said, her eyes on the road ahead of them. "We make money to amplify our lives and who we are inside. All my money goes… well, here."

The car pulled up in a parking lot outside a tall brick building with a black, metal door. Brooke got out and unlocked it, then waved for her brother to join her.

"What is this place, Brooke?" he asked, as she led him through a busy kitchen that was full of people saying hello to his sister.

Brooke turned around to the kitchen and

announced, "Brother, this is everyone. Everyone, this is Doc, my brother."

He waved nervously as he looked at the sea of faces. Then Brooke grabbed his hand and guided him towards the front of the kitchen. They emerged on the other side of a pair of swinging double doors and saw a line of people being served in a cafeteria.

"Doc," Brooke said, "can you help Dacey on the front line for a moment while I get my bags ready?"

Before he had a chance to reply, she'd smiled and trotted out of view.

"Nice to meet you, Doc," Dacey said, handing him an apron, a hairnet and a pair of gloves.

"Hey, Dacey," Doc replied. "Nice to meet you. Just tell me what I need to do."

"It's easy," she said, handing him a plate. "Just ask the next person in line what they'd like to eat today."

"Sounds good," Doc replied, as his own belly grumbled at him.

"Most of the people in line are homeless," she whispered, leaning in a little closer to him. "This might be all they get to eat today. If you give them an extra scoop, it really makes their day."

Then Dacey turned and started talking to the next person in line. Doc spotted Brooke on the other side of her with a familiar bag in her hands. Doc remembered her eating out of a similar bag when they ate together on the beach. Across the front, it said, "It's your B-Day." At the bottom, it added, "Making all the difference."

Doc put everything together in his mind: Brooke's Day – B-Day – to make a difference. He looked towards the line, which stretched out of the door. His eyes watered and his heart overflowed as he looked at the man in front of him.

"What would you like?" he asked.

The man pointed, and Doc filled up his plate until it was almost overflowing. Then he handed it to the man, who took it with his arthritic hands.

"What's your name, son?" the man asked. "I want to thank you properly."

"They call me Doc," he replied.

"Well, Doc, you're all right with me," the man said, his enthusiasm shining out of his gray eyes.

Dacey gave Doc a high-five to celebrate and handed him another plate. The work continued, with countless faces passing in front of him as he loaded up plate after plate. He made a point of always asking if they wanted a little more, which made their faces light up. They all thanked him, and a few asked him for a second plate to take with them, which he gladly provided.

Beside him, Dacey was serving an older man who'd been moved to tears.

"You don't know how hard it's been over the last week," he was saying. "Thank you so much."

She gave the gentleman a hug and then laughed and winked at Doc.

"Do you know our manager, Mr. Liang?" Dacey asked. "He's out today, but you'd love him."

"I've heard of him before," Doc said. "He works with Henry over at the golf course. They challenge people to see who can be nicest."

"Isn't he great?" Dacey asked. "I hope to be just like

him when I get older."

Then she turned and started filling up another plate. Doc looked up and saw that a familiar face was looking back at him and smiling brightly.

"Willow!" Doc said. "It's good to see you again."

"I'm sorry," she replied, looking guardedly at him as though she couldn't believe that he was calling her by her name. "You've got the better of me. I don't recognize you."

"If this was a bandage and I was still black and blue, would I be easier to recognize?" he asked, carefully putting his hand above his eye with the same broad smile. She looked quizzically at him and he could sense her sizing him up.

Soon healed him and he is no longer wearing a bandage over his eye

"Doc, is that really you?" she asked, her eyes wide with disbelief. "I've been busy, so I haven't had a chance to call you yet. But I was planning to, just like I told you I would when you gave me your number."

"It happens," Doc replied. "I'm glad to see that you've done some healing, too. What can I get for you?"

She pointed to the menu items that she wanted and he heaped them generously onto her plate. Then he handed it to Willow.

"I'm starting a new job this evening," he said. "In a couple of weeks, I should be getting a paycheck. Call me and I'll take you out to lunch. It really is good to see you."

Doc felt a tap on his shoulder and then heard Brooke's laughter in his ear.

"Come on, let's go back to the car," Brooke said.

Doc pulled off his hairnet and gloves, hanging his apron on a hook as he left through the door. The back seat of the car was piled high with B-Day bags.

"I had no idea you were doing this," Doc said.

Brooke pulled over and grabbed a bag, then ran it over to a man who was playing guitar on the street before returning to the car.

"I bought the building," she explained, "and I rent the upstairs while serving free meals out of the diner. I don't talk about it much because I'm genuinely doing it for other people. I'm not doing it for publicity, and that's why I never gave it up."

The reason people create large companies is because they spend so much of their lives working on it. If it is something you love and are genuinely inspired by, it's easy to keep growing that business

She pulled back over as she saw a couple more people and ran meals across to them before returning to the car.

"How do you feel after looking at the people in the diner this morning?" Brooke asked.

"Amazing," he said. "I'd do that every day if I could."

"That's the secret," Brooke replied, glancing towards him. "There's nothing you could possibly buy that would give you the feeling you get from helping and serving people. If you stay wealthy for long enough, you'll realize that we're here for each other. I make money to help those who can't help themselves or who just need someone to care. Being a millionaire is just a side effect of providing jobs. Money is something that people give to you because you brought value to them or connected to them what they needed. That's what sales is all about, at its heart."

She paused her monologue for a moment to hand out a couple more bags before continuing.

"I wanted you to see why I made as much as I could," she said. "It wasn't ever for me. This business was always for others, which is why I never gave up. Don't ever be jealous of someone's money because you don't understand where it came from or what's going on. A beautiful watch can be turned around and sold for more. Envy is just a lack of understanding, and one day you'll find yourself in their place if you never give up on what you love."

She got out of the car to hand out a couple more bags.

"Where was I?" she asked.

"Envy," Doc replied.

"Oh yeah," Brooke said. "Jealousy is telling you where you want to go. You just need to give yourself a chance to begin. The key to wealth is to buy things that go up in value. When we buy things that go down in value, we end up with the same amount of money, week after week. If you want to end up with more and more money over the years, you'll want to collect precious metals, real estate and other things that go up in value."

They drove along some more and then Brooke pulled up outside the food pantry, which was run by the local church. It took them a couple of trips to shuttle all the food inside, and the staff and people there erupted in applause after they'd finished unloading. Brooke beamed and led Doc back out to the car, and they pulled away with two bags of food left in the back seat.

By the time that two o'clock rolled around and Brooke had parked the car in front of the lab, Doc was feeling energized.

"Just tell me what I need to do and I'll do it," he said.

"Eat!" she said, reaching into the back seat and grabbing the last bag. "I know you're hungry."

Doc did so, tearing open the bag and biting into the sandwich.

"Most people are so intimidated that they aren't even willing to start over," Brooke said, opening up her own bag of food. "That holds them back because somewhere we believe that the past is bigger than the future will ever be. When something bad happens, most people get stuck and lock down instead of realizing that everything passes. That goes for those who get to the top and give up, too. Age is a funny thing, but don't give yourself the chance to regret. Give yourself the chance to begin and to plan for a specific future. That's the difference between dreamers and wishers."

"What is?" Doc asked, between mouthfuls.

"A dreamer asks themselves whether they'd be satisfied if that was all they did that day," Brooke explained. "They can't sit still because they're en route to their dreams. They know the small details about what they're fighting for and reverse engineer the path forward, bit by bit, more and more every day. The game of life rewards us for taking action by giving us answers on how to get to our dreams."

"Wow," Doc said. "I like that. Actions are what give us answers on how to get to our dreams. I wish you'd write a book, Brooke. You could call it Brooke's Book."

"A wisher is someone who thinks that when something gets hard, it means it's not meant to be," she replied, giggling a little. "They end up trying something else instead of sticking at it, dusting themselves off and trying again from another angle."

Doc nodded.

"The real question," Brooke said, "is when are you going to dream? It's not going to be easy, but you can't quit your way to the finish line. When a seed is planted, it grows when you water it, as long as the ground is fertile. The more you water your apple tree, the bigger it will become. Even through all the storms, if it falls over, you've got to stand it back up and take care of it. Keep watering and learning how to better care for your dream until it becomes an apple tree."

Brooke paused for a moment to pat her brother on the shoulder.

"Be careful, though," she cautioned. "If you start watering your orange trees, you're going to have fewer apples, and that's how all of life works. Your trees will die if you look away for long enough. Yet there's a law that a seed will grow into the plant that it's supposed to become. You're a seed and you're in the right soil. Your soil is what you're writing down and learning, and it's up to you to grow into what you're supposed to become, not what someone else already is. Become something just like you."

She sighed and leaned back in the driver's seat.

"Not everyone can be an Olympian," Brooke said. "And not everyone can be a scientist that changes the world, but you can. Now go get 'em, brother. You're the reason why your ancestors lived. Passion and willpower are earned by people who never give up and are felt by the ones who earn them. We just need to keep trying to make ourselves better until the world says we're good enough. Passion isn't created by those who think that they're good enough and who stop trying."

"Okay, I think I've got it," Doc said. "I'm ready."

He got out of the sports car and noticed the sound of an approaching ambulance echoing through the streets. He kept his eyes ahead of him as Dr. Ti pushed open the front door of the lab and Jessica limped forward, holding her arm delicately in front of her. It was wrapped in bloody bandages.

CHAPTER TWENTY SEVEN: KAYDEN

JESSICA LOOKED NAUSEOUS and she was holding a towel around her arm as the ambulance pulled up in front of them. The doors opened and Jimmy jumped out of the passenger seat, then circled around to the back to open the doors.

"What happened?" he asked.

"I'm not sure," Jessica replied. "I've had a sour stomach all day, and I just had an accident."

Jimmy helped her into the back of the ambulance and then took a closer look at her arm as his assistant kept it elevated.

"She's going to need stitches," Jimmy said. "We'll

take care of her."

Jimmy got back out of the ambulance and closed the back door, then nodded at his cousins.

"Brooke," he said, "I know you and Jessica are roommates. Could you contact her next of kin? We're taking her to Central Med."

"Sure thing, Jimmy," Brooke said. They watched the ambulance take off and then she turned to hug Doc. "Call me if you need me, brother. Enjoy your first day at work."

Doc and Dr. Ti watched her sports car pull out after the ambulance and then Dr. Ti led the way towards the lab.

"Crazy first day, huh?" Dr. Ti said. "Jessica cut her hand moving a tank. Luckily, we have the best insurance available, so she'll get proper care and paid as normal while she's off work."

He opened the door to the lab and gestured for Doc to head inside.

"So, Doc," he said. "Brooke's told me a lot about you. Let's get your lab coat and then I'll show you around the facility and give you a quick refresher."

They entered a larger room, their footsteps echoing in the expansive space as Dr. Ti busied himself about the lab. He gestured towards a television on the wall and started talking Doc through a slideshow of procedures.

Doc looked down at his wrist and tapped it, pausing time in the room around him.

"Hey, Soon," Doc said. "Are you there?"

"I'm here, Kayden."

"Is there any way I can show you the lab I'm

working in right now?" he asked, looking at the frozen Dr. Ti who was pointing towards his presentation. There was a knock at the door and it swung open.

"Kayden!" Soon said, stepping into view. "Or should I call you Doc?" It's a fitting name for a scientist. What can I help you with?"

"Can we poke around for a little while?"

"Well, we can have a look," Soon said.

They looked around at the different microscopes and containers, and Soon fell into deep thought.

"This is a fascinating research facility, Kayden," Soon said. "Do you mind if I take it back with me so I can take a closer look at it?"

"Go ahead," Doc said. "What do you need to do?"

The lettering on Soon's cloak slid down onto the floor and began morphing wildly into a map of the room before rushing back into the fabric of his cloak.

"I just saved this room," Soon explained. "And I explored the timeline through the lettering in my cloak, like a computer. Your world is on the verge of understanding the depths of virtual reality and will soon start bringing food and entertainment into the home. I believe that food subscription services will start to involve virtual reality in your timeline. They'll allow people from all over the world to consume food in virtual reality with their friends and family in a virtual world. Can you imagine eating Chinese in China with someone? That's where your world is about to be."

Soon smiled.

"Thank you for inviting me into your world," Soon said. "You've changed a lot, Kayden. Let's not leave Dr.

Ti hanging for too long."

He left the lab through the door that he came in by and Doc tapped his wrist. Time restarted and Dr. Ti looked back at him and paused, shaking his head.

"I thought I saw something," he said. Doc raised his eyebrows at him. "Well, anyway. Let's take a look around the lab."

Dr. Ti led the way through a set of double doors towards the cryo-chamber and Doc followed closely on his heels.

"So how far away are we from testing people?" he asked.

"We're ready now," Dr. Ti replied. "We were just waiting for you."

"Tell me about what it can do."

Dr. Ti circled the chamber with him towards a doorway to another chamber behind it. Ice crept its way over Doc's skin as his thoughts started flooding through him. The mostly steel chambers had glass viewing windows, and black hoses snaked across the white tiled floor, leading towards them.

"Right now, we're just testing submerging things in the tank and figuring out what percentages of liquids work best," Dr. Ti said.

There was a buzz from inside Dr. Ti's pocket and he pulled out his cellphone.

"Hello, Brooke," Dr. Ti said. "How's it going? Yes, I can do that. Do you want him to bring it by when he gets off?"

He walked over to Jessica's desk and pulled out a cellphone from the desk drawer, then gave it to Doc while he continued talking.

"I'm handing it to him now," Dr. Ti said. "Give Jessica my best wishes."

Then Dr. Ti cut the call and turned to look at Doc again.

"So," he said, "let's talk about the tanks in more detail and then when it gets dark, we'll head out to the parking lot. I've got a surprise for you."

Doc and Dr. Ti had a lot to talk about, and it was dark outside by the time that they'd finished brainstorming ideas and talking about the future of the lab. When the day was over and they were about to head out into the car park, Dr. Ti took Doc aside.

"Oh," he said. "I almost forgot. "Your old lab has reached out to us for a fully-funded mission to send a body into space. Perfecting the cryogenics will convince the lab to send a living human, and the scientists working on the project will be some of the first picks."

Doc's wristband turned black as he glanced over at the mice.

"A virus," Doc murmured. He looked around and leaned in closer to Dr. Ti, then added, "I can design an injectable virus that will solve all of the problems you're having with cryogenics here. As we age, we collect things we can't remove from our bodies and heal with scars and flaws. But ice destroys them anyway, like instant ageing. The virus would allow us to heal correctly and without the errors in our bodies, reversing ageing and curing age-related illnesses, like a jellyfish being reborn."

"Interesting," Dr. Ti said. "What would it involve?"

"We just need to consume an algae like Chlorella," Doc explained. "It'll bond to the heavy metals in our bodies and remove them, because naturally we can't, even by detoxing. Our intestines simply reabsorb any metals that our bodies try to remove. The beauty about this is that we can survive on algae and, with some testing, create a self-sustaining bubble that uses sunlight to grow the algae in a tank I'll design. We won't be far from a full suspended animation pod after that. With just the algae and the virus alone, I can double the current life expectancy."

"If we can produce human results on ageing, the lab will be funded for life," Dr. Ti replied. "Getting clearance to send someone into space would be no trouble at all. We'd like Jessica to be here though, because the tank is mostly her domain. How soon could you have your virus working in mice?"

They continued to talk as the sun slipped completely from the sky, discussing an omni-directional braking system, the first restriction device of its kind and one that astronauts desperately needed in space. Being able to add it into an astronaut's suit would assimilate gravity and remove any extra gym equipment altogether. The variable pressure design would allow resistance in every direction, changing the face of workouts, rehab and space travel.

"We needed you here ages ago, Doc," Dr. Ti said, smiling at him as they walked out towards the parking lot. "The company provides vehicles because we go from lab to lab and work with moving things like the chambers. I've got you the keys to this truck right here, and you're welcome to take it home for the night."

"Awesome!" Doc exclaimed. "Thanks, Dr. Ti."

He took the keys and climbed into the truck, closing the door behind him. He pulled Jessica's phone out of his pocket and placed it on the passenger seat. Then he cranked the truck into reverse and waved goodbye to Dr. Ti before backing slowly out of the parking lot.

What's something I need to remember? Doc thought.

A slip of paper slid out of his wrist and a grateful smile crossed his face. He pulled over and parked the car, then went into a thrift store to pursue his forgotten goal. Sifting through the clothes, he found the perfect outfit for his dad, a blue t-shirt and a pair of khaki pants like the ones his father always wore. He paid for it with the money he'd earned from the museum and walked out of the store with the outfit.

His stomach growled. Grateful to have some money for once, he stopped off for some food and put the Styrofoam plates on the passenger seat before pulling out. He was cruising along when he heard Jessica's phone buzzing into life beneath the plates. He reached over and picked it up, trying to remember the password.

0204, he thought. *It's a good job I asked her.*

Once he'd stopped at a set of lights, he unlocked the phone and started scrolling through the missed calls. He noticed that they all came from the same number.

I'd better tell them she was in an accident at work.

He dialed the number, noticing as he did so that the light had turned green. He heard a voice from the phone.

"Jessica, let me explain!"

But he'd lost his grip on it, and a small car had darted in front of the truck that was crossing the intersection. He crashed into the car and tears began to flow as goosebumps crawled up his back and across his arms.

The scene stopped, Jessica's phone slipping from his hand as he loosened his grip on the wheel. Then the vehicles slammed to a stop and he reached over to cut off the engine. The dark roads around them were empty. Smoke was rising from the truck.

That was the call from Jessica, he thought dimly, trembling as he looked over at the car. A deep haze settled over his mind as he remembered the orb buzzing and the echoing call from his sister.

"No!" he cried, as the world filled with silence. He got out of his vehicle and watched as Cyrus fell out of the other car. "No! Oh my god, it was my brother!"

Time started to slow down as Doc started to understand how his brother had saved him and figured out how to get into space. Infact, Doc had been living it like it was all himself. He looked up and spotted an ambulance, which rushed over and pulled up by the accident. His imagination played out Jimmy getting out of the vehicle with a pale face and a tortured expression.

"That's my family!" Jimmy bellowed, losing his composure for a moment before his professionalism set back in again. "Somebody help me!"

The medics started to race over and the scene faded out into a sandy mist, revealing the room that they were in. Cyrus coughed and sat up, touching his wristband. He locked eyes with Doc and their vision flipped as they instantly swapped bodies.

"Doc, we made it," Kayden said.

"Have you been living as me the whole time?" Doc asked. Doc's brother Kayden, nodded. "So you know what I was going through when I lost Jessica, don't you?"

Only Soon, Monty, & Aurora (The Originals) ever called him Kayden... He received the name "Kayden" on pg 34 Because it was the last thing he remembered hearing. Why? The echoes from the EMT's during his last moments on Earth

There was a pause as a shared understanding emerged between the two of them.

"I really did love Jessica when I lost her," Doc said. "Did you ever believe that one day we'd be on the planet the orb fell from, bro? I remember being upstairs and spending the day with Bobo. I called him back up to the house before you all went out on the boat that day. I remember unpacking boxes with mom upstairs and watching the orb fall from the sky in the video that dad shared when you all got home. That night, I saw the glow from my window, and now here we are. Living in each other's shoes so that we have clarity on why we are the way we are."

Doc's song: "If he was me" was for Jessica, which is why she stepped in after he finished singing it

Kayden burst into tears.

"I'm so grateful to be talking to you again," he replied. "I didn't know you'd been through so much heartache. We'll always gravitate towards our dreams and who we really are. Regret is the pain that takes the magic out of life. I wish we could have accessed this kind of experience before now. Clarity can bring us all together."

A door opened in the wall and Soon walked into the white room. The brothers looked towards him and then to Soon's wristband, which was glowing green.

"It's good to see you both understanding each other a little better," Soon said. "I've almost got you both back home."

A blank expression settled on both their faces as they looked towards Soon.

"Well," Soon continued, "clarity is the beginning of change. Now that your wristbands are fully functional and you understand more about what will happen in your life, how far will you go? It's time for your real story to begin."

Doc stumbled as sand rose through the floor. Everything misted away and Doc landed on his back, looking out over an ocean. Soon was standing out in the water in a familiar dream. Doc dug his fingers into the sand and looked down in disbelief as he felt himself shrinking down into a child.

"Soon!" he yelled, listening to the high-pitched tone of his voice. The white room opened up into the scene in his dreams and he lay on the beach, looking out at Soon in the water.

"That doesn't have to be the way your life ends, Doc," he said. "In fact, through your new thoughts and ideas, you're going to change the world. Welcome home."

TO BE CONTINUED...

WHERE DID MASTER SOON COME FROM?
THE WRITTEN LEGACY CONTINUES

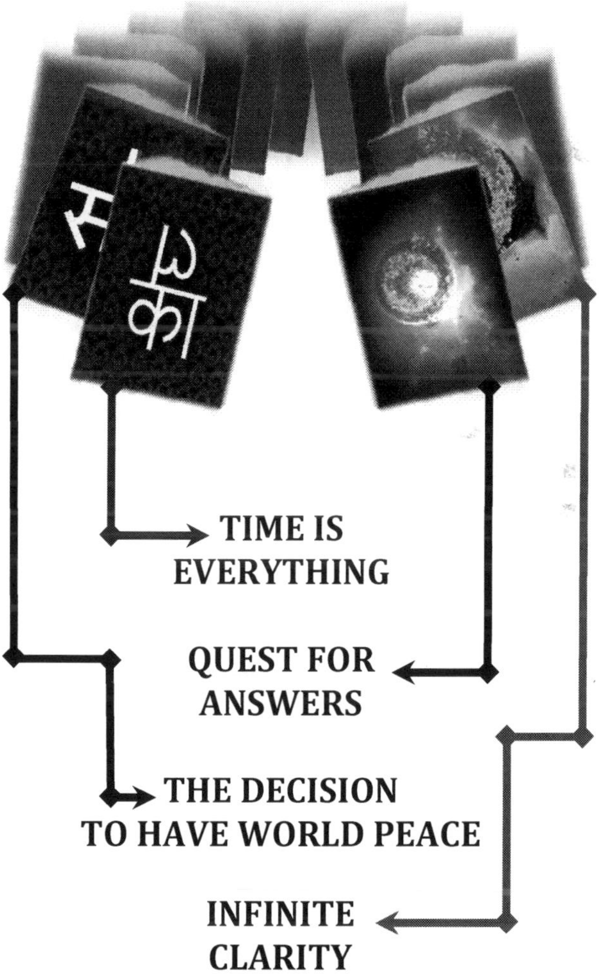

JOIN THE CONVERSATION

THANKS FOR READING THE COLOR GONE! Whether you loved the book or you hated it, I want to hear your thoughts. Please do leave a short review on Amazon and/or Goodreads – and be sure to share it with me on your social networking site of choice! I love to learn from my readers' feedback, and I share my favourite reviews with my social media followers.

While you're at it, why not give me a follow to hear the latest book news as and when it happens? And feel free to reach out to me. I'd love to see where your book ends up as it travels and is signed by fellow readers.

http://www.RianMileti.com
http://www.TheColorGone.com

Made in the USA
Monee, IL
29 August 2022

4a98e0d7-c568-474a-94af-4b2bbc062b2eR02